STORYBOOK COLLECTION

MARVEL

NEW YORK

THE ORIGIN OF THE AMAZING SPIDER-MAN: GREAT POWER...............1

THE ORIGIN OF THE AMAZING SPIDER-MAN: GREAT RESPONSIBILITY...............17

THE DIABOLICAL DOCTOR OCTOPUS...............37

BEWARE THE GREEN GOBLIN...............53

IN THE GRIP OF THE SANDMAN...............69

THE AMAZING PETER PARKER...............85

BIRTH OF THE LIZARD...............97

THE RHINO'S RAMPAGE...............111

CAGED BY KRAVEN THE HUNTER...............125

THE MENACE OF MYSTERIO 139

A WEEK WITH THE WEB-SLINGER 151

REVENGE OF THE GREEN GOBLIN 163

30,000 VOLTS OF ELECTRO 177

CRY OF THE VULTURE 191

THE TALE OF THE LIZARD'S RAGE 205

THE CLAWS OF THE BLACK CAT 219

SEE SPOT PUNCH 235

THE MANY FACES OF THE CHAMELEON 249

ATTACK OF THE SINISTER SIX 265

WHAT MAKES A HERO? 285

"The Origin of the Amazing Spider-Man: Great Power" adapted by Michael Siglain. Illustrated by The Storybook Art Group. Based upon the Marvel comic book series *Spider-Man*.

"The Origin of the Amazing Spider-Man: Great Responsibility" adapted by Michael Siglain. Illustrated by The Storybook Art Group. Based upon the Marvel comic book series *Spider-Man*.

"The Diabolical Doctor Octopus" adapted by Nachie Castro. Illustrated by The Storybook Art Group. Based upon the Marvel comic book series *Spider-Man*.

"Beware the Green Goblin" adapted by Tomas Palacios. Illustrated by The Storybook Art Group. Based upon the Marvel comic book series *Spider-Man*.

"In the Grip of the Sandman" adapted by Scott Peterson. Illustrated by Craig Rousseau and Hi-Fi Design. Based upon the Marvel comic book series *Spider-Man*.

"The Amazing Peter Parker" written by Clarissa Wong. Illustrated by Craig Rousseau and Hi-Fi Design. Based upon the Marvel comic book series *Spider-Man*.

"Birth of the Lizard" adapted by Clarissa Wong. Illustrated by Todd Nauck and Hi-Fi Design. Based upon the Marvel comic book series *Spider-Man*.

"The Rhino's Rampage" adapted by Elizabeth Rudnick. Illustrated by Craig Rousseau and Hi-Fi Design. Based upon the Marvel comic book series *Spider-Man*.

"Caged by Kraven the Hunter" adapted by Kevin Shinick. Illustrated by Craig Rousseau and Hi-Fi Design. Based upon the Marvel comic book series *Spider-Man*.

"The Menace of Mysterio" adapted by Clarissa Wong. Illustrated by Todd Nauck and Hi-Fi Design. Based upon the Marvel comic book series *Spider-Man*.

"A Week with the Web-Slinger" written by Tomas Palacios. Illustrated by Craig Rousseau and Hi-Fi Design. Based upon the Marvel comic book series *Spider-Man*.

"Revenge of the Green Goblin" adapted by Steve Behling. Illustrated by Todd Nauck and Hi-Fi Design. Based upon the Marvel comic book series *Spider-Man*.

"30,000 Volts of Electro" adapted by Matt Manning. Illustrated by Craig Rousseau and Hi-Fi Design. Based upon the Marvel comic book series *Spider-Man*.

"Cry of the Vulture" adapted by Elizabeth Rudnick. Illustrated by Craig Rousseau and Hi-Fi Design. Based upon the Marvel comic book series *Spider-Man*.

"The Tale of the Lizard's Rage" adapted by Clarissa Wong. Illustrated by Todd Nauck and Hi-Fi Design. Based upon the Marvel comic book series *Spider-Man*.

"The Claws of the Black Cat" adapted by Brendon Halpin. Illustrated by Todd Nauck and Hi-Fi Design. Based upon the Marvel comic book series *Spider-Man*.

"See Spot Punch" adapted by Nachie Castro. Illustrated by Craig Rousseau and Hi-Fi Design. Based upon the Marvel comic book series *Spider-Man*.

"The Many Faces of the Chameleon" written by Bryan Q. Miller. Illustrated by Craig Rousseau and Hi-Fi Design. Based upon the Marvel comic book series *Spider-Man*.

"Attack of the Sinister Six" adapted by Scott Peterson. Illustrated by Todd Nauck and Hi-Fi Design. Based upon the Marvel comic book series *Spider-Man*.

"What Makes a Hero?" written by Tomas Palacios. Illustrated by Craig Rousseau and Hi-Fi Design. Based upon the Marvel comic book series *Spider-Man*.

Printed in the United States of America

First Edition

3 5 7 9 10 8 6 4 2

G942-9090-6-12269

ISBN 978-14231-4292-8

Cover illustrated by Pat Olliffe and Brian Miller
Storybook designed by Jennifer Redding

www.marvel.com

MARVEL

The Origin of the Amazing Spider-Man™

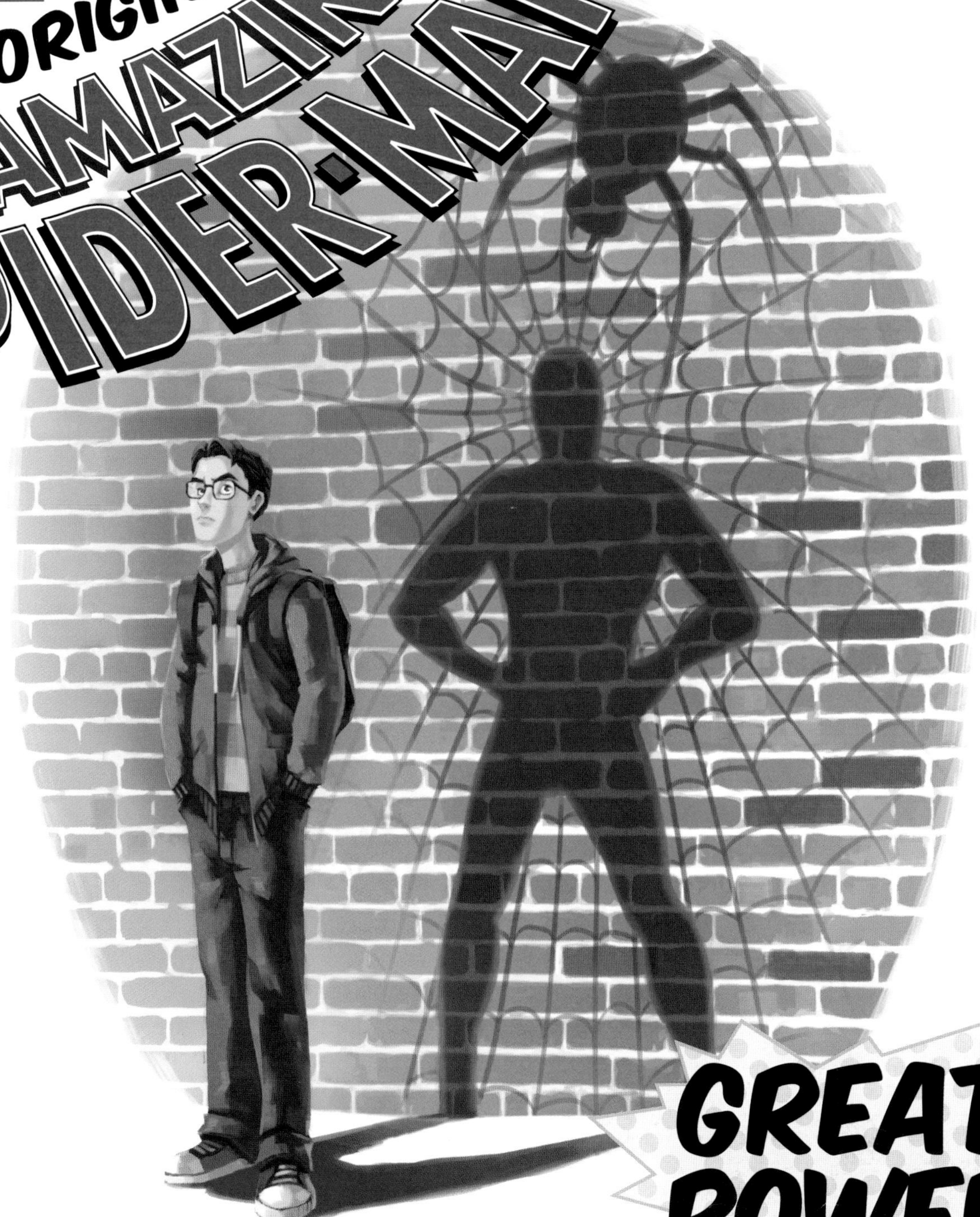

Great Power

Peter Parker was an average teenager. He lived in Queens, New York, with his uncle Ben and his aunt May, and attended Midtown High School. Peter enjoyed school, and his favorite class was science. He loved to learn, study, and experiment, and his teachers were all very proud of him.

But Peter didn't have many friends at school. The other students couldn't understand why Peter liked learning so much. They bullied him and called him names. And that made Peter feel sad and lonely.

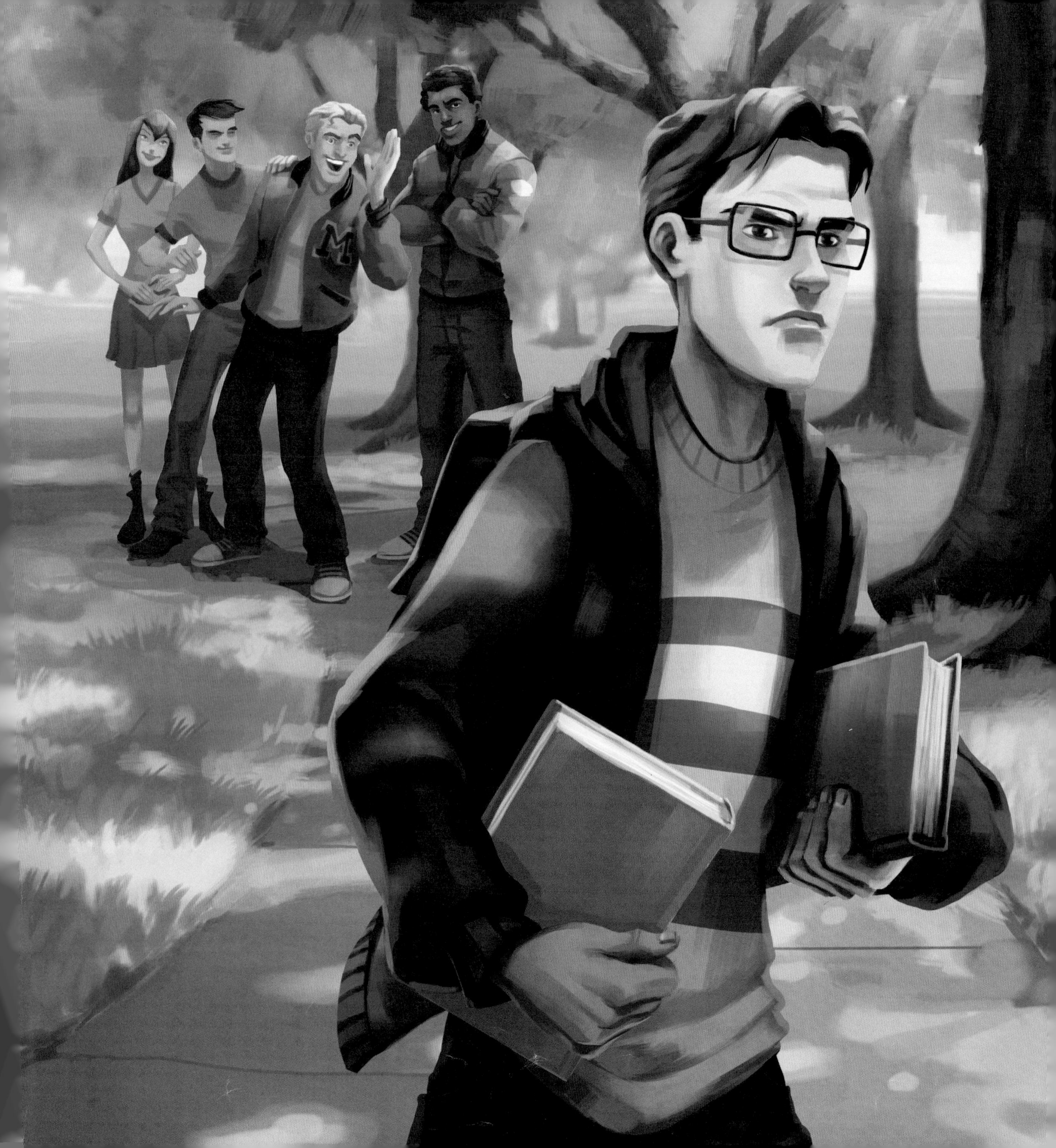

Whenever Peter felt unhappy at school, he knew he could find happiness at home with Uncle Ben and Aunt May. They were always there to comfort him and to help him, and that always made him smile.

Another thing that made Peter smile was his upcoming field trip to the Science Hall. There, he would learn all about radioactive waves, and how scientists could work with dangerous radioactivity. Peter was very excited!

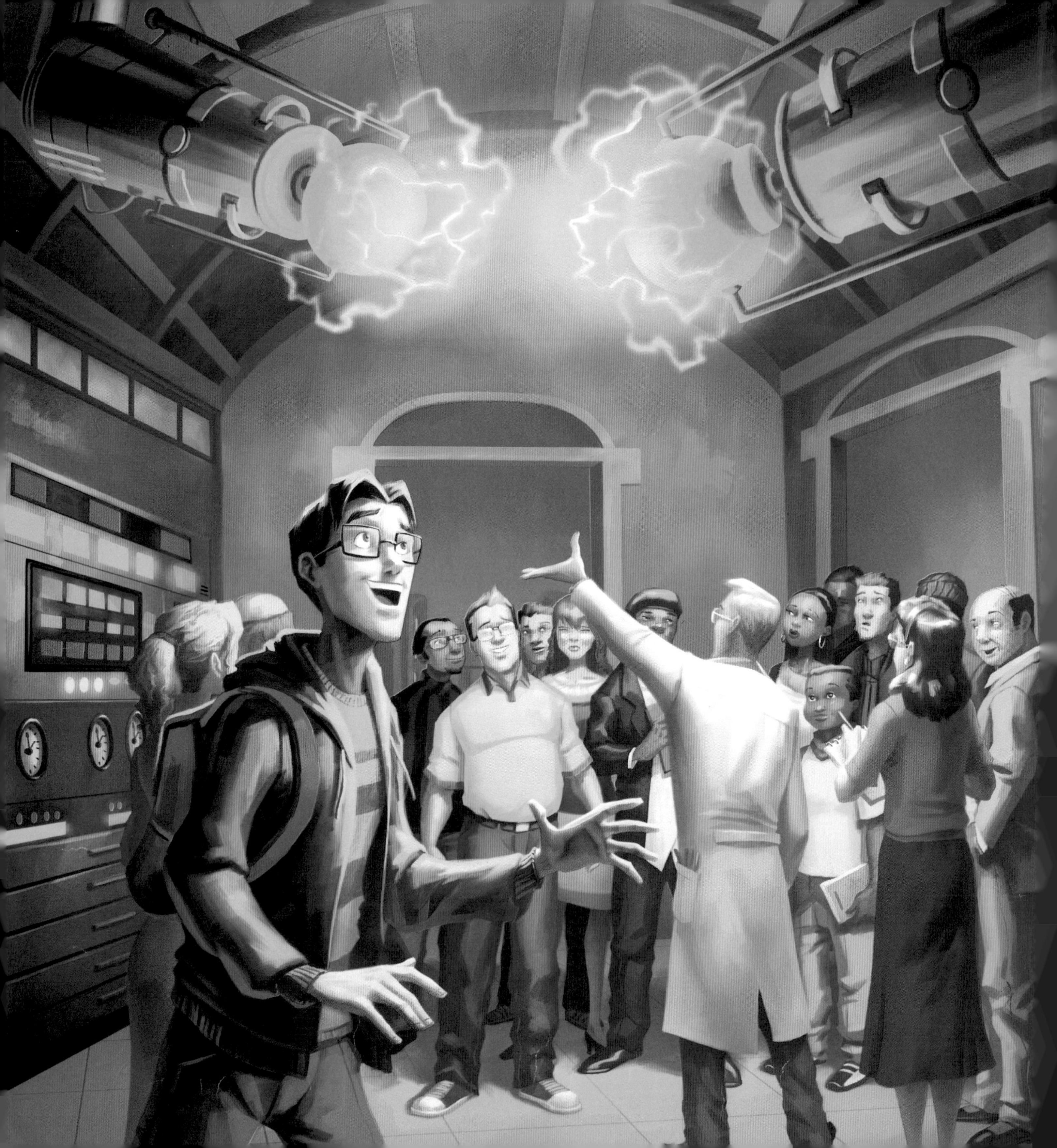

At the Science Hall, Peter and his fellow students looked on in amazement. The demonstration was about to begin, and Peter was about to see how scientists controlled a radioactive wave.

But something else was also looking on. Unseen by Peter, the other students, or the scientists was a big black spider. And it was descending right into the rays!

Peter was so taken by the experiment and the brilliant scientists that he didn't notice the spider pass through the radioactive waves. He didn't even notice the glowing arachnid as it fell toward him.

Peter was distracted, thinking about how much he wanted to grow up to be like one of these scientists. If he could do that, Uncle Ben and Aunt May would be so proud. But then something happened that would forever change Peter's life. . . .

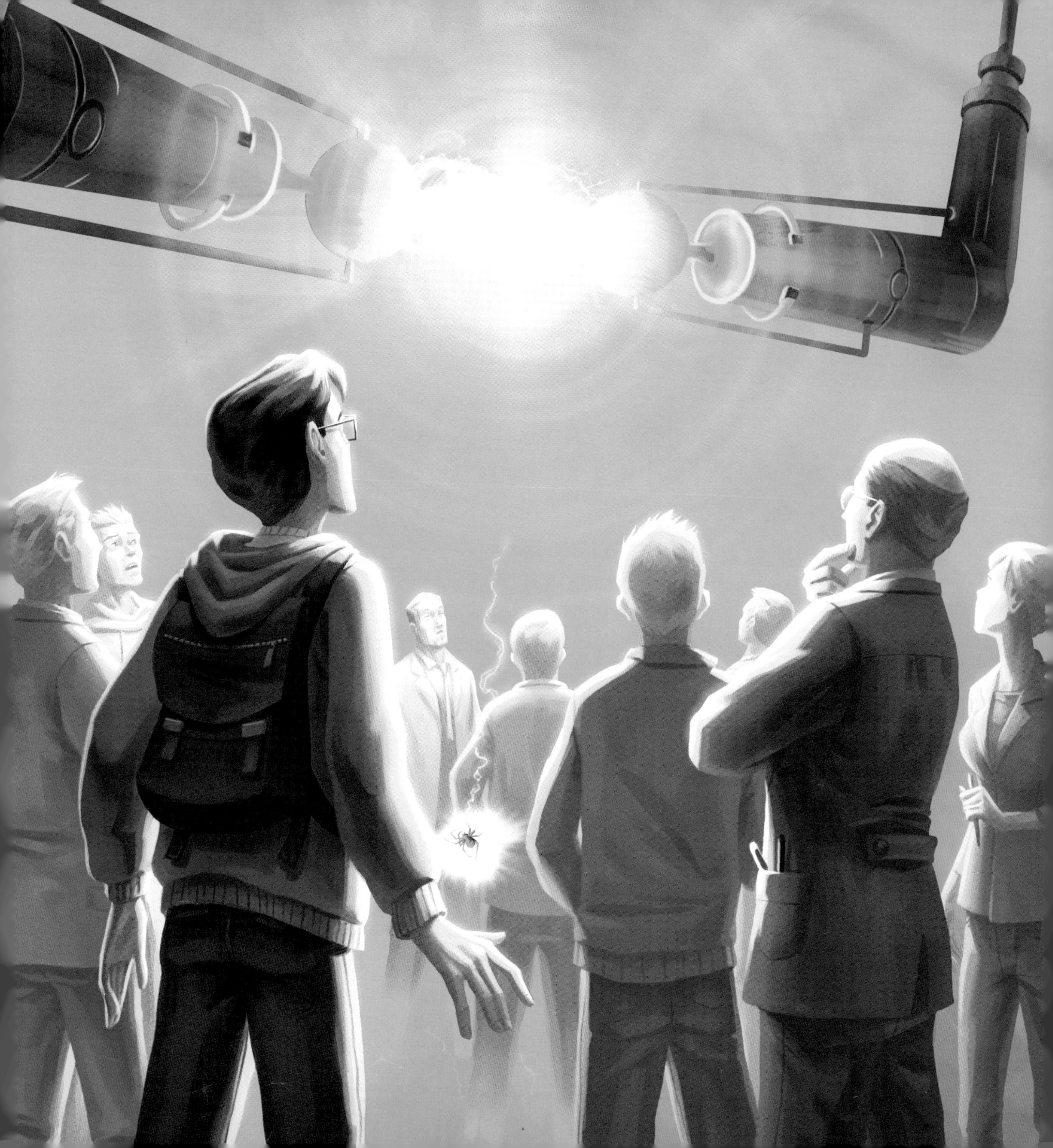

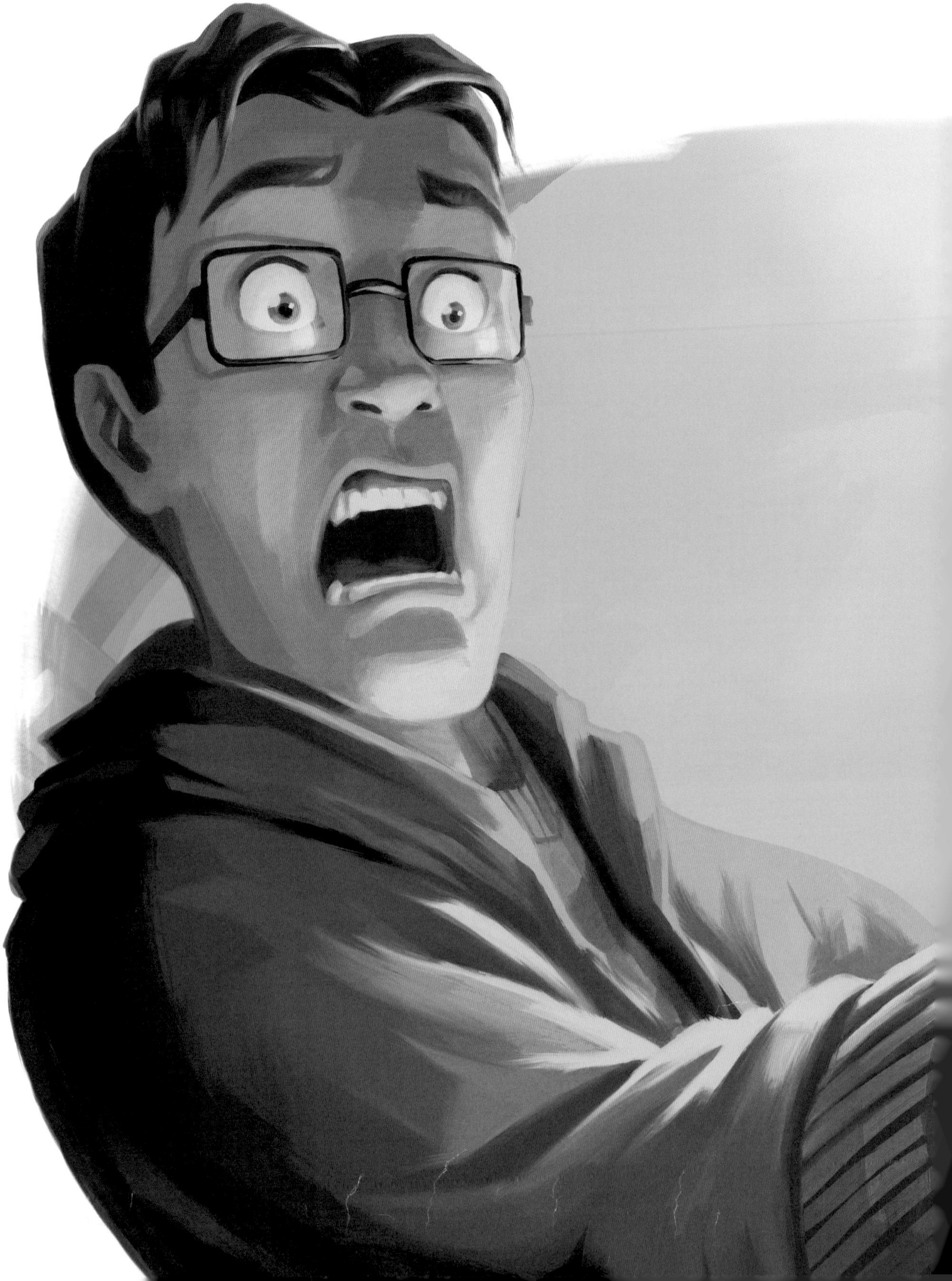

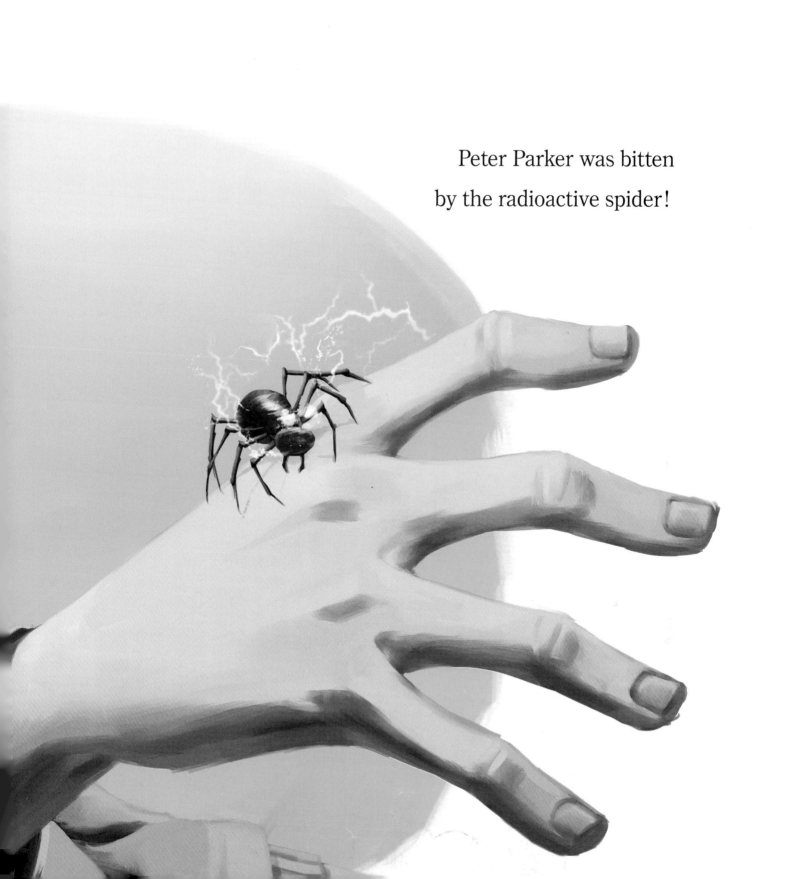

Peter Parker was bitten
by the radioactive spider!

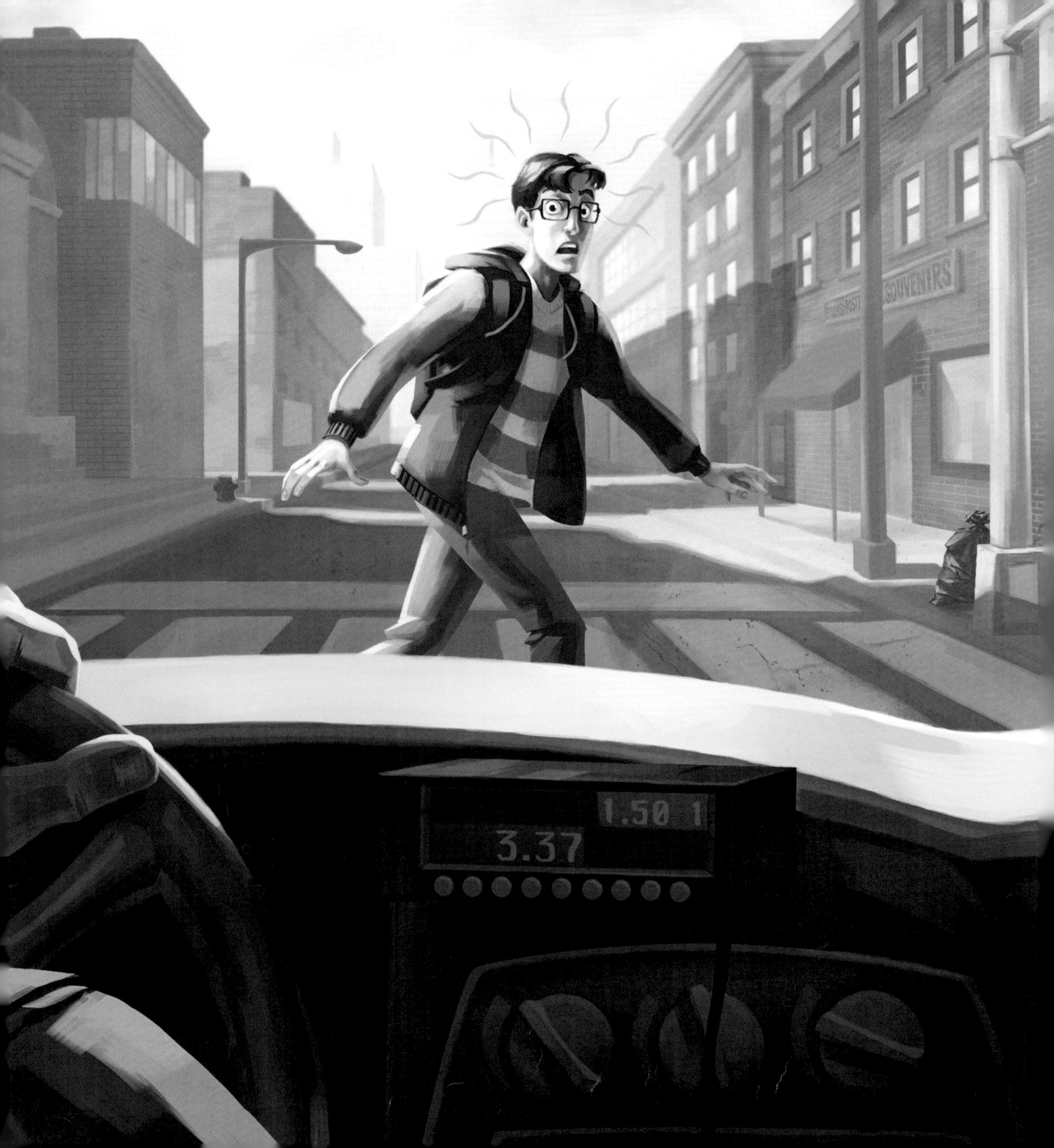
SOUVENIRS
1.50 1
3.37

Peter didn't tell anyone about the spider bite. He suddenly didn't feel well and rushed out of the Science Hall. His heart was racing, and he felt very strange. He just wanted to go home.

But when Peter started to cross the street, he felt a weird sensation. It was almost as if his *whole body* was tingling, telling him to react. To move. To do something.

So he did. Just in the nick of time, Peter Parker jumped out of the way of an oncoming taxi. . . .

And landed on the *side of a building!* Peter couldn't believe it!

Not only was he clinging to a brick wall, but he could actually

climb straight *up the building*, just like a spider!

Peter also had increased strength. When he reached the roof,

he crushed a chimney with his bare hands!

Peter felt that same tingly sensation in his head again, and it told him to jump. With remarkable strength, Peter leaped from rooftop to rooftop, covering great distances in a single bound. Then that same sensation told him that the easiest way to get back to the street was to climb down a thin clothesline, the same way a spider would climb down its silken web.

Peter stood in an alleyway in awe of his newfound abilities. He realized that he must've gotten these powers from the radioactive spider's bite back at the Science Hall.

Peter Parker was still a teenager who enjoyed science class and lived with his uncle Ben and aunt May in Queens, but from this moment on, he was anything but average. Peter Parker was amazing!

MARVEL

THE ORIGIN OF the AMAZING SPIDER-MAN™

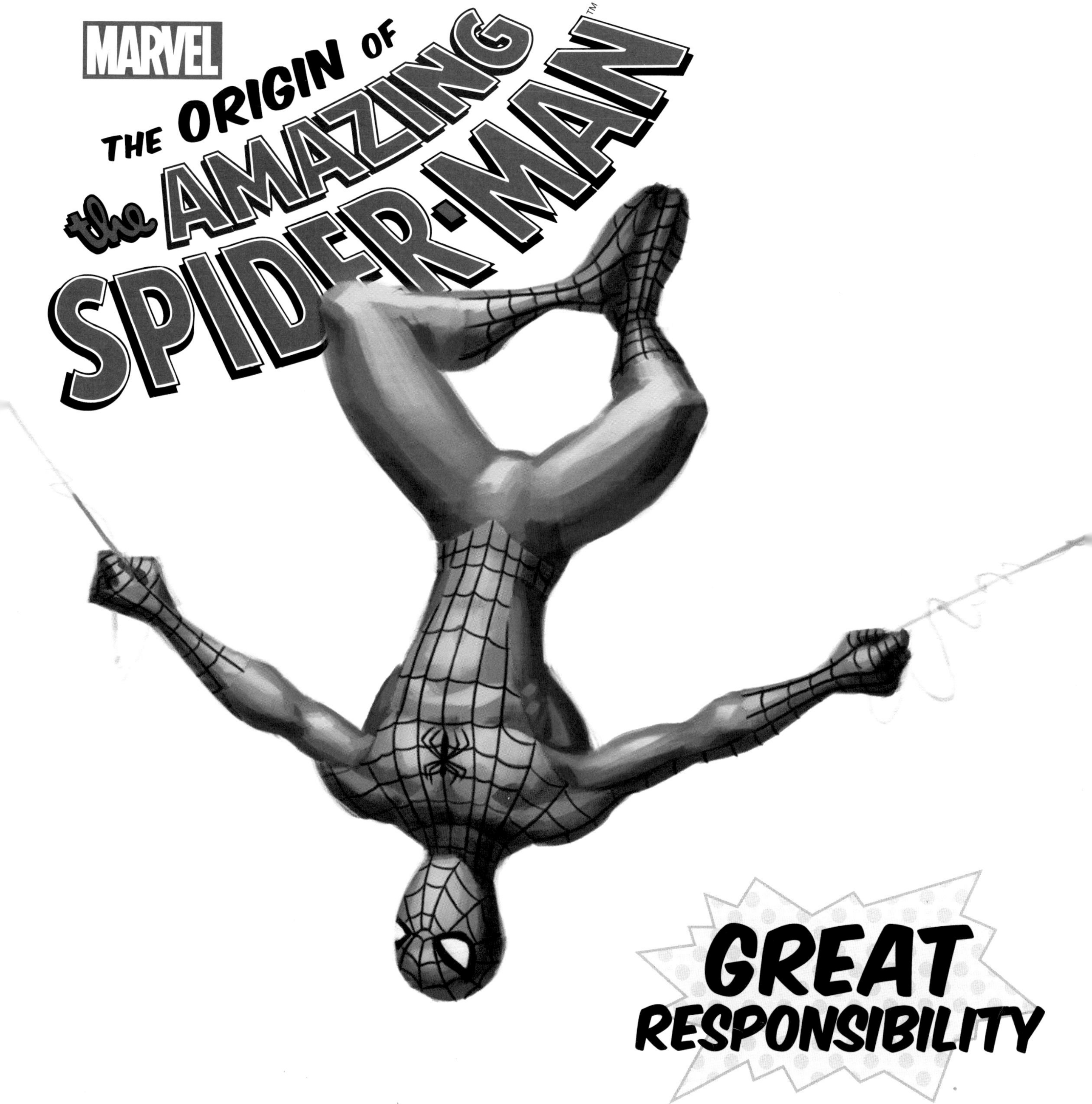

GREAT RESPONSIBILITY

Peter Parker was a normal teenager until he was bitten by a radioactive spider. Now, Peter could cling to walls, climb up buildings, and jump from rooftop to rooftop with incredible speed and strength.

But Peter needed to test his newfound abilities. He saw the perfect opportunity to do so at a wrestling match.

Peter wore a disguise so that no one would recognize him, and faced off against a professional wrestler named Crusher Hogan. Crusher was big and strong, but he was no match for Peter Parker and his sensational strength!

Peter was well paid for winning the wrestling match, and he decided to use his special abilities to earn some extra money. But he was still unsure of his powers. He was afraid to tell anyone about them, so he if he was going to use them, he would need a disguise.

Peter thought long and hard about a good stage name and costume. He finally decided to use the radioactive spider as his inspiration, and soon Peter Parker had a new identity. . .

The Amazing Spider-Man!

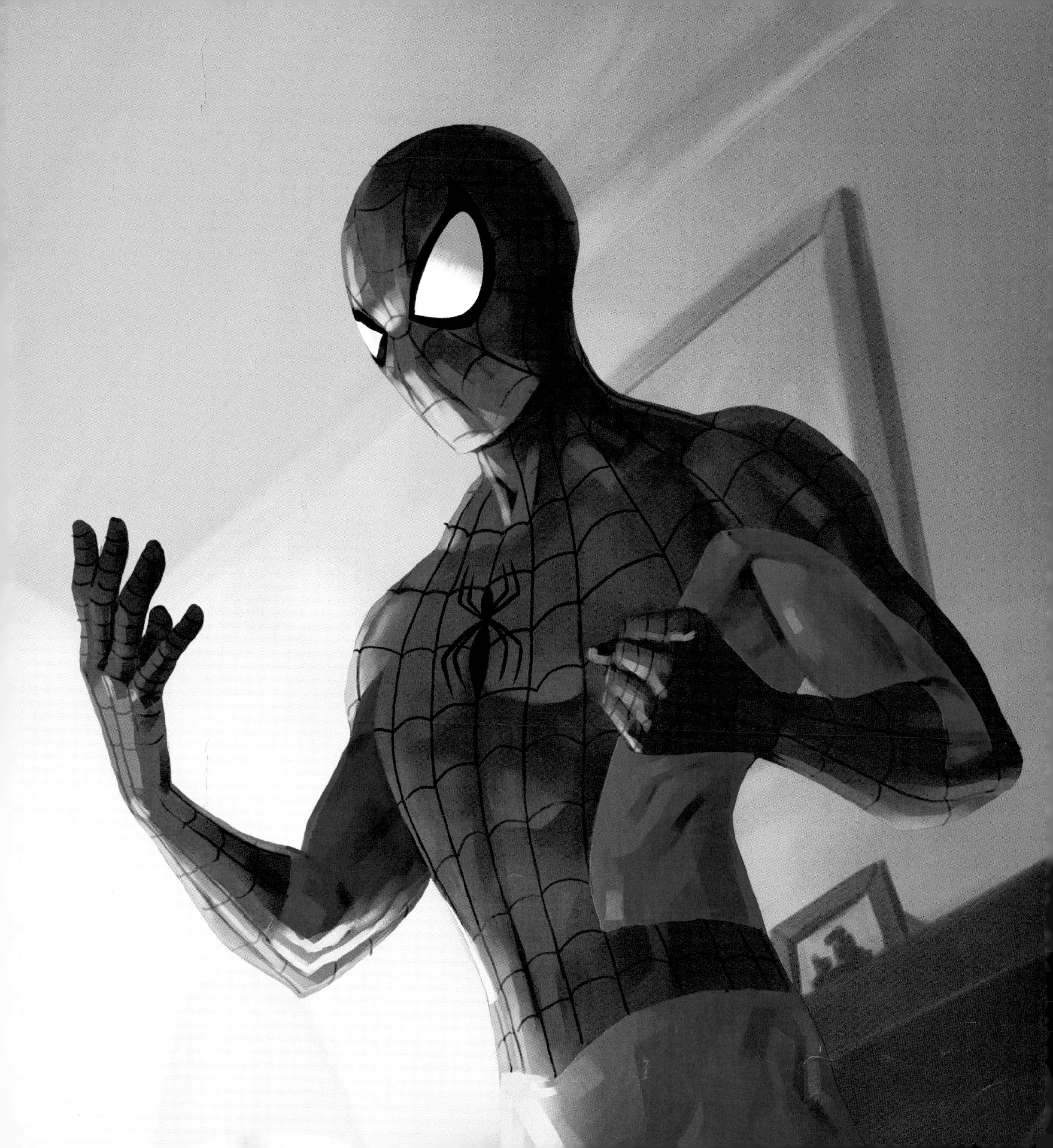

Soon, the Amazing Spider-Man was a television sensation!

Peter was having the time of his life!

He was also enjoying his time at home with Uncle Ben
and Aunt May. Peter's Uncle Ben saved up enough money to buy
Peter a special microscope for his science experiments. Uncle
Ben told Peter that science was power and that "with great
power comes great responsibility."

Peter was thrilled! He used his microscope and his
chemistry set and worked hard to create a very special fluid.
It was as strong and as sticky as a spider's web!

Peter then created devices that could spin the fluid into a web or shoot it in a line across the room. Peter called these his web-shooters.

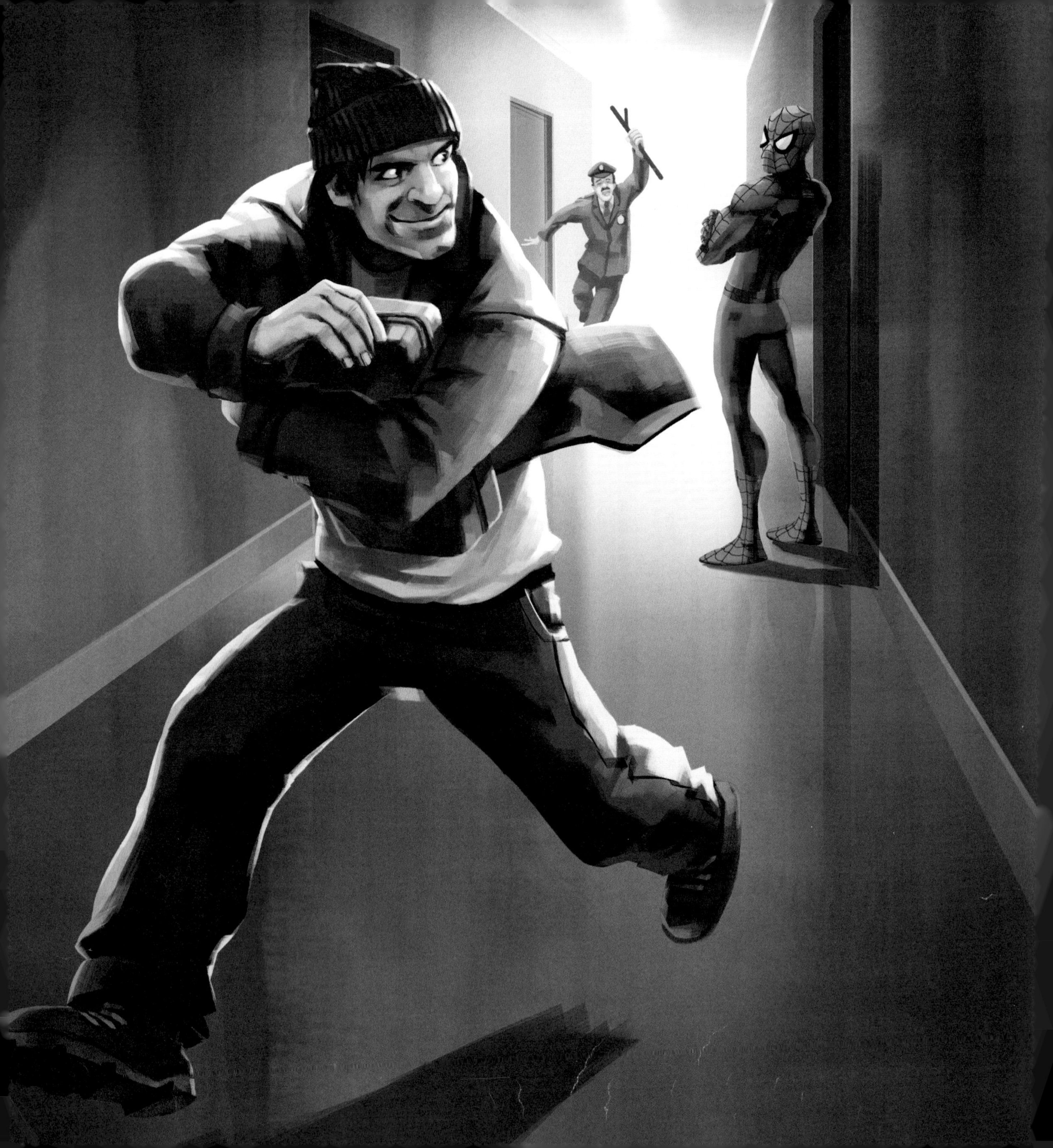

With his cartridges of web fluid and his cool new web-shooters, Peter's Spider-Man costume was finally complete. Now he really did have all the abilities of a spider — and he was going show them off for the world to see!

Peter performed on many television shows and became very popular. After one show, while he was daydreaming about fame and fortune, a security guard called out to him. The guard wanted Spider-Man to help stop a robber who was getting away. But Peter did nothing. He was only concerned about himself.

That night, when Peter returned home to Forest Hills,
Queens, he saw police cars parked in front of his house.
Something was wrong!

The police told Peter that Uncle Ben was killed by a criminal. The police had the crook cornered at an abandoned warehouse by the waterfront.

Peter was upset. He didn't want the criminal to get away, so he ran upstairs to change into his Spider-Man costume.

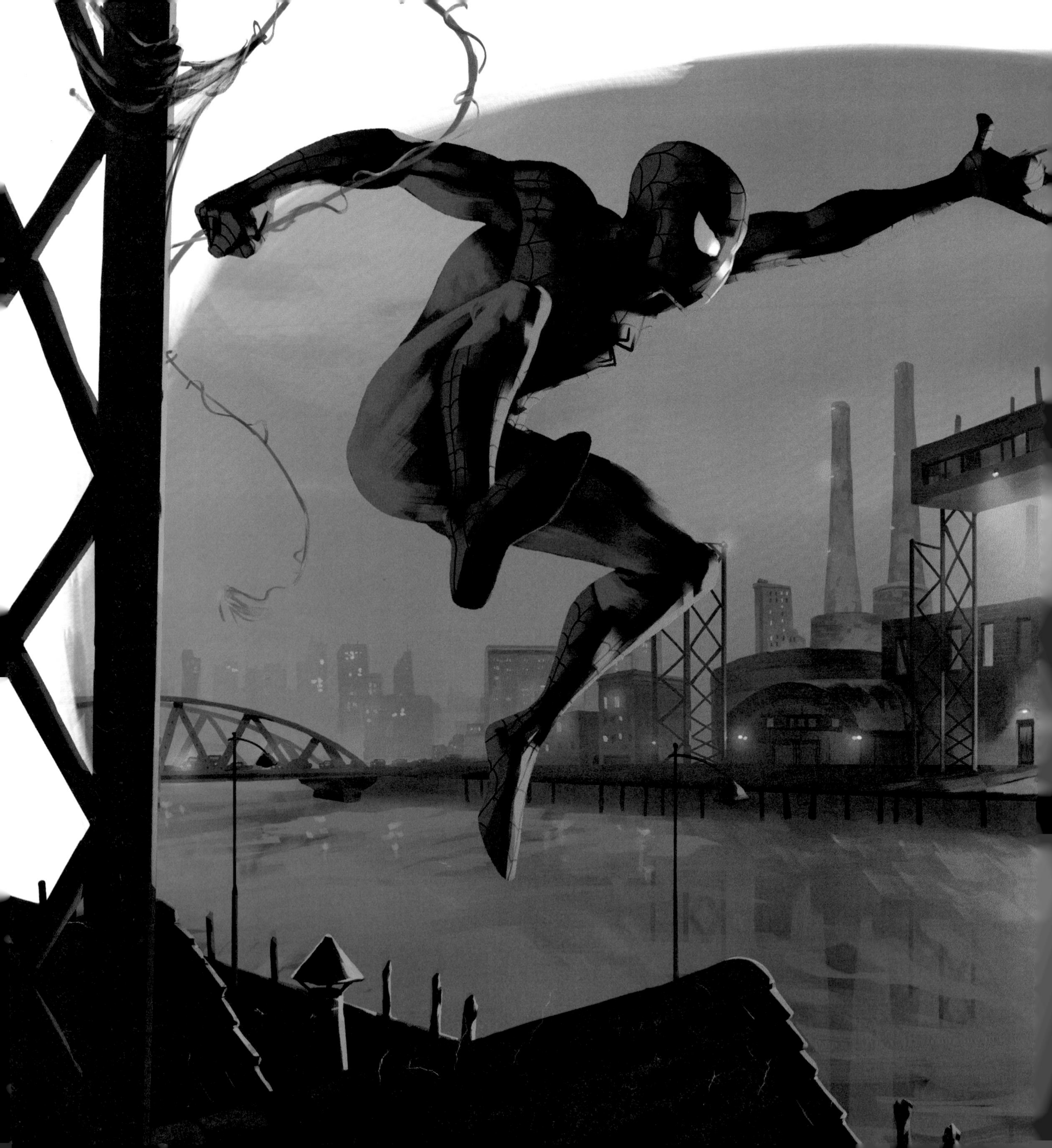

Using his wondrous webs and his super spider-strength, Peter raced to the warehouse to find the crook!

As Spider-Man, Peter landed inside the old warehouse, surprising the criminal!

Spider-Man quickly
shot a web at the
criminal's gun, then
yanked on the web,
pulling the gun out
of the crook's hand.
Then, using his spider-
strength, Peter knocked
out the criminal with
one mighty punch!

The robber's hat
fell from his head, and
Peter's eyes went wide
in disbelief.

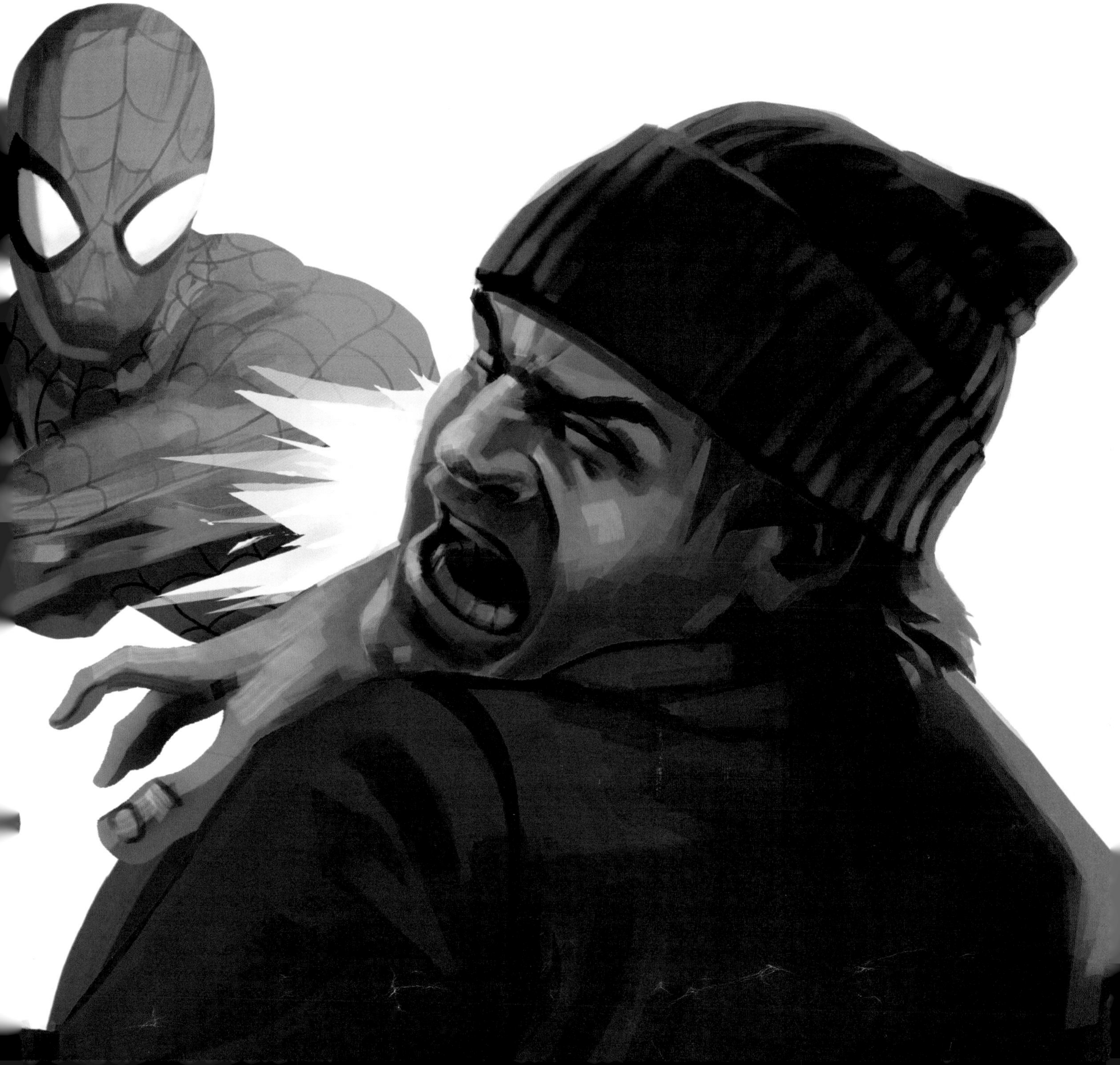

Peter was shocked to see that the criminal who killed Uncle
Ben was the same man that he let run by him at the television
studio. Peter was upset that he had acted so selfishly.

Peter used his webbing to attach the crook to a streetlamp for the police to find. Then he thought about Uncle Ben. He remembered what he had told him earlier: with great power comes great responsibility.

From that point on, Peter Parker vowed to always use his powers for good as the Amazing Spider-Man!

MARVEL

The Amazing Spider-Man™

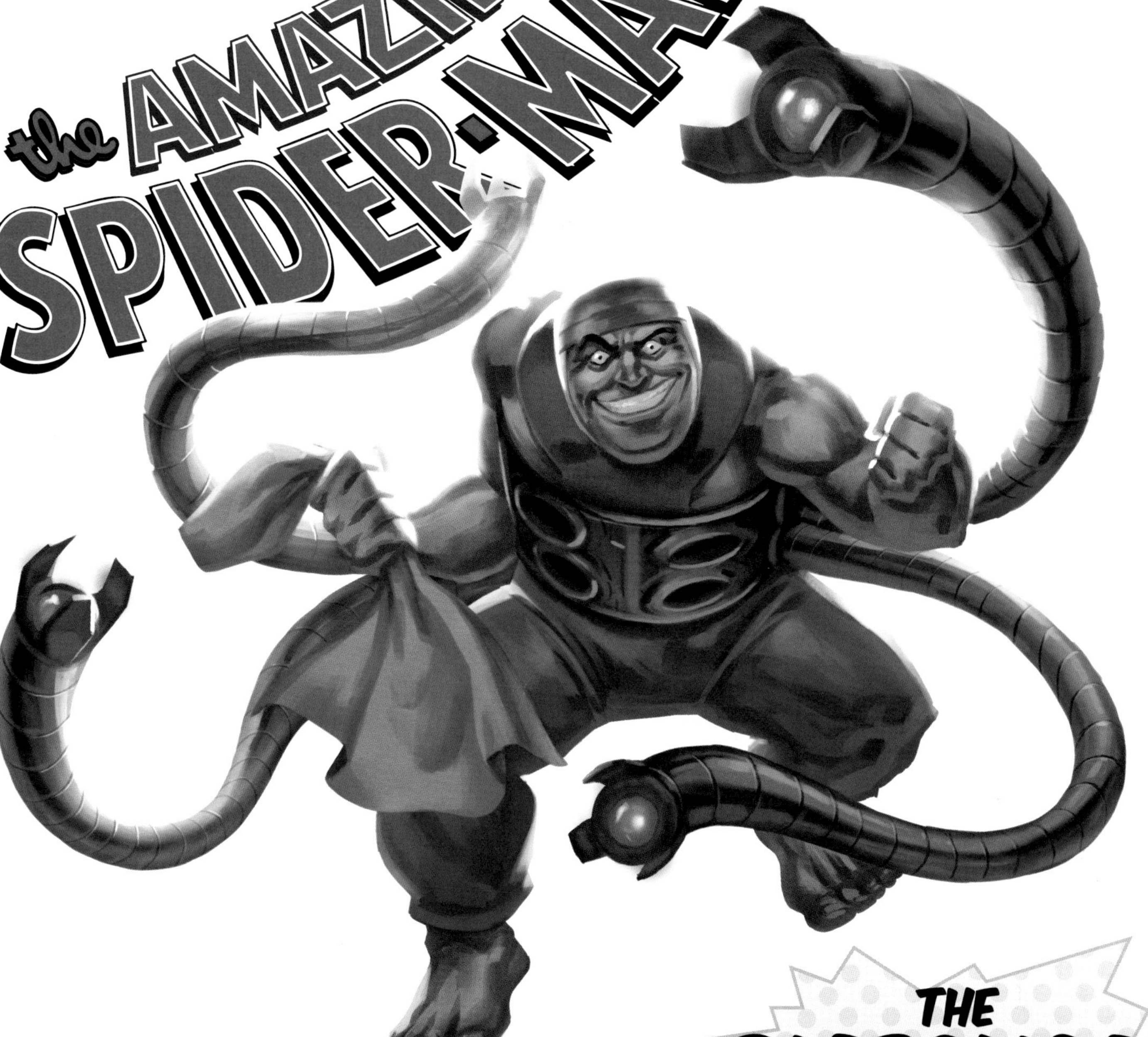

The Diabolical Doctor Octopus

For the first time in a long time, Peter Parker felt like things were going his way. He had made it through another long week at Midtown High School. He broke up two robberies as the Amazing Spider-Man. And on top of that, he was on time for work! Peter walked into the busy lobby of *The Daily Bugle* with pictures from his latest adventure as Spider-Man. But little did he know, an experiment was happening across town that would change his life forever — an experiment that would create one of Spider-Man's greatest villains!

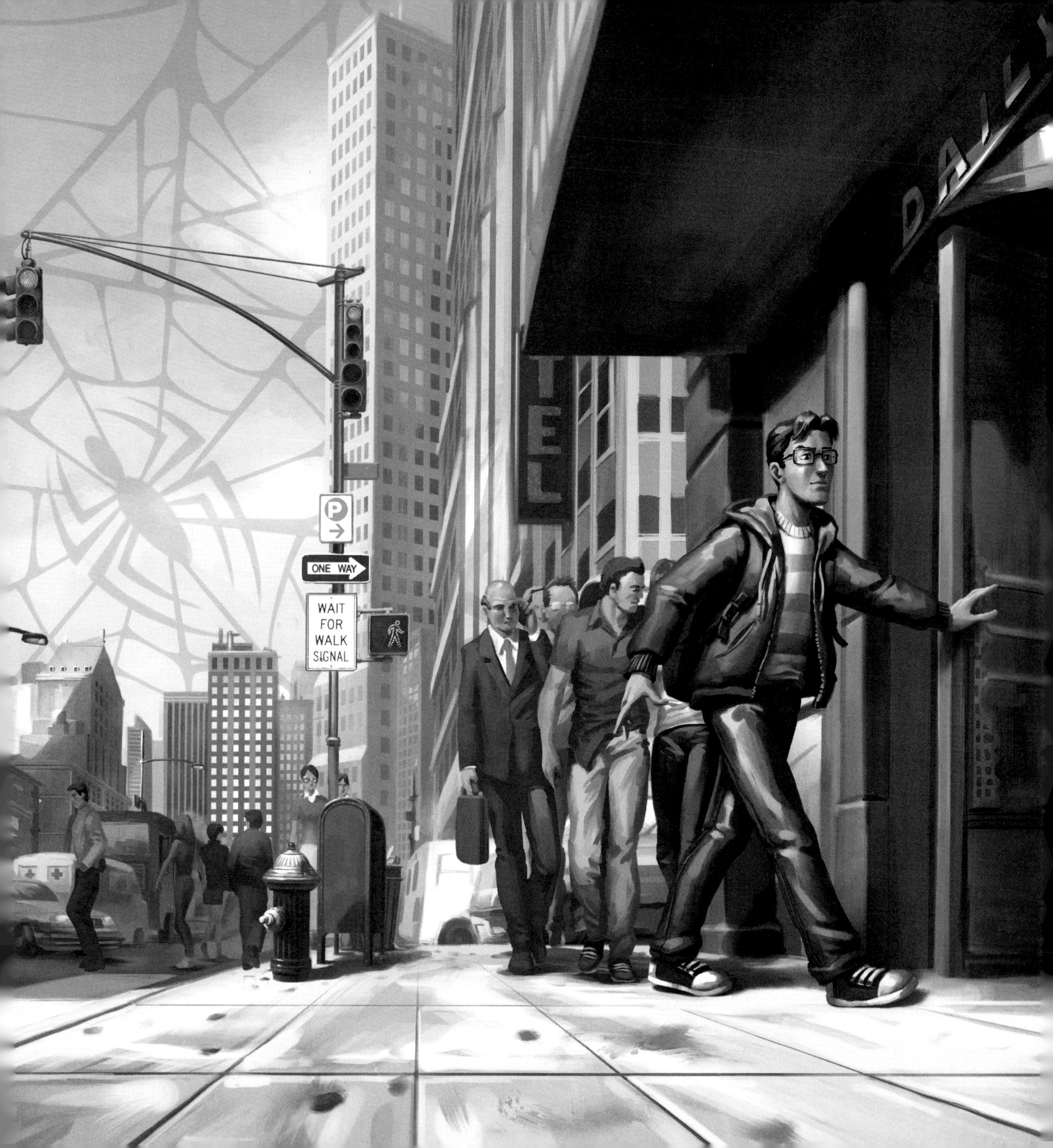
P
ONE WAY
WAIT FOR WALK SIGNAL

In a laboratory uptown, four mechanical arms were delicately handling dangerous chemicals. The robotic arms were attached to a giant belt connected to the brilliant scientist Dr. Otto Octavius. Because of the way the arms looked, he was given the name "Dr. Octopus." But no one called him this when he was around. Dr. Octavius was a brilliant man, but he also had a short temper!

Dr. Octavius' experiment was at its most delicate point. He was combining a series of radioactive chemicals that, when mixed properly, would help create a new power source! He was complimenting himself on a job well done, when the computers started showing something was wrong. "No!" Dr. Octavius yelled. "This can't be!"

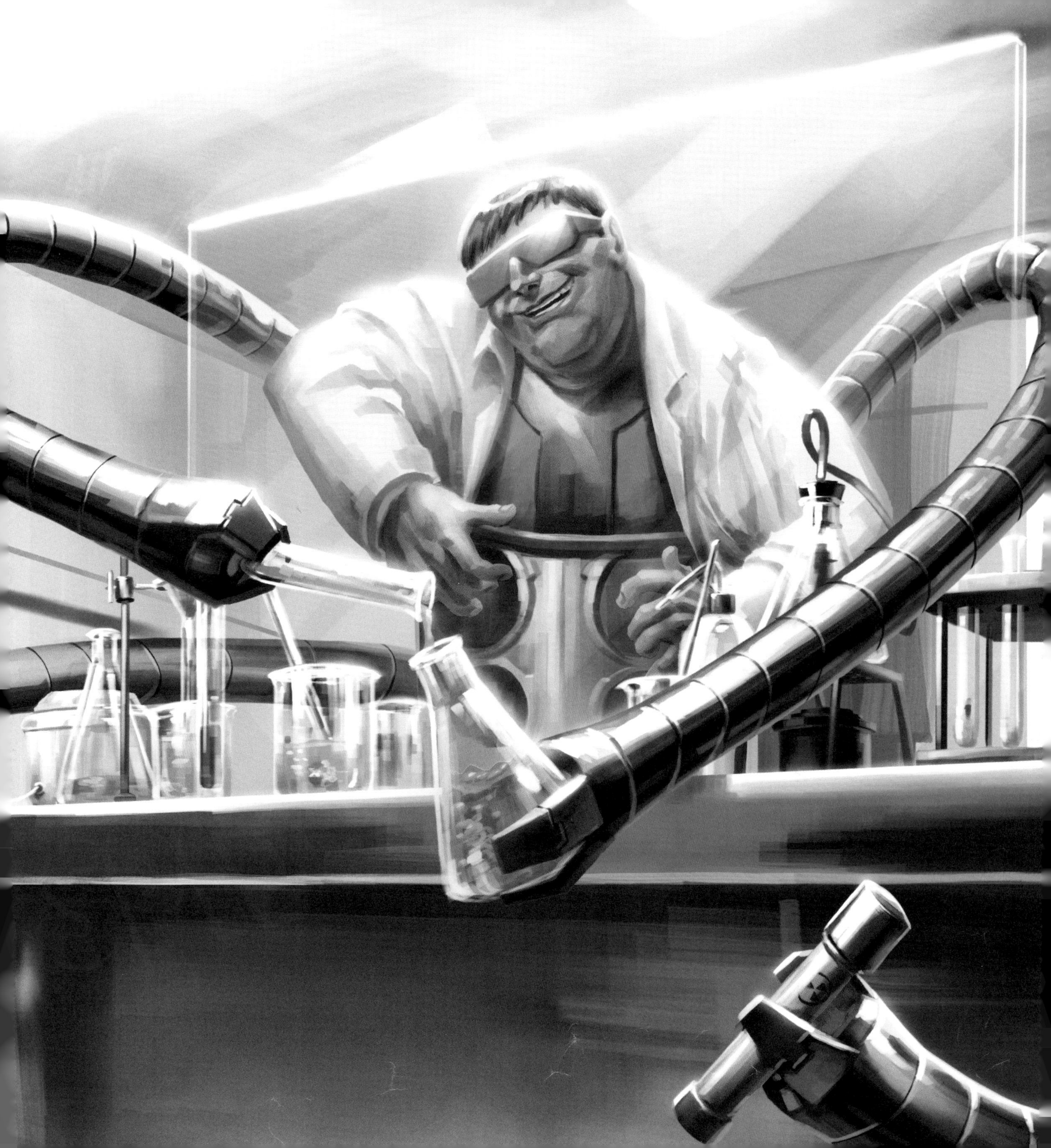

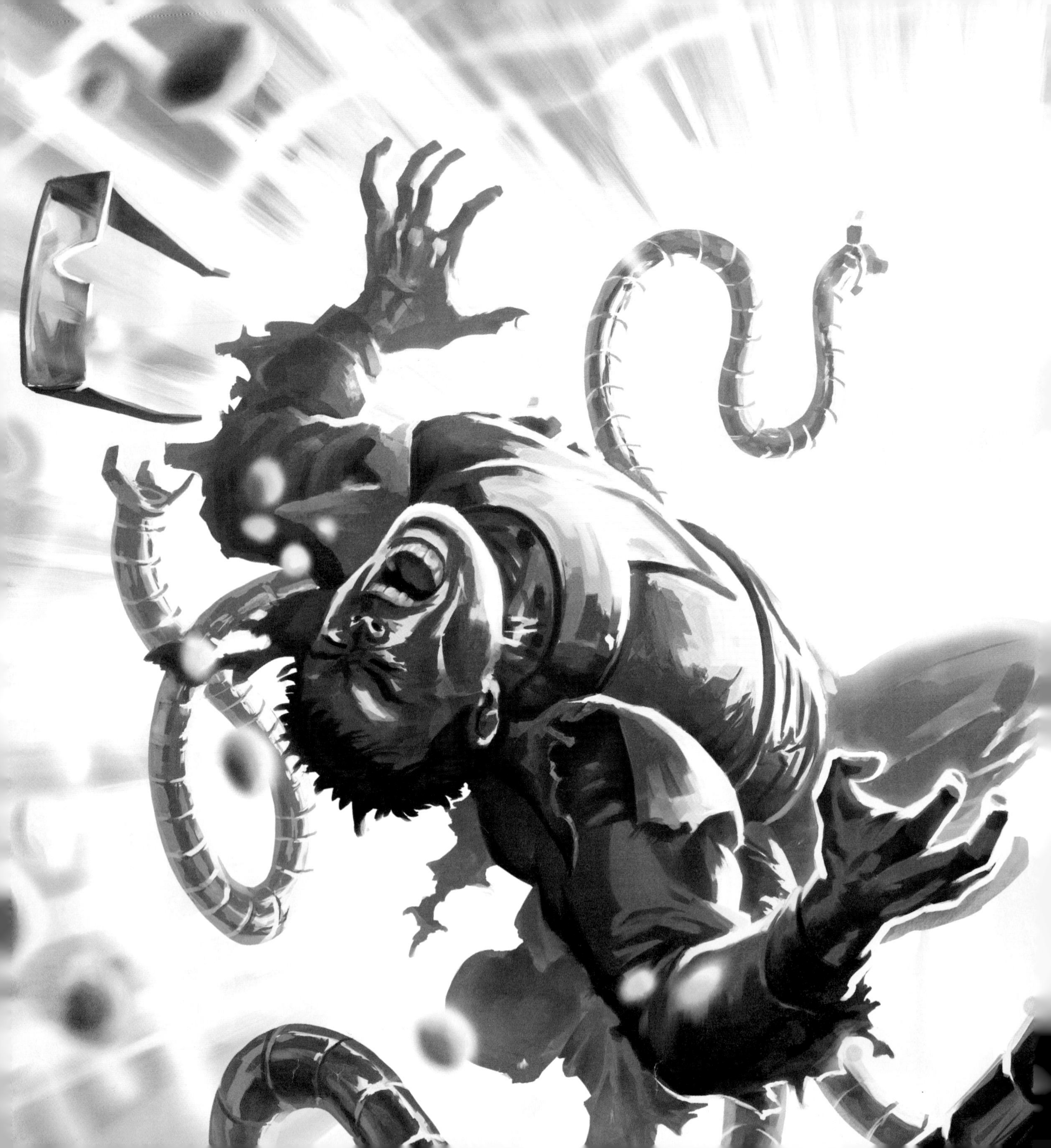

Suddenly there was a giant explosion! The blast knocked Dr. Octavius across the room.

When he woke up, Dr. Octavius had no idea where he was. He looked down and realized his mechanical arms were still attached. Two doctors quickly appeared in his room. They explained that the force from the explosion had permanently attached the arms to his body! But Dr. Octavius stopped paying attention. Fools, he thought. Why am I being held here by people who are clearly not as smart as me?

As Dr. Octavius became angrier, his mechanical arms started to come alive. It was incredible! He felt like he had a greater control than ever before. He moved them as if they were his own arms and legs! The doctors tried to get him to lay back down, but with a burst of strength, he used his mechanical arms to pull himself straight out of the bed.

"You can't keep me here!" he roared. "Nothing can keep me from my work!"

"Parker!" yelled Peter's boss J. Jonah Jameson. "There's been an accident at a lab uptown. Some egghead scientist blew himself up and busted out of the hospital. The police are chasing after him and I need pictures for tomorrow's front page!"

Peter was happy to get more work. He needed the money to help Aunt May. "Sure thing, Mr. Jameson," he said. "But do you think I could get a raise?"

Jameson cut him off. "Kid, you're lucky I'm giving you a job!" Peter sighed, grabbed his camera, and headed out the door.

Peter arrived at the laboratory where Dr. Octavius had worked. "Run" yelled someone fleeing the building. "Doctor Octopus has gone mad!"

"Doctor Octopus?" thought Peter. "Well, we'll see if Doc Ock can stand up to the friendly neighborhood Spider-Man!" He changed into his Spider-Man costume and climbed up the side of the building.

Inside, Doc Ock was terrorizing the helpless scientists. I have to save them, Spidey said to himself. He only had a few seconds to act!

Spider-Man burst through the window, startling Doc Ock! The villain whirled around, his arms ready to attack. "Spider-Man!" yelled Doc Ock, picking up a chair with one of his arms and throwing it at Spidey. "Do you think I'd let a wall-crawling freak stop my genius plans?"

Spidey dodged the projectile and quickly moved between Doc Ock and the hostages. "I don't think you're really in a place to call anyone a freak. . ." But Spider-Man had underestimated just how fast Doc Ock's robotic arms were! Before he knew it, Doc Ock had grabbed Spidey and thrown him out the window!

Spider-Man crashed to the ground, stunned! Wow! He's strong! Spidey thought. Maybe I'm not strong enough to defeat him. . . .

Suddenly, the captured scientists ran from the building. Those people wouldn't have escaped if I hadn't been going toe-to-toe with Doc Ock, he thought.

Spider-Man couldn't give up. He picked himself up and climbed back into the building. But Doc Ock had set up a series of traps! Spidey was able to dodge and disable the machines with the help of his spider-sense, but Doc Ock grabbed the hero with his mechanical arms!

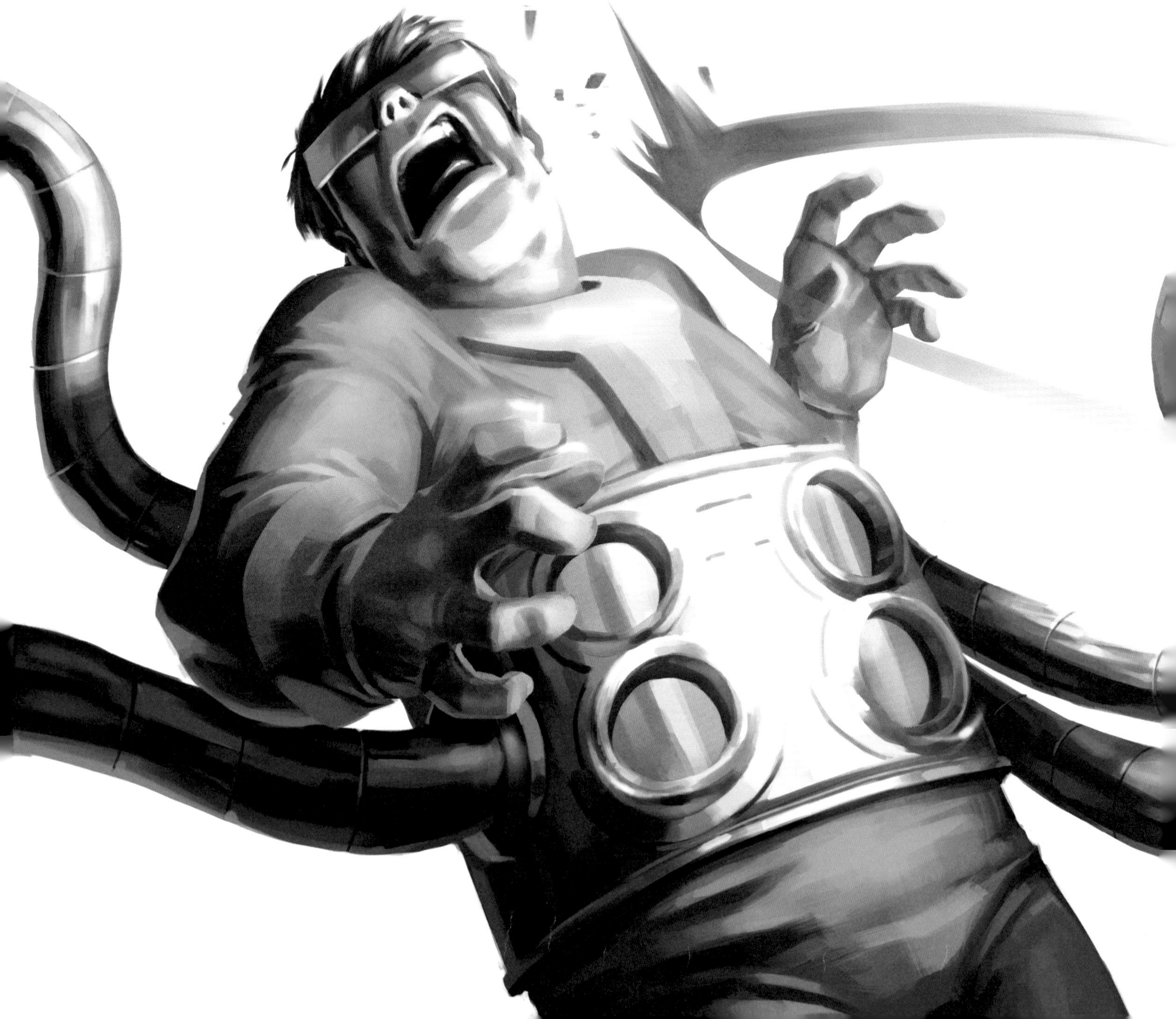

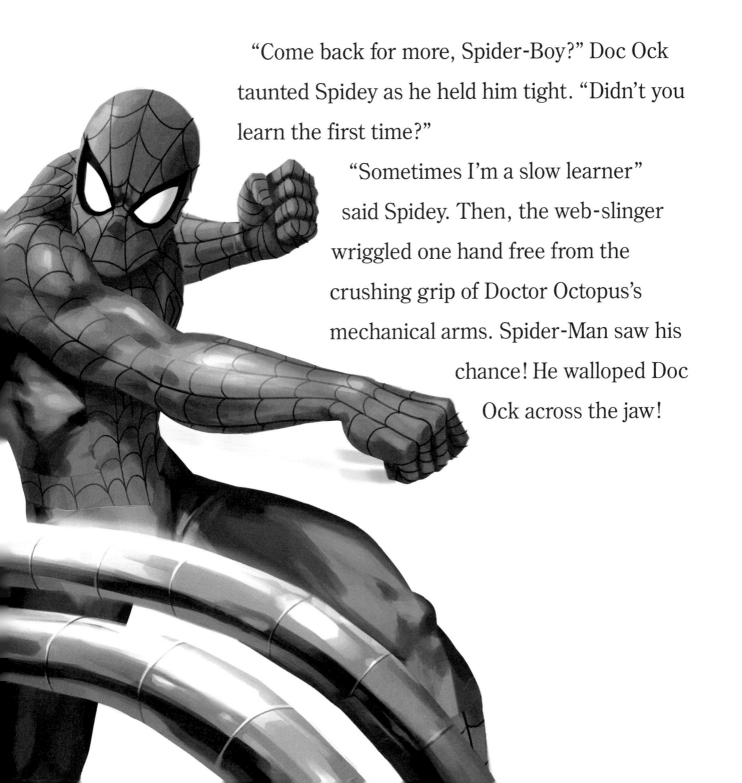

"Come back for more, Spider-Boy?" Doc Ock taunted Spidey as he held him tight. "Didn't you learn the first time?"

"Sometimes I'm a slow learner" said Spidey. Then, the web-slinger wriggled one hand free from the crushing grip of Doctor Octopus's mechanical arms. Spider-Man saw his chance! He walloped Doc Ock across the jaw!

Spider-Man had done it! While Doc Ock was stunned, he used his webbing to tie up the villain. Then the wall-crawler hung Doctor Octopus from the ceiling and headed out to get the police. Spider-Man had even managed to get some pictures for *The Daily Bugle* before the police arrived. It was a job well done for both Peter Parker and the Amazing Spider-Man!

MARVEL

the AMAZING SPIDER-MAN™

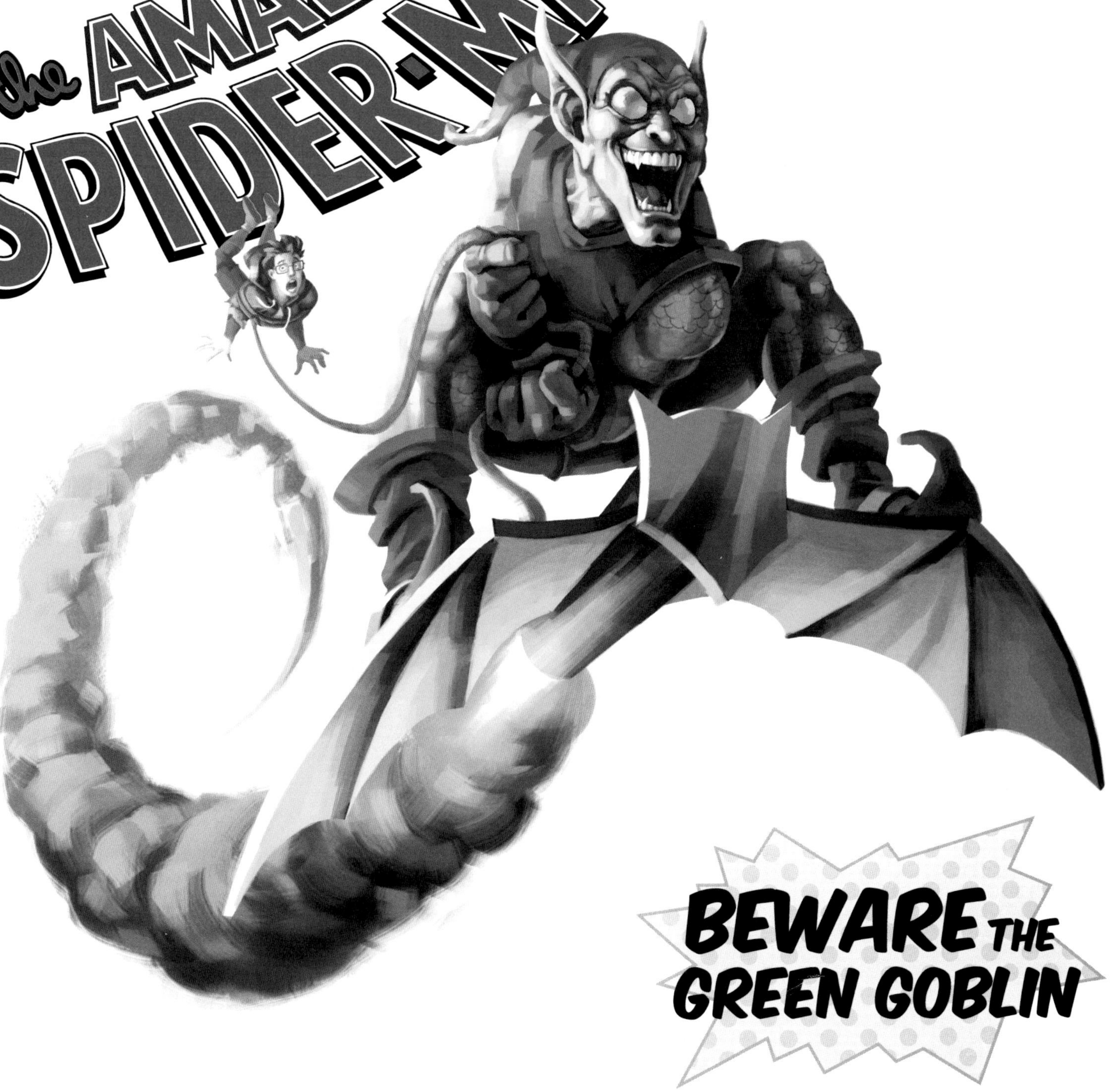

BEWARE THE GREEN GOBLIN

For Peter Parker, being a high school student meant studying in the library, hanging with his friends, and sometimes dealing with the school bully.

"What are you reading, bookworm?" said Flash Thompson as he yanked *The Daily Bugle* from Peter's hands. This made Peter very upset. *If Flash knew I was also Spider-Man, he'd think twice about being a bully,* Peter thought.

Suddenly, Peter's best friend, Harry Osborn, ran over. "You won't believe this!" he said. "I just heard on the radio that the Enforcers broke into the Empire State Building!"

Peter fought the Enforcers once before and knew the police would need all the help they could get. Peter dashed into an alley behind the school...and seconds later, the Amazing Spider-Man was swinging from skyscraper to skyscraper, high above the streets of New York City!

Peter loved being Spider-Man and saving the day. He felt like he was ready for anything. But today, he also felt that someone was watching him....

When Spider-Man arrived at the Empire State Building, the Enforcers were waiting!

Montana tried to snare Spidey with his lasso. "Gonna catch me a Spider-Man!" he cried. But Spidey was quick! He dodged the lasso and leaped out of Montana's reach. "Get 'em, Ox!" cried Montana.

Next, Ox tried to throw a large garbage can at Spider-Man. But before it could hit Spidey, he spun a web and flung the garbage can back at Ox, knocking him to the ground!

Suddenly Spidey's spider-sense tingled. When he turned around, he saw Dangerous Dan toss a strange grenade at him. But Spider-Man leaped over the green explosion and knocked out the villain!

"Sorry, boys, the party's over," Spider-Man called out as he tied up the Enforcers with his spider webs. "But don't worry, you'll have a long time to think about your next get-together — in prison!"

As he swung away, Spider-Man yelled to the police, "They're all yours, officers!"

Spider-Man landed in an alley and quickly put on his regular clothes over his Spider-Man costume. But not quickly enough.

The Green Goblin had quietly followed Peter back to Aunt May's house in Forest Hills, Queens, and had seen him change into Peter Parker. He now knew Spider-Man's secret identity!

"Spider-Man!" the Green Goblin hissed to Peter. "So nice to finally meet you!"

What happened to my spider-sense? Peter thought. I bet that strange gas from Dangerous Dan's grenade had something to do with this!

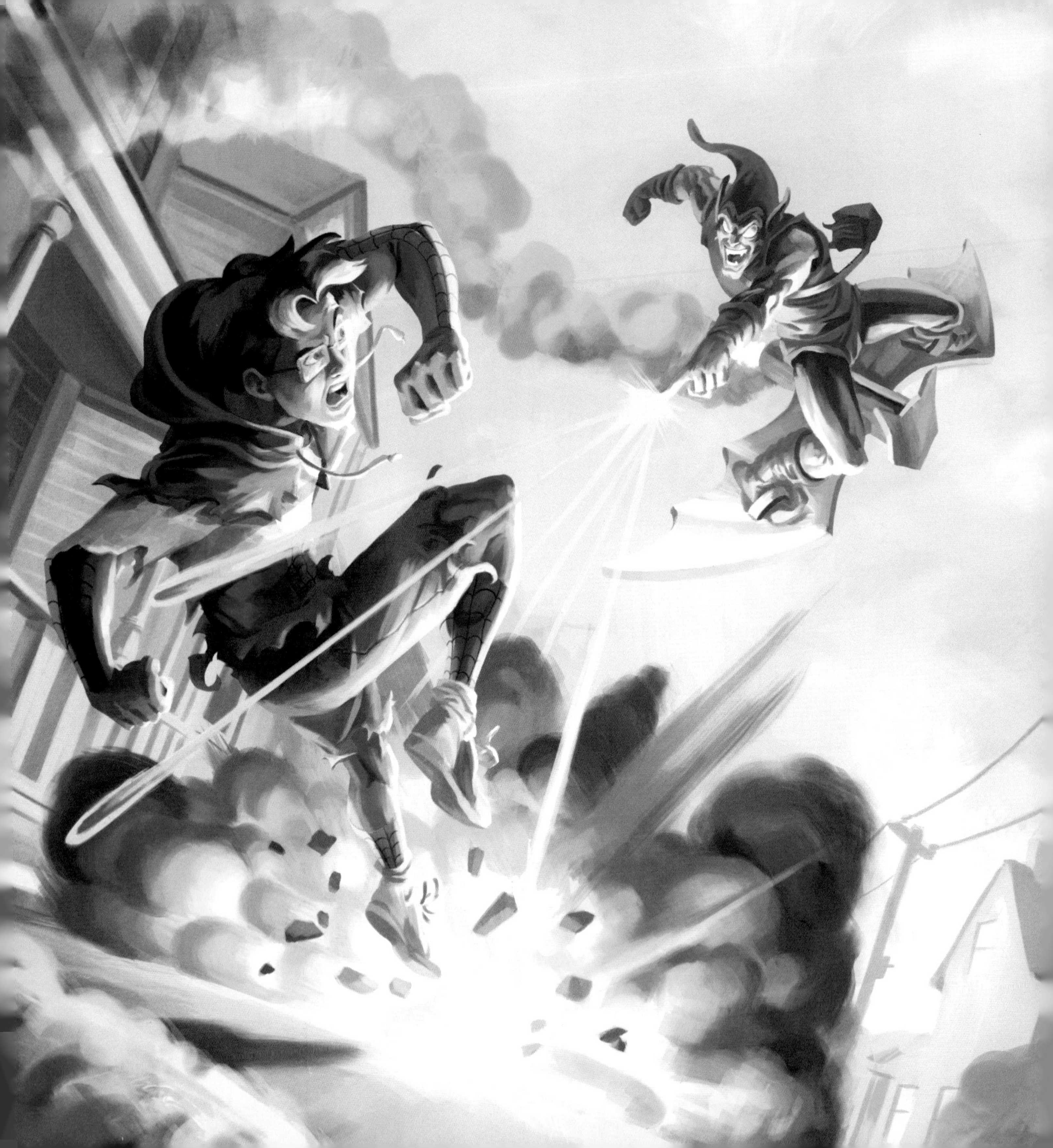

Suddenly, the Green Goblin attacked! He swooped down on his goblin glider and tossed several pumpkin bombs at Peter. Some pumpkins contained green gasses, while another spread black smoke. Others were small explosives. Peter dodged as many pumpkin bombs as he could, but without his spider-sense to warn him of danger, Peter tired himself out and was easily defeated.

"You're coming with me, web-head!" the Goblin hissed as he captured Peter!

Peter soon found himself inside the Goblin's secret lair.

"Hello, Peter Parker. . ." said a familiar voice. When Peter looked up, he could not believe his eyes. The Green Goblin was Norman Osborn—his best friend Harry's father!

Peter had to escape. But the only way to do that was to distract the Goblin long enough so he could break free.

"So, how'd you become a Halloween costume, Green Goober?" Peter said. This made Norman very angry.

"I'll tell you exactly how I became the Green Goblin!" Norman hissed.

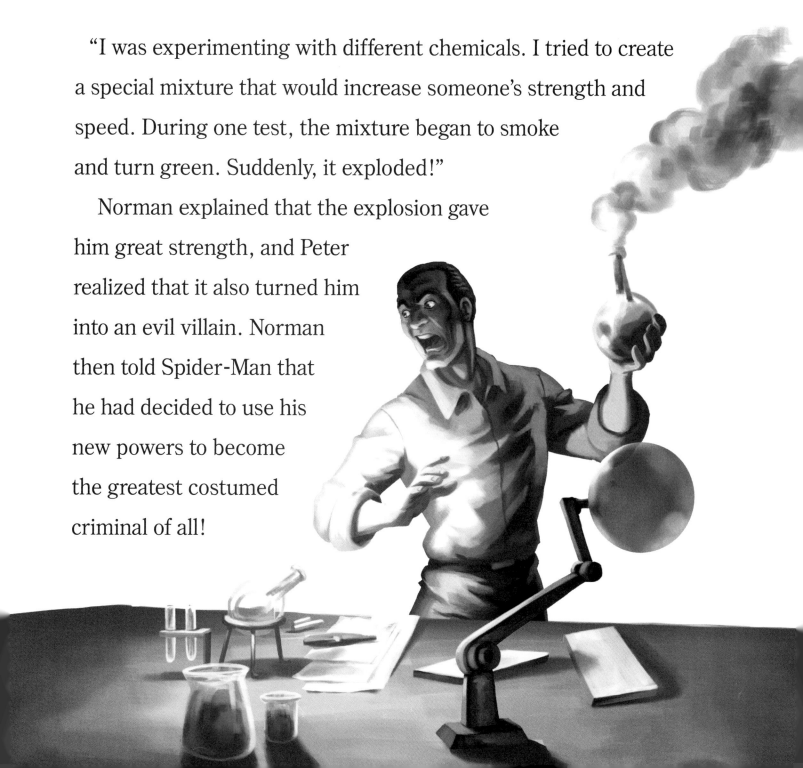

"I was experimenting with different chemicals. I tried to create a special mixture that would increase someone's strength and speed. During one test, the mixture began to smoke and turn green. Suddenly, it exploded!"

Norman explained that the explosion gave him great strength, and Peter realized that it also turned him into an evil villain. Norman then told Spider-Man that he had decided to use his new powers to become the greatest costumed criminal of all!

Norman flashed a sinister smile. His story reminded him just how strong he really was. And now, he wanted to prove it!

Norman put his Green Goblin mask back on and turned to Peter. "Time to stop you once and for all!" He pulled a lever and freed Peter from the chair so that he could defeat Spider-Man. This was Peter's chance! He quickly put on his mask.

It was web-slinging time!

The Green Goblin tossed several pumpkin bombs at Spider-Man. They exploded all around the web-slinger, but this time he was ready! He flipped and twisted out of harm's way.

"You may be quick, Spider-Punk, but I'm quicker!" the Goblin said.

Spidey spun a web and shot it at the Green Goblin's face. "Can it, Gobby!" Spider-Man said.

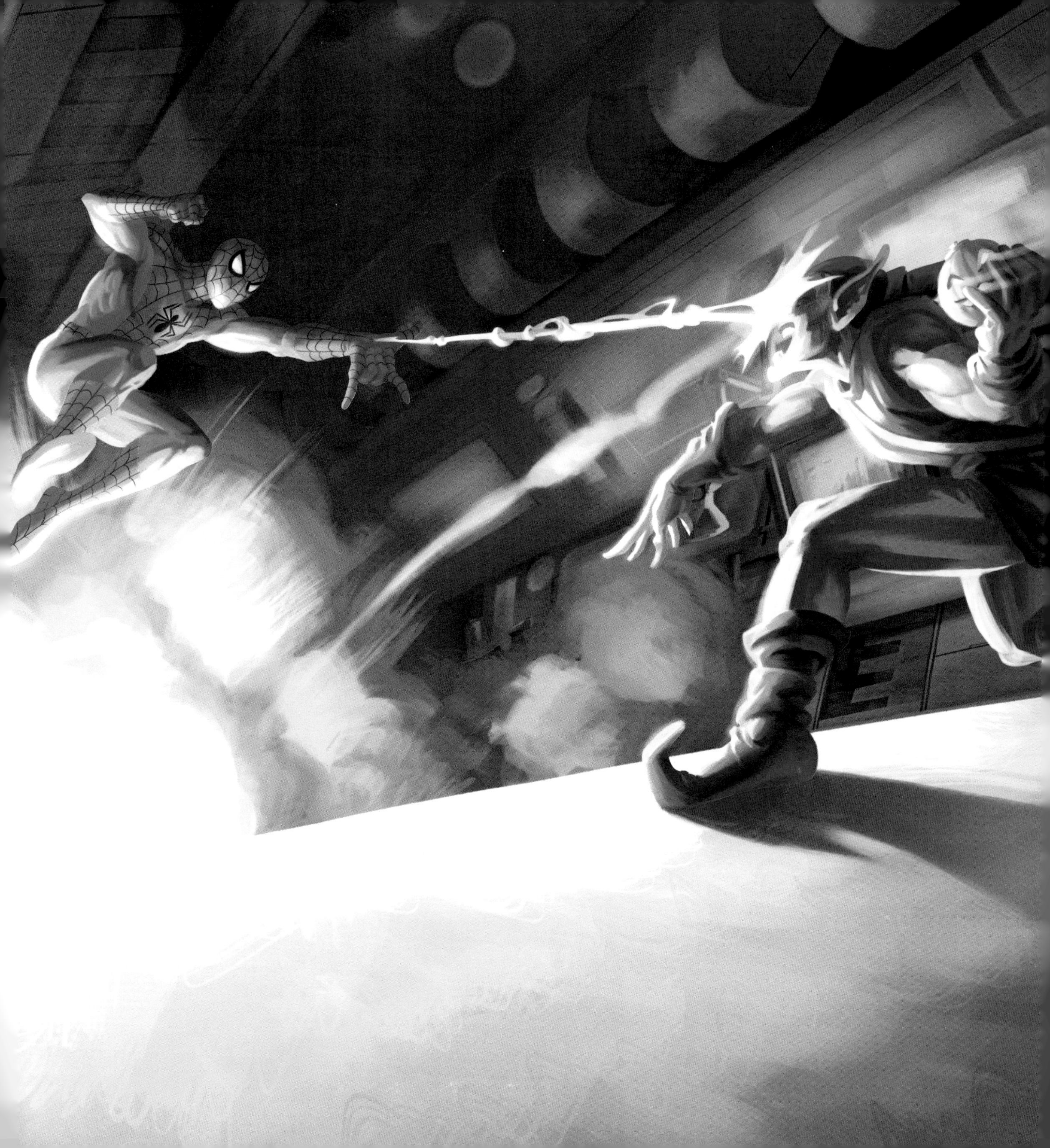

Blinded by the web, the Green Goblin stumbled backward. He knocked over several vials of dangerous chemicals. Suddenly a huge explosion rocked the lab!

"No — not again!" the Green Goblin cried.

When the smoke cleared, Spider-Man knelt down to the fallen Green Goblin and removed his mask.

"What happened?" asked a confused Norman Osborn. "Where am I? And who are you?"

He doesn't remember anything! Spider-Man thought. My secret identity is safe!

Norman Osborn would
no longer cause chaos
and mayhem as the Green
Goblin. Spider-Man had
saved his best friend's
father, his own secret
identity, *and* the city!

Well, Spider-Man
said to himself,
all in a day's work for —

"Help!" cried a voice from
the streets below. "That guy stole my purse!"

Spider-Man shook his head. I guess a Super Hero's
work is never done! Peter thought before exclaiming,
"Spider-Man to the rescue!"

MARVEL

the AMAZING SPIDER-MAN™

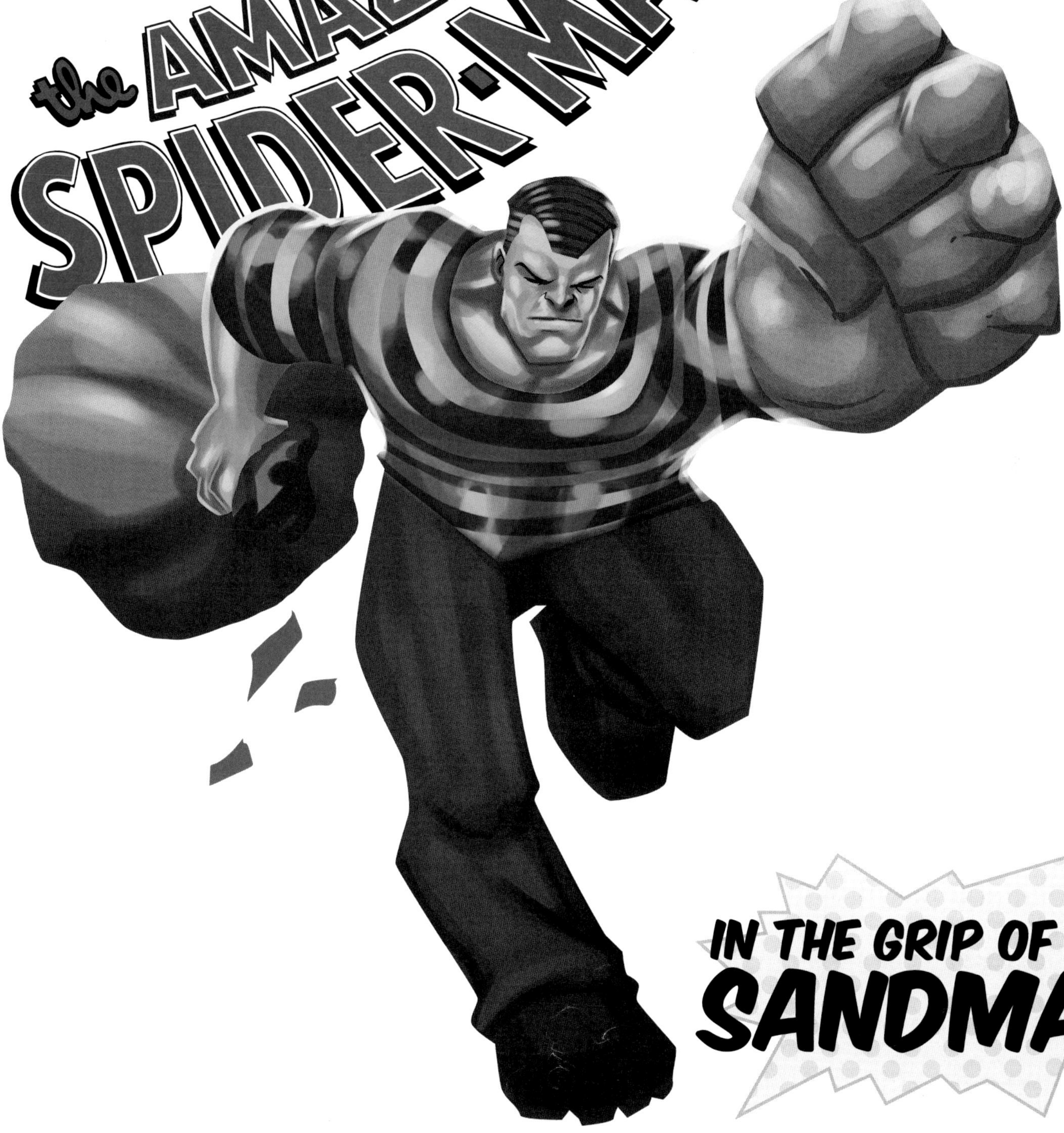

IN THE GRIP OF THE SANDMAN

The sound of police sirens caught Spider-Man's attention. Living in New York City, you heard sirens all the time. But until Peter Parker had become Spider-Man, he barely even noticed them. Now he always noticed. Because each siren might mean it was time for Spider-Man to come to someone's rescue.

Spider-Man saw several police cars rushing down the street. Then he saw a man running across a rooftop.

I'll bet he's the one the police are after, Spider-Man thought. Well, maybe the friendly neighborhood Spider-Man should pay him a little visit.

Spider-Man swung down and landed in front of the man. "Hi, there," he said. "I'm . . . hey, I recognize you! You're —"

"The Sandman," the man said with a growl. "And, yeah, the police are after me in nine states. Now get out of my way."

"No can do," Spider-Man said. "You're what we people in the Super Hero business call a bad guy. Also, you're big and everything, but it's highly unlikely you could — huh?"

Spider-Man threw a punch and his entire arm passed through the Sandman's chest.

"And *that's* how I got my name." The Sandman laughed. "But it's not *always* that way. See?"

The Sandman hit Spider-Man so hard, the web-slinger fell off the roof.

Spider-Man shot a web and swung back to the rooftop. Then he realized his mask was ripped.

Great, he thought. I can't chase the Sandman like this — everyone will see my face! I have to keep my identity a secret.

Later, at home, Peter repaired his mask.

"Ah, the life of a Super Hero," he grumbled. "Instead of chasing villains, I'm practicing my needlework."

Meanwhile, across town, the Sandman was also keeping busy — but in a much-less-legal way.

They think these banks are so tough to break into, he said to himself. But if air can get in, so can sand.

Turning his body into tiny grains of sand, he slipped through the tiniest of cracks and into the vault.

While he raided the vault, the Sandman remembered how he'd gotten his power. Once upon a time, he'd just been a petty criminal named Flint Marko.

One night, he managed to escape from prison. But in his rush to get away, he didn't notice he was going right into a dangerous area where scientific tests were being performed.

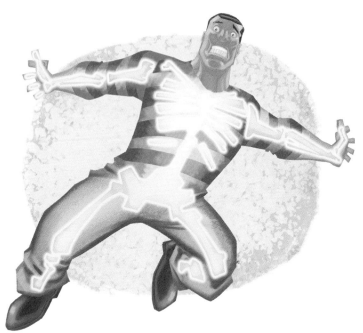

He walked right into the middle of one test. After being caught in an explosion, he was surprised to be alive.

He was even more surprised he could turn his body into sand . . . and back again.

"That should do it!" Peter said, putting the last stitch in his mask. Just then, he heard a news bulletin.

"Attention! The Sandman has been seen at the First National Bank of New York!"

"And right on time!" Spider-Man said.

Bullets may not hurt me and regular jail cells may not be able to hold me, the Sandman said to himself, but I still get tired.

The Sandman saw a school close by. "Perfect," he said, pushing his way in. "I always used to get plenty of sleep in school."

Spider-Man was hot on Sandman's trail and saw him enter Midtown High School.

Everything is going to depend on speed and timing, Spider-Man thought. My only chance is to catch him by surprise.

"Miss me?" Spider-Man said, putting everything he had into one giant uppercut.

It wasn't enough.

"Hey, that was pretty good," the Sandman said, rubbing his jaw. "This really is just like being back at school. Except that I didn't used to be able to do. . .this!"

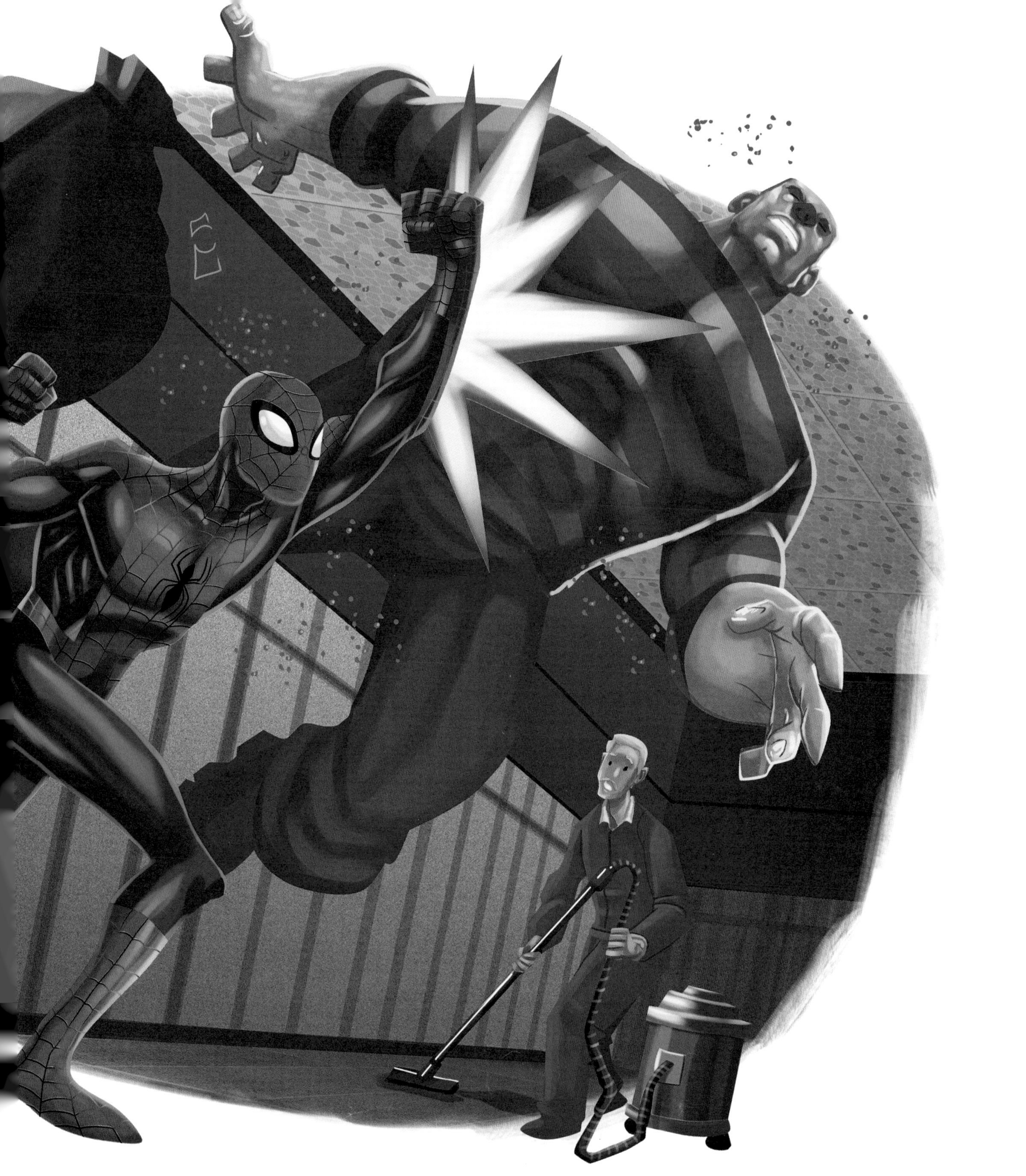

"Turning your fists into sledgehammers?" Spider-Man said, as he jumped out of the way. "That's pretty handy.

"All right, that was terrible, even by my standards," Spider-Man admitted.

Spidey looked around. His strength wasn't enough, and no web could hold sand. Was there something in the school he could use?

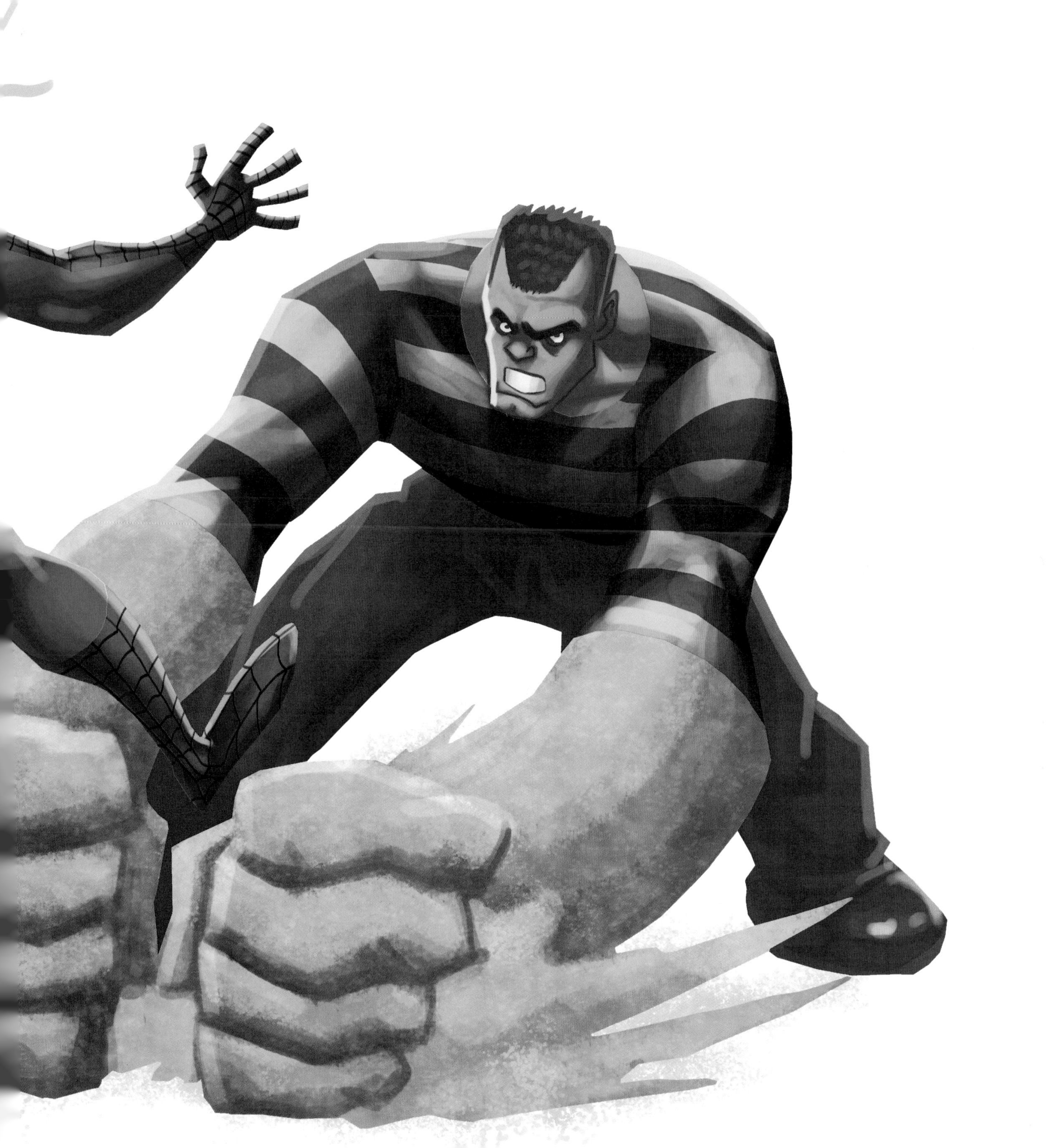

Ah-ha! he thought, spotting a janitor.
Spider-Man suddenly dropped to the floor and
swept the Sandman's legs out from underneath
him. "What can I say?" he asked. "I
get a kick out of bad jokes."

Spider-Man leaped over the fallen Sandman and shot a web at the janitor's vacuum. "Let's just make a clean sweep of it, shall we?" he said, flipping the switch.

"Hey. . .no!" the Sandman screamed as he was sucked into the machine.

"And with that," Spider-Man said, turning off the vacuum, "I give this school a clean bill of health."

"That was amazing!" the captain of the football team yelled.

"You're amazing," the school's head cheerleader purred.

"Please," Spider-Man said. "Nothing any. . . well, totally amazing Spider-Man couldn't have done."

"Man, Peter Parker's going to be sorry he missed this" one of the kids said.

"You kidding?" another student replied. "If he'd been here, he would have just been terrified!"

Spider-Man shook his head. No one could see it, but beneath the mask, Peter Parker was smiling.

MARVEL

THE AMAZING SPIDER-MAN™

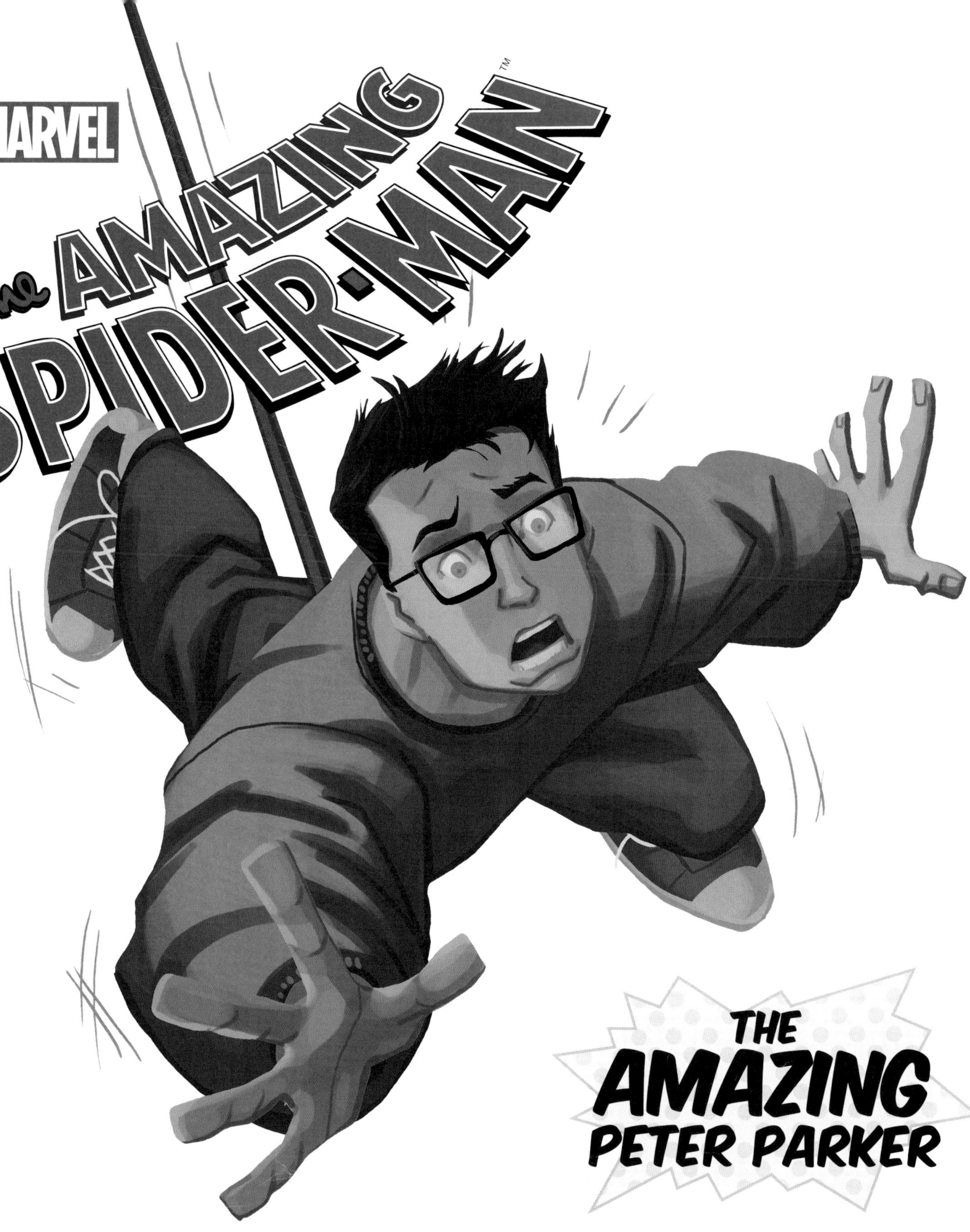

THE AMAZING PETER PARKER

After spending the night before last defeating the city's latest Super Villains, it seemed almost unavoidable that Peter Parker would sleep through his alarm clock. Rushing to the bus stop only to watch the school bus drive away, Peter quickly changed into his Spider-Man costume. Web-slinging through the streets, Peter managed to catch up to the bus.

That was a close call. I can't be late for my math test! Peter thought as he sighed to himself with relief under his mask.

But getting to school in time was the least of Peter's troubles. Flash Thompson was Spider-Man's number one fan—but Peter Parker was his number one target. Unfortunately for Peter, their teacher, Mr. Baer, did not notice Flash trying to cheat off of Peter's test.

And Peter's troubles continued in his English class. But his teacher, Ms. Roseman, had her back turned.

In gym class, Peter was unlucky enough to be on the same rock-climbing wall as Flash. Peter groaned to himself as Flash teased him.

"What's wrong, Puny Parker? Why so slow?" Flash taunted.

"Cut it out, Flash!" Peter said as he tried to stop the bully. Peter resisted using his powers because if he did — oh, boy! With Peter's super spider-strength, he could knock out Flash with his little finger!

Peter couldn't take it anymore, and by the time Flash was done laughing, Peter was already at the top of the rock wall.

"How did you do that?" Flash gasped as he looked up in shock.

But watching Flash's reaction didn't feel as good as Peter thought it would. Geez, why did I do that? I just showed off my wall-crawling ability to the whole class! All I need to do is shoot a web across the gym and then everyone would *know* I'm Spider-Man. Oh, well, what comes up must come down. . .Peter thought, and he let go of the wall.

Falling in midair is only half as much fun without my Spidey costume, Peter thought.

"Ha! Look at Puny Parker! He can't do anything right." Flash laughed. Soon everyone in the gym looked up to see what was going on.

"Parker, stop looking like you got caught in some spider web and pull yourself together!" the coach shouted from below.

Peter was back to acting like the clumsy kid everyone knew him to be.

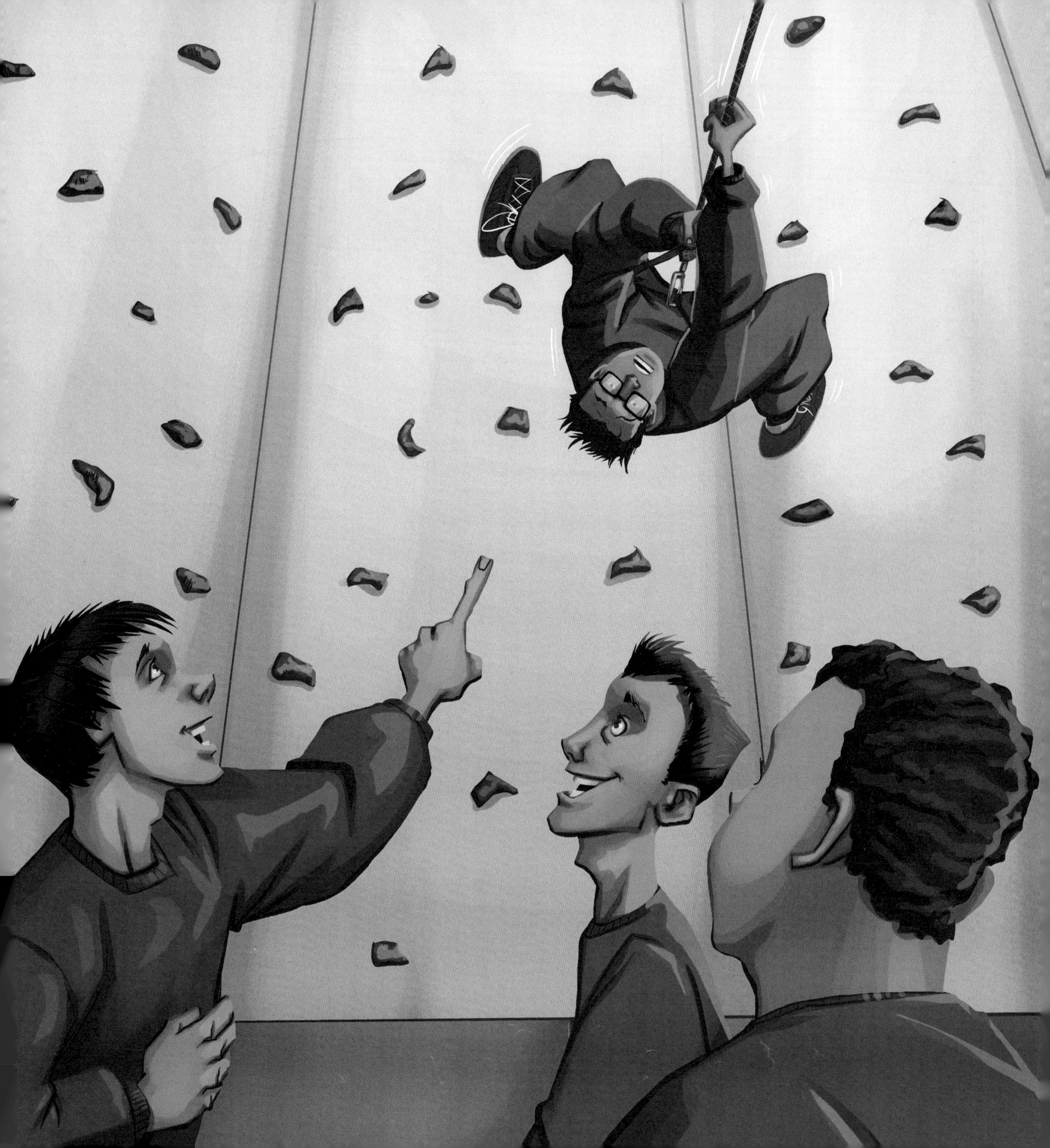

As Peter walked down the hallway later, he couldn't help but wish his classmates actually knew who he really was outside of school. If they did, then they wouldn't be laughing at him. Instead, he would be the coolest, most popular kid in school. Cheerleaders would actually look at him. And Flash Thompson would be the one they laughed at.

As Spider-Man, Peter outsmarted top-notch evil scientists, such as Doc Ock and the Green Goblin. But somehow Flash Thompson, a clown who didn't even have a diploma yet, found a way to get under his skin. But Peter couldn't let this bully get the better of him.

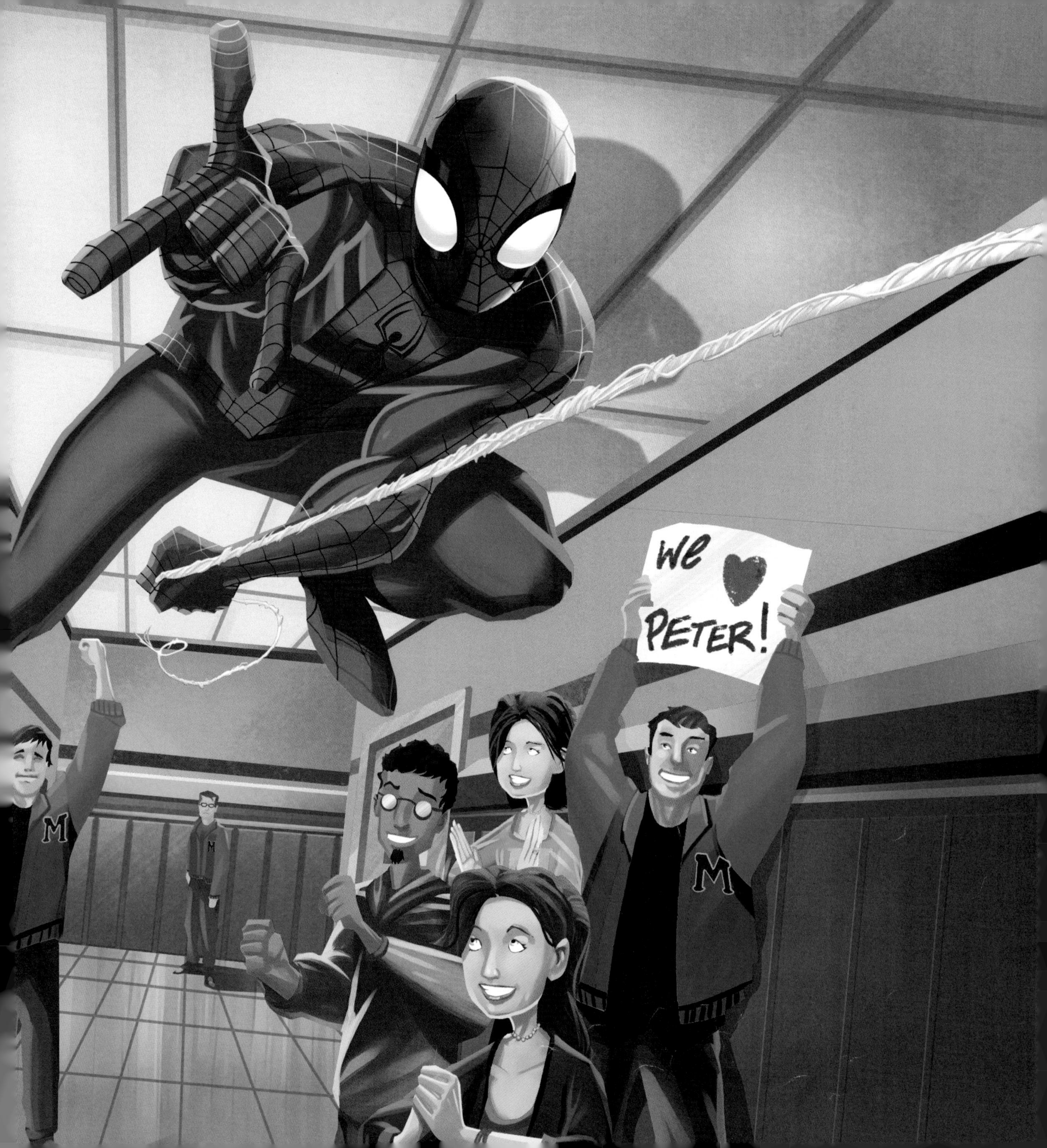
WE
PETER!

Battling the city's most evil villains while looking like a fool in gym class is all part of being a Super Hero, Peter thought. Peter realized how dangerous it would be if everyone knew his secret identity. His foes might try to hurt Aunt May — all because he wanted to use his super powers in school. He would rather have Aunt May safe and sound than have himself be popular. His family was more important and valuable than his status in high school.

Flash continued to bully kids even after school had ended. "What kind of junk are you reading?!" Flash said as he ripped a newspaper away from Harry Osborn.

"Chill out, Flash, I was only reading the comics!" Harry said.

"Liar! I know you were really reading about Spider-Man being a menace! Spider-Man is amazing! I totally would be an awesome sidekick for Spider-Man. I'm not clumsy like Parker over there." Flash laughed.

"But the real question is if Spider-Man would want *you* as his sidekick! I think Peter has a better chance than you, Flash!" Harry smirked.

Flash was shocked by Harry's insult and was determined to change Harry's mind.

Watching Flash and Harry argue, Peter grinned. He knew Spider-Man didn't need a sidekick. Besides, Peter had been pretty amazing all along, with or without his Spider-Man costume, and that's all that mattered.

MARVEL

the AMAZING SPIDER-MAN™

BIRTH OF THE LIZARD

Everyone was talking about a strange creature lurking in the Florida Everglades. It was called the Lizard, and it could walk and talk like a man! But no one could get a picture of the monster.

This Lizard fellow doesn't seem as tough as the Super Villains Spider-Man has battled, Peter Parker thought as he read *The Daily Bugle*. J. Jonah Jameson, Peter's boss at *The Daily Bugle,* would give him a huge, fat check in return for a photo of the Lizard. "Hmm, I got an idea. Get ready for your close up, Lizard!" Peter said. Soon he was off to Florida.

That's odd. My spider-sense is going off, but there's no danger, Spider-Man thought once he arrived in the swamp. He spotted a woman at a house nearby. Hoping she would have information about the Lizard, he web-swung over.

"Excuse me, have you seen an eight foot lizard?" Spider-Man asked the woman. She gasped, surprised by Spider-Man's visit, but frantically replied, "The Lizard? He's my husband, Dr. Curtis Connors!"

The name sounded familiar. Dr. Connors was a famous scientist and expert on lizards, especially the kind that could lose a limb and then grow a new one. Dr. Connors' wife explained that he had lost his own arm in an accident and was determined to create a serum using reptilian DNA that would grow back the arm he lost. And once he did, it seemed like the happiest moment of his life!

"I've really done it! This is the greatest medical feat of all time!" Dr. Connors said as he beamed with excitement.

But that all quickly changed once Dr. Connors realized he not only grew a new arm, but also sharp claws, rough, scaly skin, and a long green tail!

"What have I done?" he exclaimed in horror.

As he desperately tried to discover an antidote to change himself back, he became less like Dr. Connors and grew more like a cold-blooded lizard. Ashamed of his failure, he ran away into the darkness of the swamp.

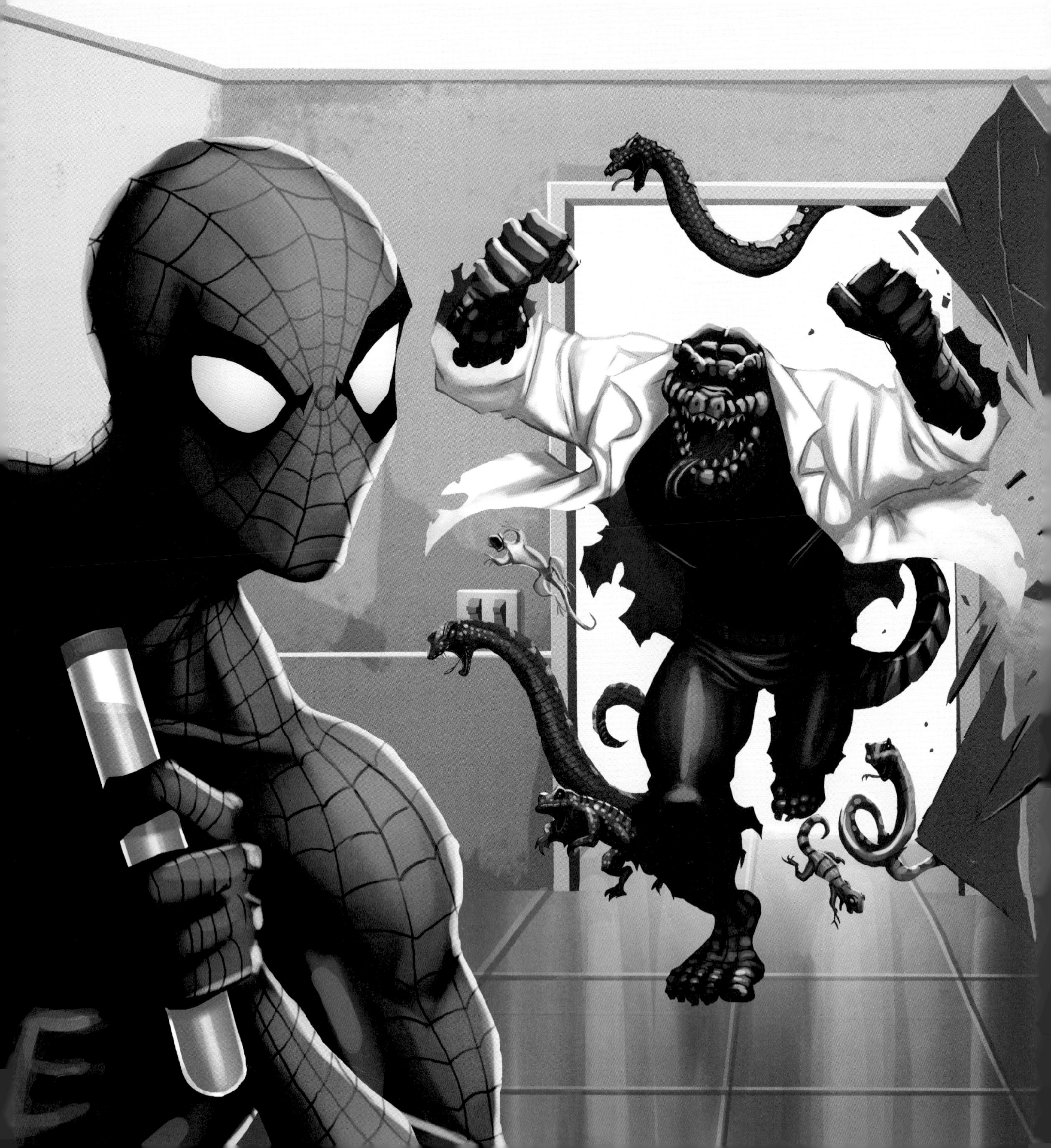

"I know I can find a way to cure Dr. Connors and turn him back into a human. . ." Spider-Man told the doctor's wife. Flash Thompson doesn't call me a science nerd for nothing! he thought as he studied Dr. Connors' notes.

"Just make sure not to hurt the Lizard, Spider-Man. . .after all, he's still my dad," Billy, Dr. Connors' son, told Spider-Man. But then Billy yelled, "Look!" It was the Lizard—and he bought a few scary looking reptile friends, too.

"What are you doing in my lab? And what are you doing with my family?" the Lizard yelled. Clearly he was very angry.

"Calm down, big guy. I'm just trying to help you out!" Spider-Man replied.

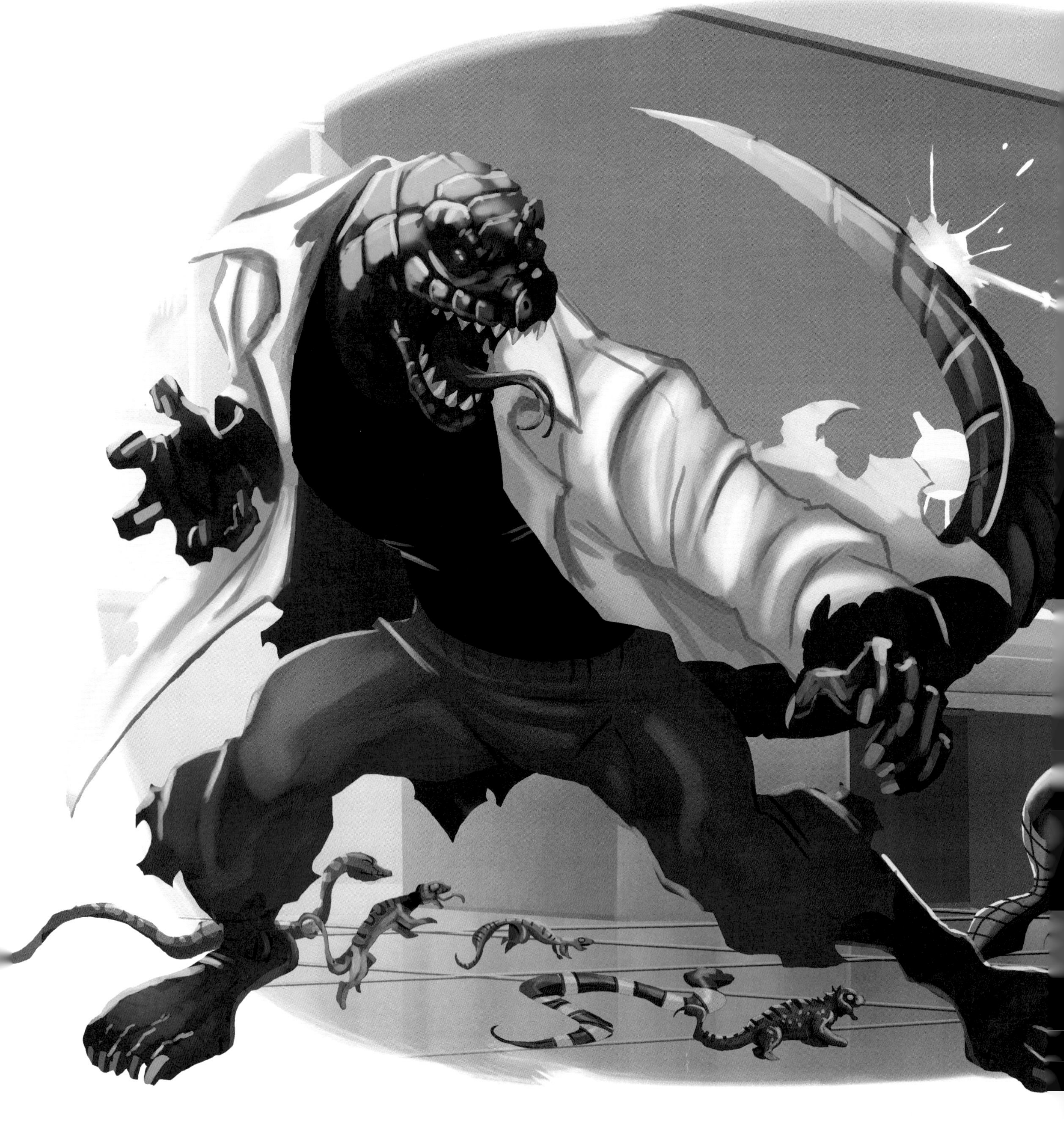

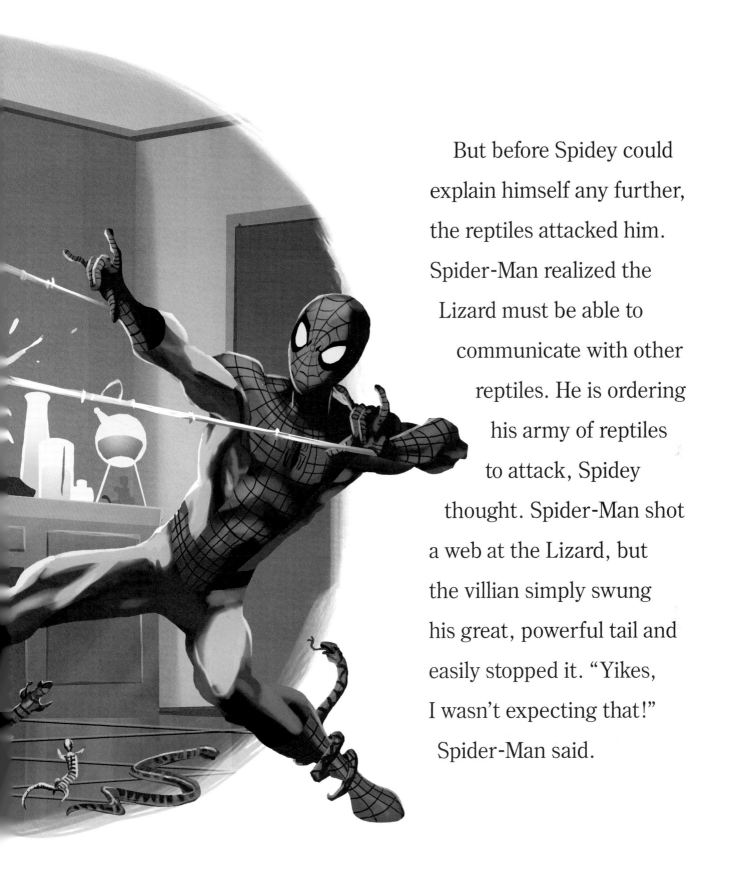

But before Spidey could explain himself any further, the reptiles attacked him. Spider-Man realized the Lizard must be able to communicate with other reptiles. He is ordering his army of reptiles to attack, Spidey thought. Spider-Man shot a web at the Lizard, but the villian simply swung his great, powerful tail and easily stopped it. "Yikes, I wasn't expecting that!" Spider-Man said.

Suddenly, the Lizard hurled a desk at Spider-Man like it was a baseball. "You've been lifting weights, haven't you?" Spidey asked as he jumped out of the way. Spider-Man tried punching the Lizard, but his reptile skin was as hard as armor. *Oof.* I think I just heard a few bones crack! Spider-Man thought.

"Now, it's time to finish you off!" the Lizard growled.

This is my only chance to save the Doc! Spider-Man thought.

"Here, I've got something that'll taste better than a spider!"

Spidey said. Acting fast, he took out a test tube and poured the

antidote into the Lizard's mouth.

The snakes that had wrapped around Spider-Man suddenly loosened and returned to the swamp. The Lizard was growing weak. The antidote was working! "Hey Lizard, smile for the camera!" Spider-Man said as he snapped a quick photo of his foe. And it was just in time, because Dr. Connors was back!

"Look, I'm human again!" Dr. Connors shouted with excitement.

As Billy and Mrs. Connors hugged Dr. Connors, the doctor thanked the spectacular Spider-Man. "You saved me. Without you, we would never be a family again. This is the happiest day of my life. Thank you. We'll never forget you!"

Back in New York, Peter was excited to show Mr. Jameson his photo of the Lizard. "So what do you think?" Peter said. But Peter didn't expect what happened next.

His boss simply shook his head and ripped the photo into millions of pieces. "You're wasting my time, Parker! How could you get such a close-up shot of the Lizard? This is a fake!" JJJ shouted. JJJ was stubborn, and Peter couldn't convince him otherwise. Well, at least I was able to help out Dr. Connors and his family, Peter thought, smiling to himself. That was more important than any giant check JJJ could have given him.

MARVEL

THE AMAZING SPIDER-MAN™

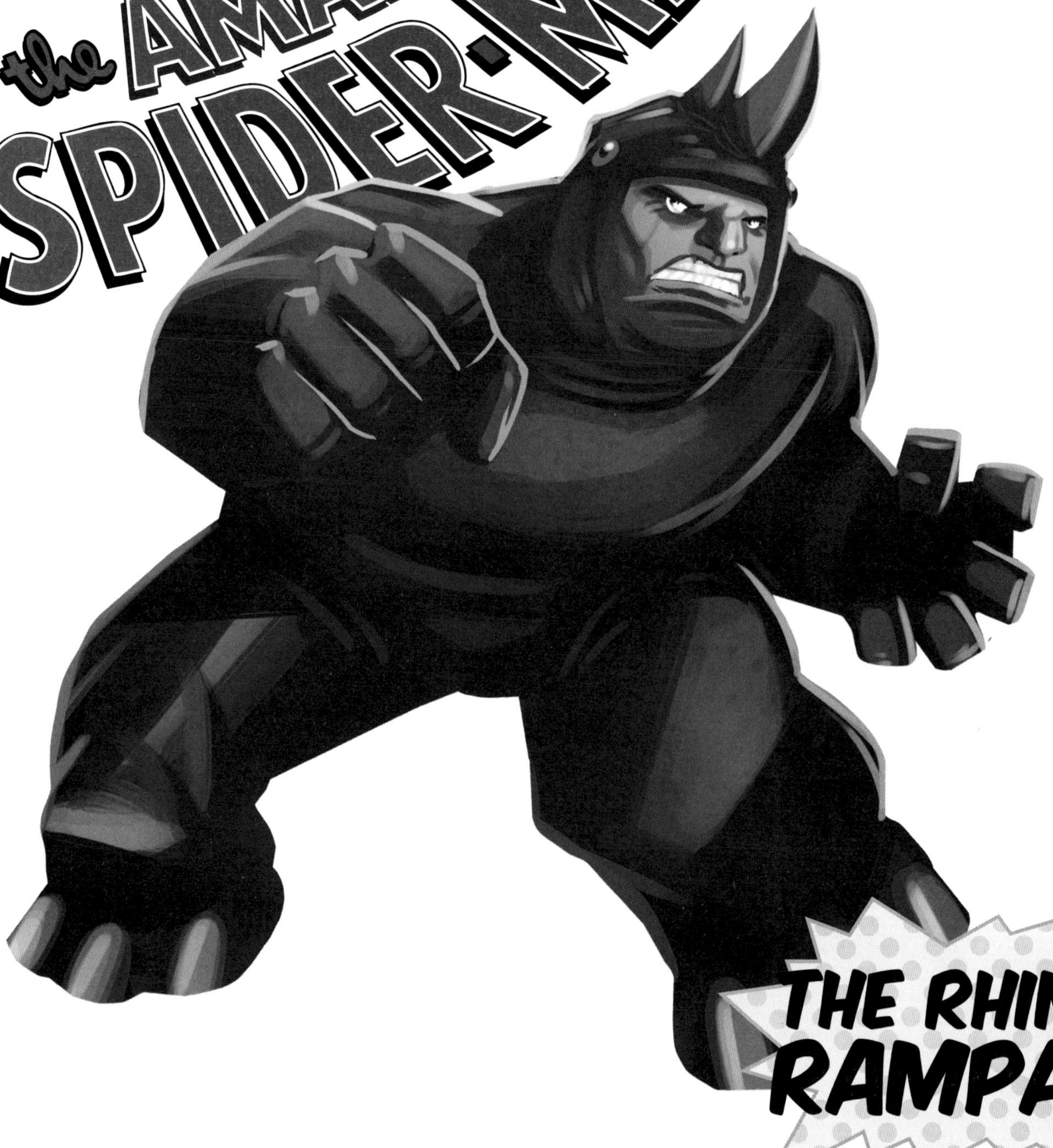

THE RHINO'S RAMPAGE

Peter Parker held up his Spider-Man costume. It was ripped from his last battle, and it needed a few repairs. Peter was about to fix it when he heard a loud knock at the door.

"Peter, dear, can I come in?" Aunt May said.

"Um, hold on, Aunt May!" Peter shouted nervously. He had to hide the costume before his aunt saw it! He threw it under the bed just as she walked in.

"Shouldn't you be getting ready?" his aunt asked.

Peter was confused. Then he remembered. He was supposed to have dinner at Mrs. Watson's and meet her niece, Mary Jane.

Soon, Peter stood in Mrs. Watson's living room, waiting.

Suddenly the doorbell rang.

Mrs. Watson turned and said, "Peter, I'd like you to meet my niece."

Peter's jaw dropped. Mary Jane was beautiful!

"Hi, tiger," Mary Jane said, as she smiled and walked through the door.

Aunt May and Mrs. Watson went to start dinner. Peter was still trying to figure out what to say to Mary Jane when a news alert flashed across the television screen.

"We interrupt this program to bring you important news," the anchor announced. "The Rhino is attacking Corona Park!"

The Rhino was one of Spider-Man's most dangerous foes! Alexsei Sytsevich was a crook who volunteered for a dangerous experiment. He had a strange chemical applied to his skin, which created a whole new skin on top of his — one that was as thick as a Rhino's and twice as strong! It had taken all of Spider-Man's strength to get him into prison in the first place. And now he was free — again!

"Oh, my gosh!" Mary Jane shouted, startling Peter out of his thoughts. "Flushing Meadows is so close. Wouldn't it be amazing to see the Rhino in person!"

Peter smiled. That wasn't a bad idea at all. He could stop Rhino and still go on his date with Mary Jane.

Minutes later, they arrived in the heart of Flushing Meadows, Queens. While Mary Jane raced forward, Peter held back. He had to figure out a way to change into his Spider-Man costume without Mary Jane learning his secret identity!

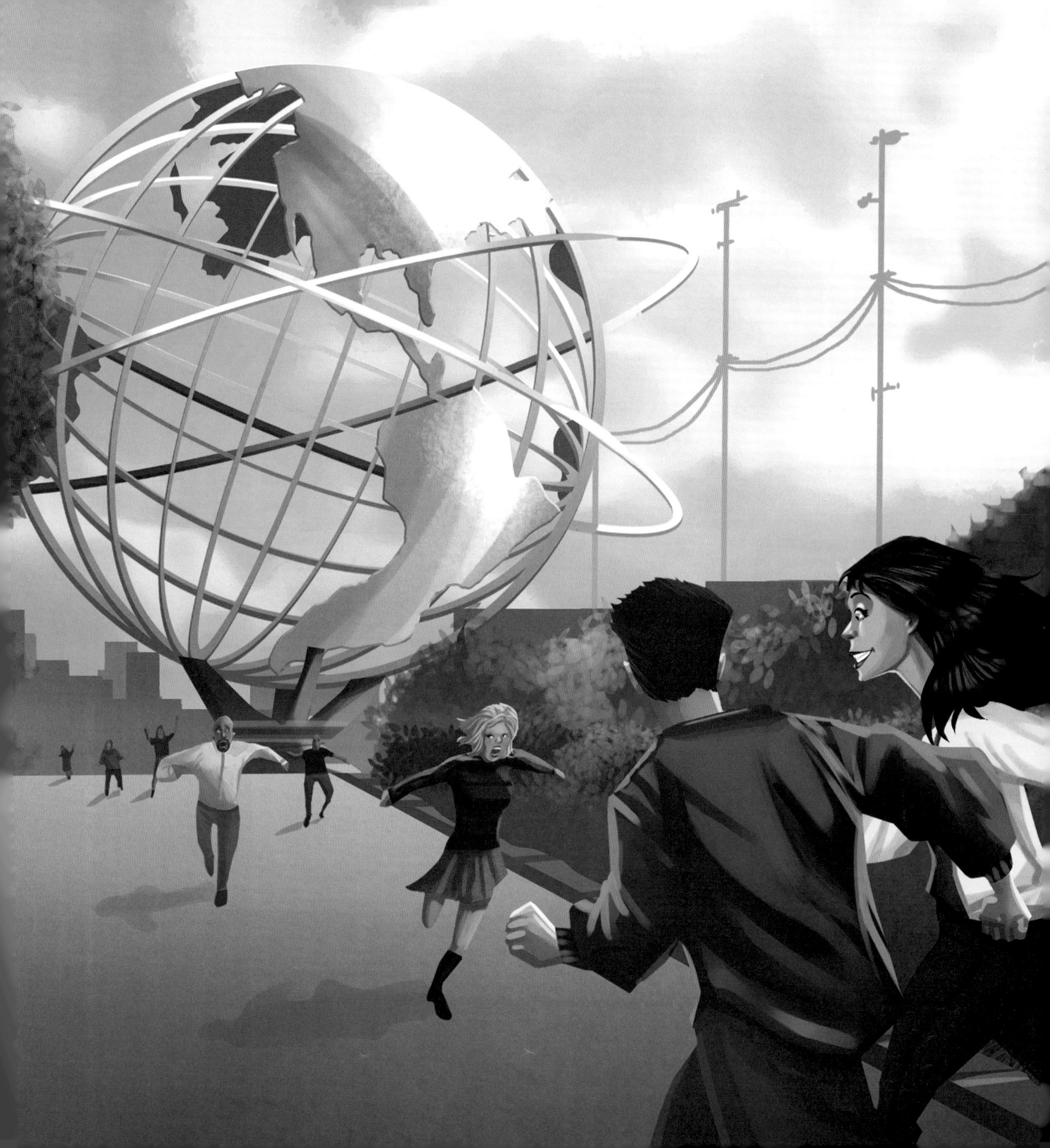

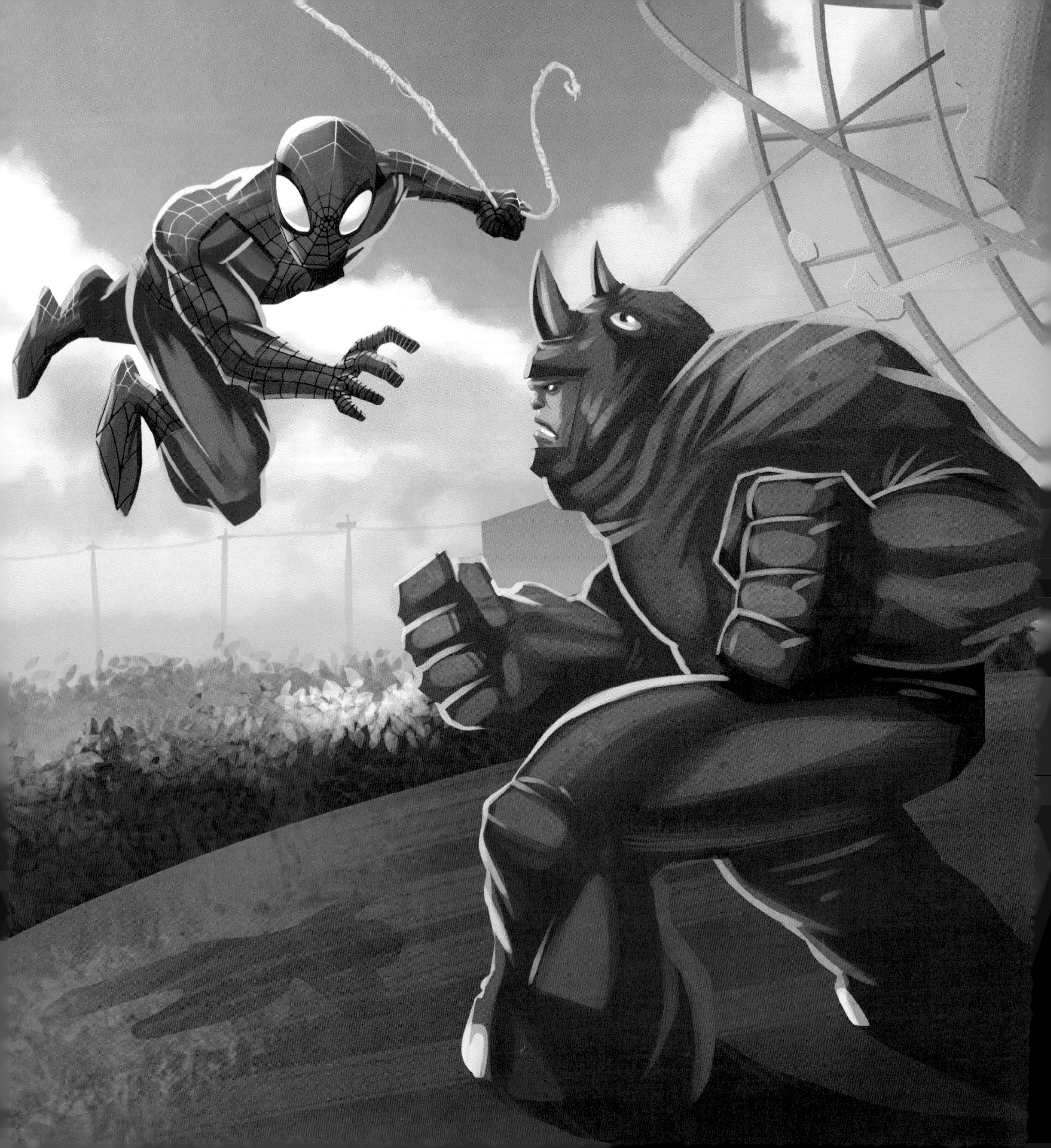

Peter told Mary Jane that he needed to get some pictures for *The Daily Bugle* and raced off to change into his Spider-Man costume!

Scaling one of the towers in the middle of the park, Spider-Man scanned the area. It didn't take him long to find the large beast. Using his webs, Spider-Man swung down in front of the Rhino.

"If you're trying to find your way back to jail," he said, "I'd be happy to take you."

The Rhino took a step back, surprised by Spider-Man's sudden arrival. He wasn't going to get beaten again. Raising his arms, the Rhino swung up at Spider-Man, knocking the wall-crawler back!

The Rhino threw another punch, and Spider-Man staggered. It was like being hit with cement block. Shaking it off, Spider-Man shot a web and swung up onto the top of the giant stainless steel Unisphere depicting the Earth. Spidey needed to think of something — and fast!

Spider-Man decided to use his speed to his advantage. The Rhino charged at the wall-crawler, who quickly jumped up, causing the Rhino to hit his head.

But the Rhino just shook it off. Then, before Spider-Man could stop him, the beast landed a mighty blow and thundered off. He'd escaped — for now.

During the fight, a piece of the Rhino's hard skin had flaked off. It was just the clue Spider-Man needed!

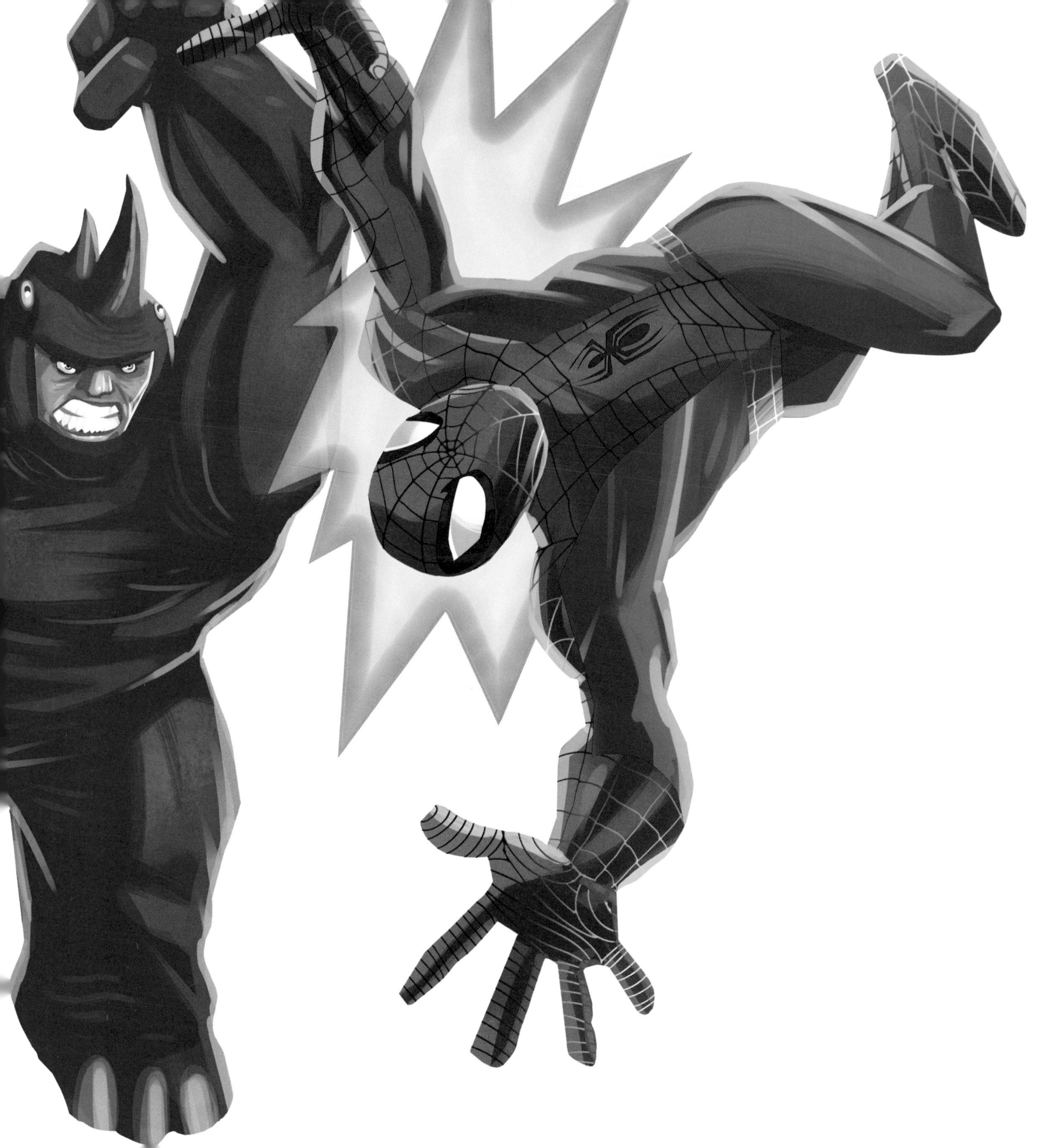

Peter did a quick change and returned to Mary Jane.

"Did you get your pictures?" she asked, still smiling.

"Yup, and I'll tell you all about it," he promised, "if you let me take you out tomorrow."

"I think that can be arranged," she said, her voice teasing.

As Peter and Mary Jane started to walk home, he began to smile. At least one thing was going well. Now if he could just defeat the Rhino in time for him to actually have a normal date tomorrow night, everything would be perfect.

A short while later, Spider-Man crawled through the window of Dr. Curtis Connors' office. The doctor had just moved to New York. Dr. Connors had helped him in the past, and Spider-Man hoped he would help him again now. Holding out his hand, Spider-Man showed the doctor a sample of the Rhino's tough skin.

"There's no way to stop him while he's protected by this," Spider-Man said. "Can you help me?"

The doctor nodded and got to work. In no time, the two created a special chemical that could stop the Rhino. Spider-Man coated his webs with the chemical so he would be ready for his next fight with the Rhino.

All Spider-Man had to do now was find him!

Using his powerful spider-sense, the webbed wonder found the Rhino trying to break into a nearby hospital.

The Rhino attacked Spider-Man! Spidey ducked and fired his web-shooters. It was a direct hit, but nothing happened!

Then the Rhino charged at Spider-Man and the two went crashing out the window to the ground below. The special chemical finally took effect and the Rhino's tough, grey skin started to dissolve.

Just then, Spider-Man delivered a powerful punch to the Rhino's jaw, knocking him out!

Later, the cops arrived to arrest the defeated Rhino. Spider-Man waited until he was sure the Rhino was captured for good and then quickly raced home for his date with Mary Jane.

Peter changed back into his regular clothes and called Mary Jane. They were going out for a night on the town. And this time, Peter hoped no Super Villains would get in the way!

MARVEL

the AMAZING SPIDER-MAN™

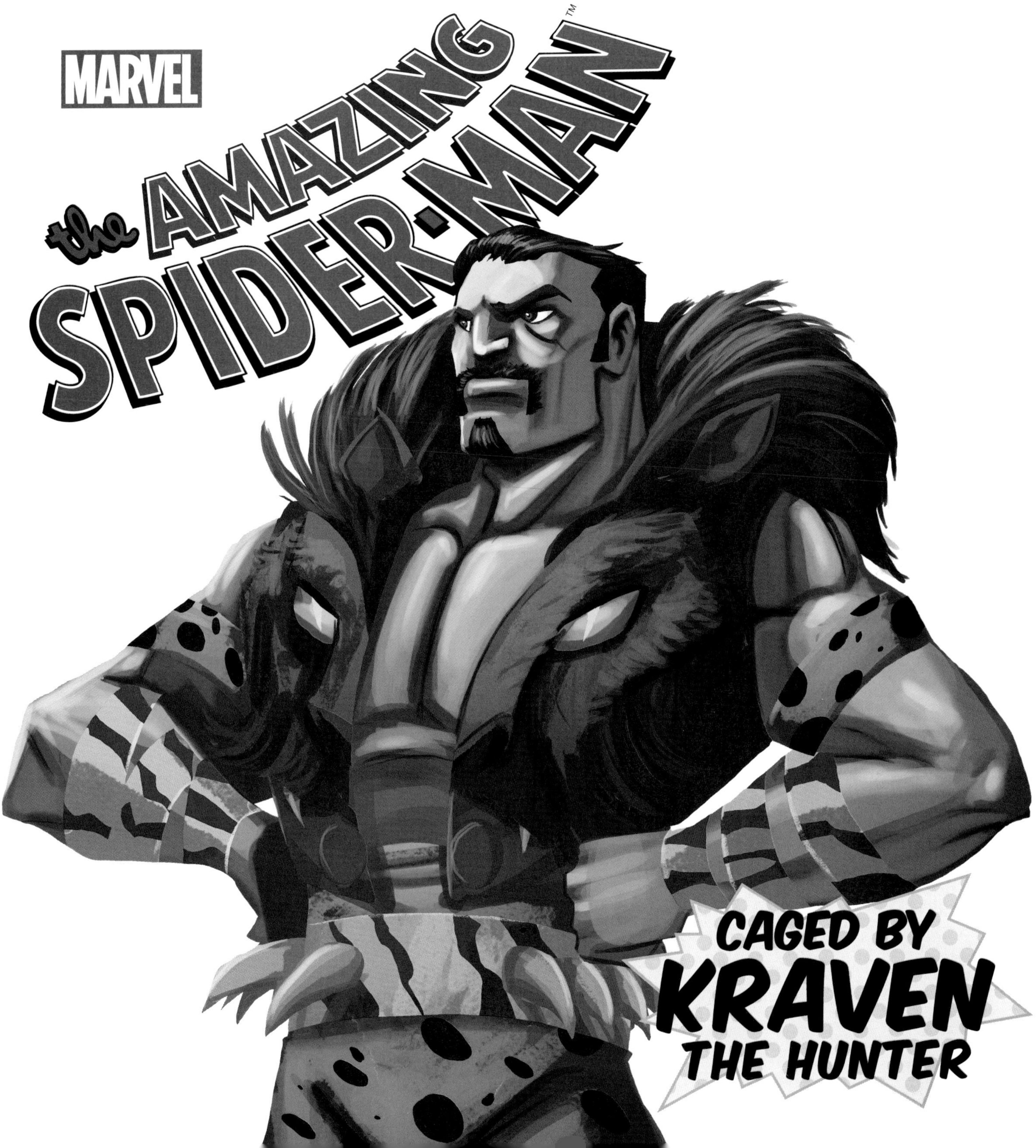

CAGED BY KRAVEN THE HUNTER

Peter Parker was having a great day. As fun as it was being the Amazing Spider-Man, sometimes a regular Saturday was even better, especially if he got to spend it at the zoo with Mary Jane Watson.

"Getting so close to these wild animals is exciting," she said.

But Peter took a step back. "This might be a little too close," he whimpered. Peter liked pretending to be scared of things he wasn't in order to protect his secret identity. But suddenly something happened that really did make him worry.

My spider-sense is tingling, thought Peter. It looks like Spider-Man won't have the day off after all. Peter wished he could spend more time just enjoying the zoo, but he knew that with great power came great responsibility.

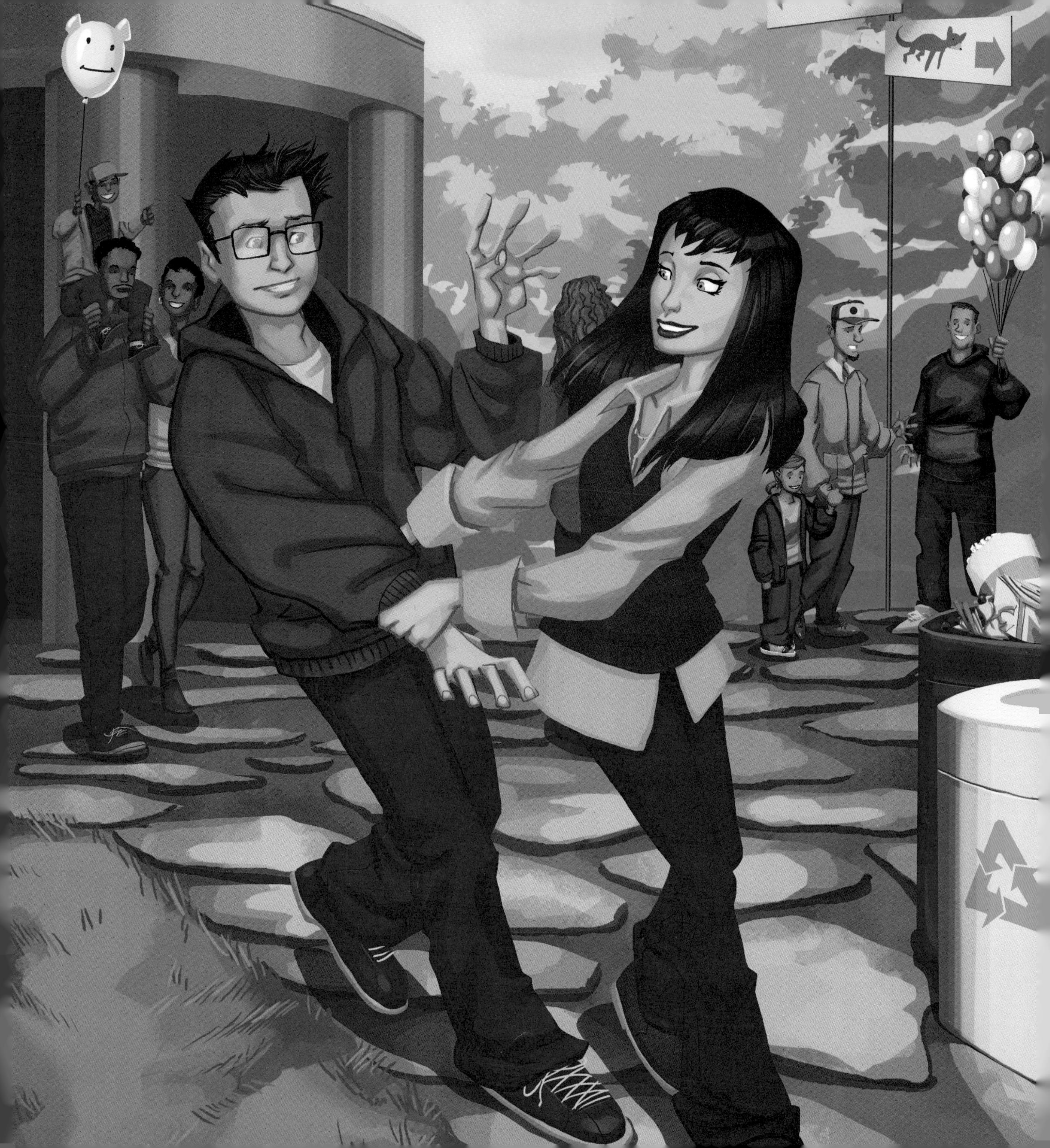

"Somebody help!" screamed the janitor. "A gorilla's gotten loose!" And what a giant gorilla it was! He was three times the size of a man, with enough power to crush a nearby hot-dog cart. Peter realized that even though the animal was probably just confused, he could still accidentally hurt someone.

With everyone looking at the beast, Peter snuck away to change into his costume. He hoped that Mary Jane wouldn't notice him leaving. But he was certain that if the gorilla wasn't enough of a distraction, she'd surely be distracted by the sight her friendly neighborhood Spider-Man.

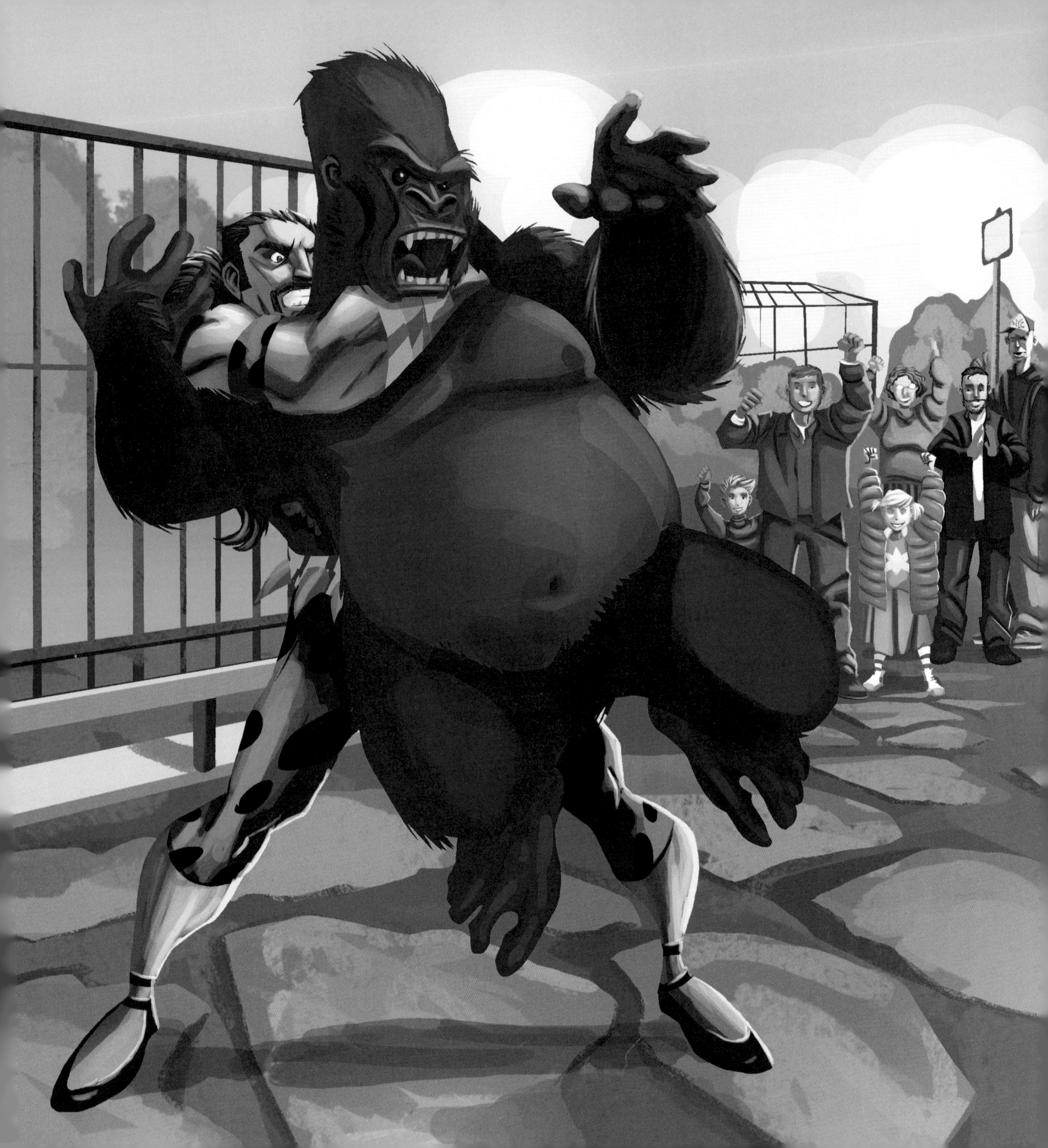
NYC

But when he returned, Spider-Man found somebody else already on the scene. It was Kraven the Hunter, the greatest hunter alive. And within a matter of seconds, he showed the powerful primate who the king of the jungle *really* was.

The crowd applauded as Kraven quickly subdued the gorilla with a choke hold and dragged him back into his cage. Emerging from the lair, Kraven locked the door behind him as flashbulbs popped and reporters took pictures of this newly crowned hero.

Like a leopard returning from a kill, Kraven stood triumphant.
His clothes were dirty and he smelled like the jungle. A reporter
shouted, "What are you doing in America, Kraven?"

With the growl of a wildcat the hunter responded, "I have defeated every animal there is, so today I hunt the most dangerous creature alive. . .man. But not just any man. . . Spider-Man!"

Spidey couldn't believe his ears. Hunt me? he thought. There must be a mistake. This great hunter didn't come all this way just to squash a spider, did he? Surely he must have me confused with some other charming, handsome, and radioactive web-head.

But with that, Kraven lunged at Spider-Man with
the force of a tiger. Luckily the wall-crawler
jumped out of the way just in time.

"Whoa! You must be lost, pal. The auditions for *The Lion King* are downtown," Spidey cracked. But even though he was joking, Spider-Man could feel how strong Kraven was. He had the strength of an elephant and the speed of a panther. Unfortunately, he also had something else.

This Spider-Man is tougher than I imagined, thought Kraven. I will have to cheat by sticking him with this poison venom that I stole from a snake. "You can't win Spider-Man," roared the hunter. "I have the secrets of the jungle on my side!"

But before Kraven could inject Spidey with the poisonous venom, the hero swung into action.

"That's fine with me." Spidey laughed. "Because all I need are the secrets of a spider!"

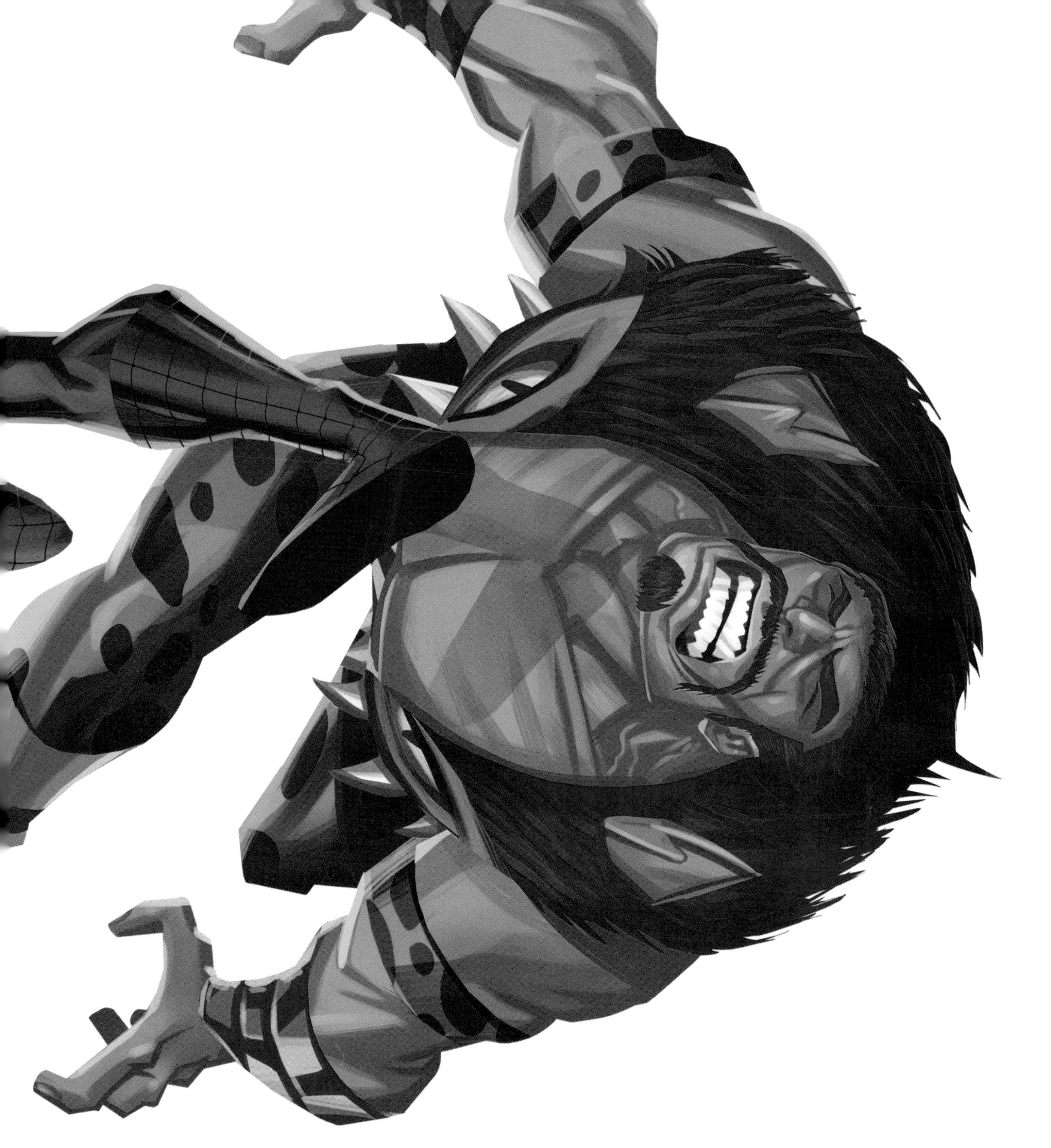

Spider-Man did it! He captured the greatest hunter alive.

"Sorry I had to ruin your birthday," said Spidey.

"My birthday!" cried Kraven. "Why would you think it's my birthday?"

"Well," said Spidey, "you look like a monkey. And you smell like one, too."

With that, Spider-Man had to change out of his costume and get back to Mary Jane. Even with the unexpected arrival of a Super Villain on a Saturday afternoon, it was still a great day for both Peter Parker and the Amazing Spider-Man.

MARVEL

the AMAZING SPIDER-MAN™

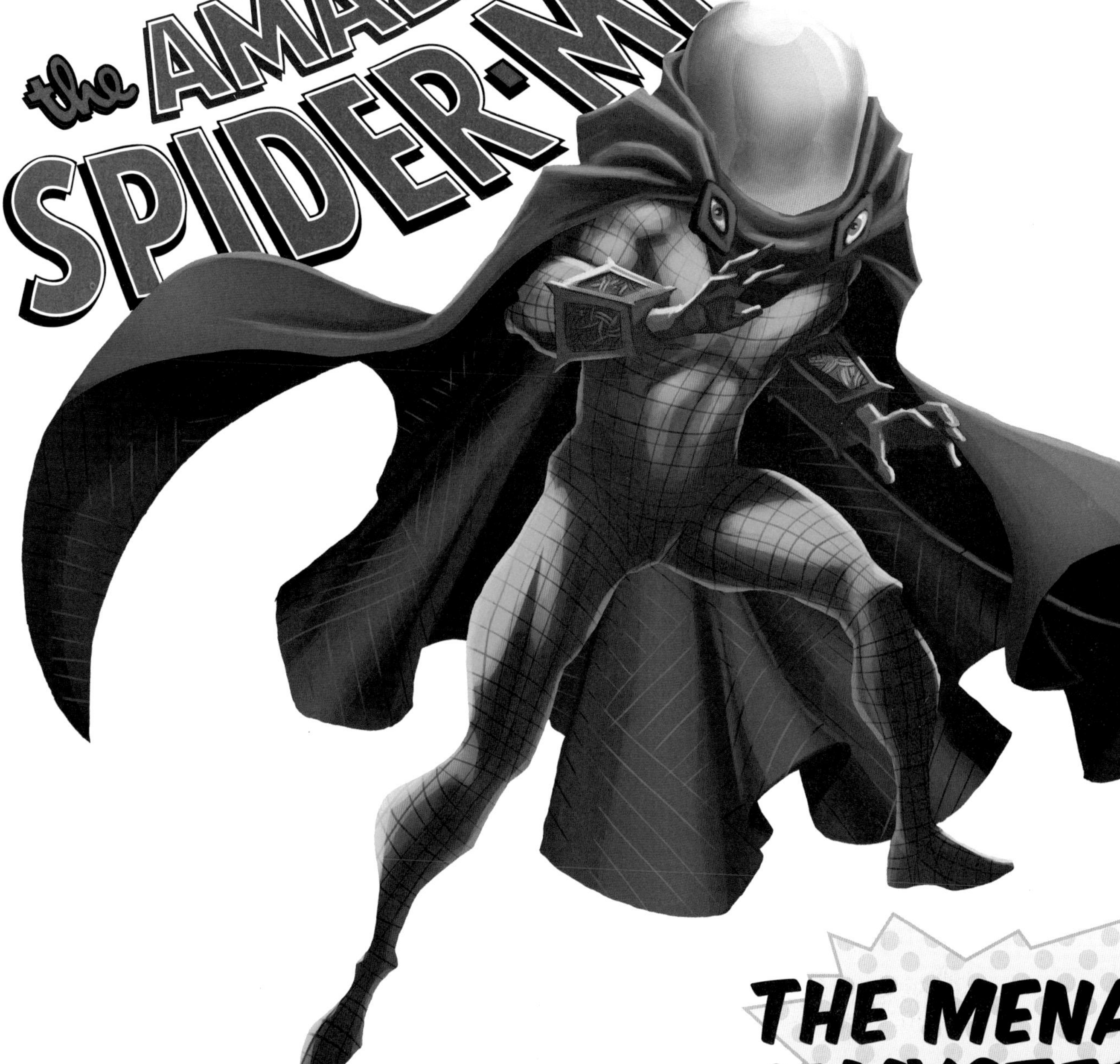

THE MENACE OF MYSTERIO

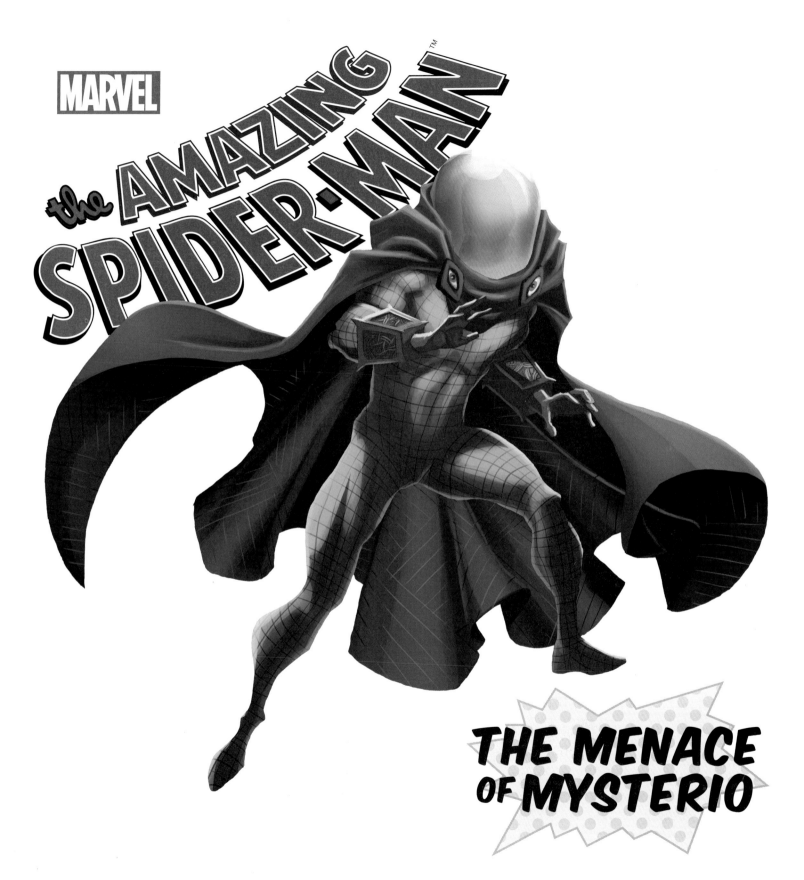

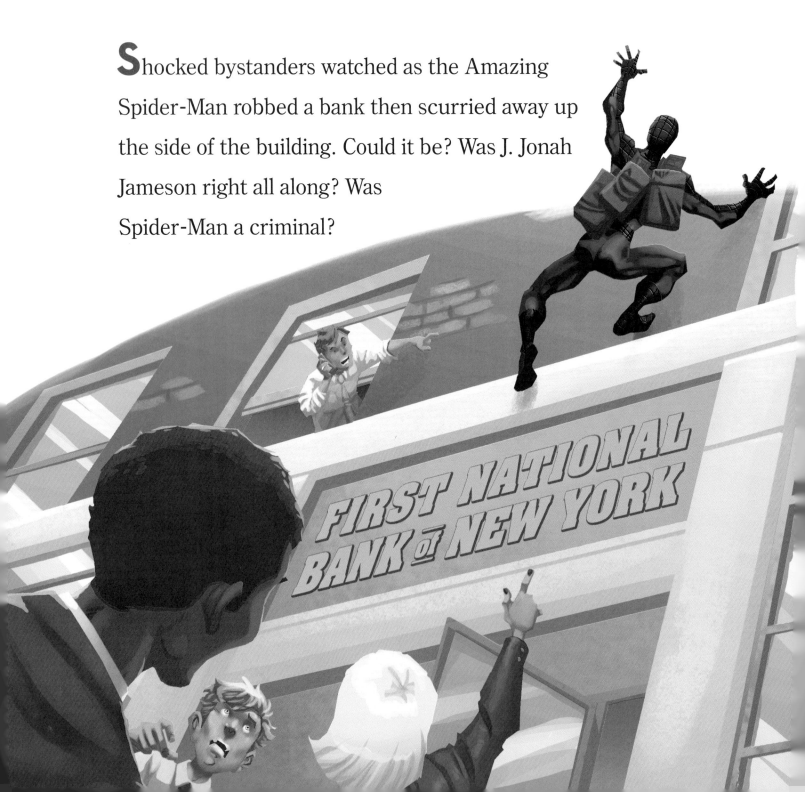

Shocked bystanders watched as the Amazing
Spider-Man robbed a bank then scurried away up
the side of the building. Could it be? Was J. Jonah
Jameson right all along? Was
Spider-Man a criminal?

Of all the people in New York, Peter Parker was the most surprised to learn about Spider-Man's bank robbery. Peter knew for certain that Spider-Man was innocent. But who would set up Spider-Man?

Peter rushed to *The Daily Bugle* to find his boss, J. Jonah Jameson, talking to a mysterious figure. His name was Mysterio, and he promised JJJ he would get rid of Spider-Man tomorrow morning at the Brooklyn Bridge.

Once Spider-Man arrived at the famous bridge, a cloud of smoke appeared and a booming voice announced, "I am Mysterio—I am the one who will single-handedly destroy you!"

As the two began to battle, Mysterio's strange powers dissolved Spidey's webs in midair. Then, just as Spider-Man was about to attack the villain, Mysterio disappeared into thin air!

When Peter returned to *The Daily Bugle,* he couldn't believe his eyes. Mysterio was shaking hands with JJJ!

"I always knew Spider-Man was a criminal!" J. Jonah Jameson said, grinning from ear to ear.

But just as Mysterio was leaving, Peter slyly placed a homing device on his cape. As Spider-Man, Peter planned to follow Mysterio back to wherever he came from!

The homing device led Spidey to an old TV studio. But as soon as Spider-Man was inside, the menacing Mysterio appeared. "Is it true? Am I about to defeat Spider-Man two times in a row? Roll the cameras!" The evil villain cackled as he attacked.

Spider-Man was down, but wasn't going to give up without a fight! Plus, he had to ask Mysterio about something he suspected all along — whether or not Mysterio was really the Spider-Man imposter.

"Of course it was me,"
the villian hissed. "Who else
would have the genius to improve
upon your powers?" Mysterio said with an evil laugh.

"You see, before this, I was a special-effects and makeup artist. But when the movies changed and started using effects created on computers, I knew I had to change, too. . . That's when I started using my skills to copy yours. And the best part of all was how you got all the blame!

"As Mysterio, I will defeat Spider-Man and become the greatest hero the world has ever known!" Mysterio proudly exclaimed. "Are you ready for your close-up, Spidey?"

But before Mysterio knew it, Spider-Man jumped into action

"So you're a copycat, huh? Let's see if you can copy this!" Spider-Man said.

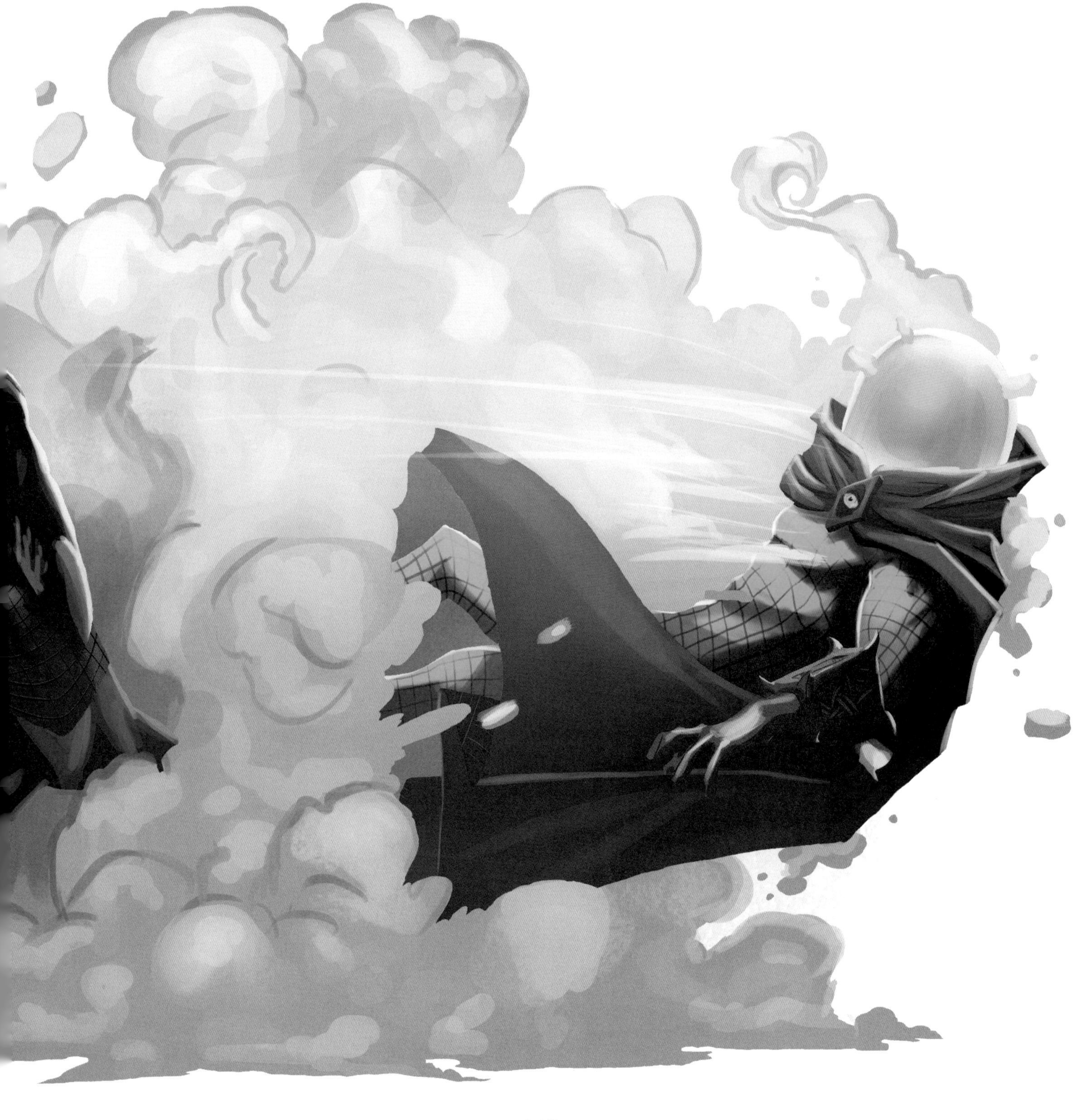

Mysterio, realizing he had underestimated the Amazing Spider-Man, tried to escape.

But instead of escaping, Mysterio ran through a set for a science-fiction TV show!

In front of a live studio audience and surprised camera crew, Spider-Man slammed Mysterio from above with all of his super spider-strength. "It's time for your curtain call!" Spider-Man announced to the villain.

The next day, Peter was happy to see his friends cheering for Spider-Man. But he was even happier to see the headline of *The Daily Bugle*. For once, Spider-Man wasn't JJJ's public enemy number one. Spidey made sure to thank J. Jonah Jameson in person. . .and that was better than any standing ovation!

MARVEL

the AMAZING SPIDER-MAN™

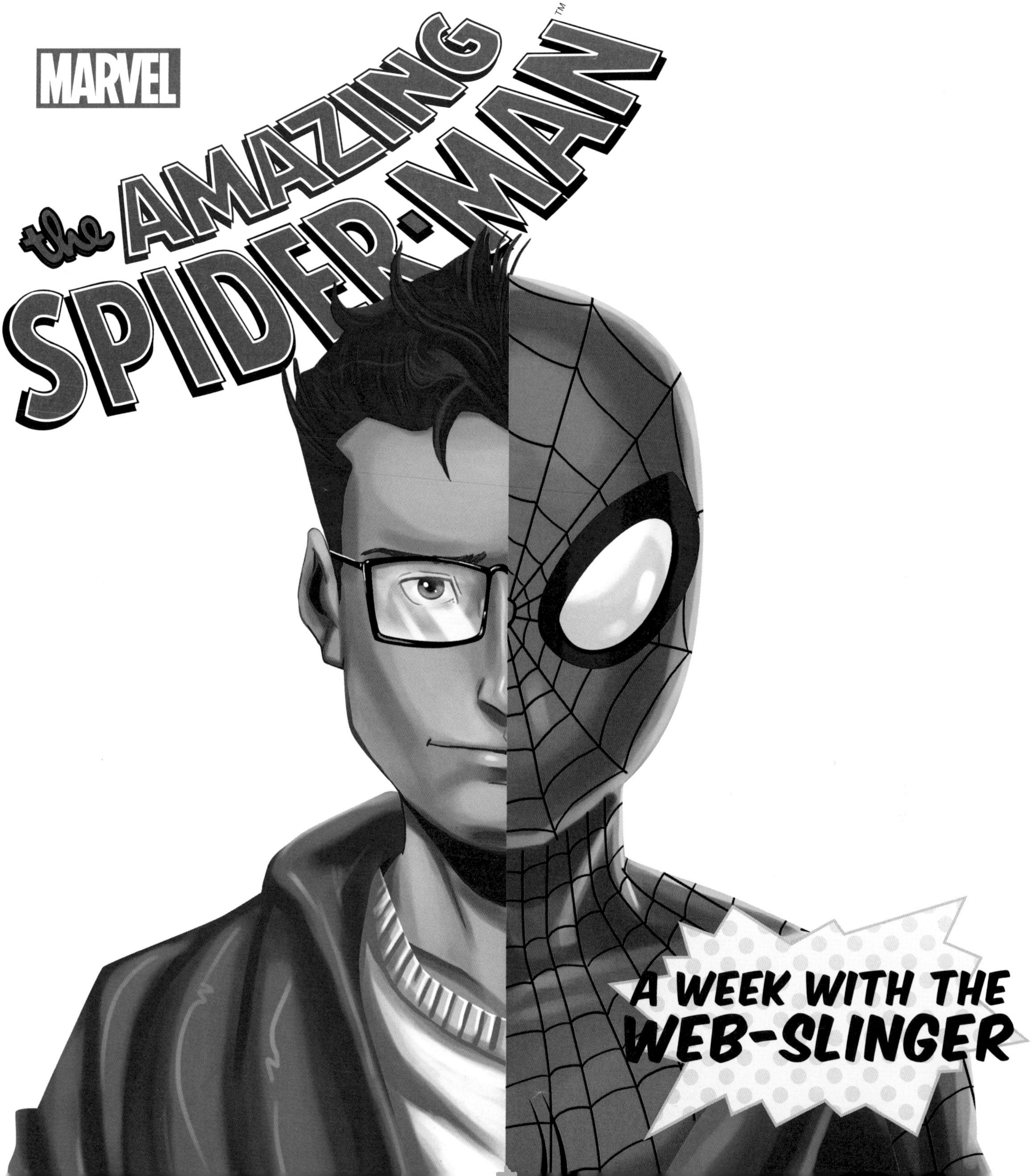

A WEEK WITH THE WEB-SLINGER

MONDAY—Peter Parker read the assignment that his history teacher at Midtown High passed out to the class. A five page report on the outcome of the Civil War and its effects on America. Peter smiled. It was only Monday and his assignment was due in one week. Plenty of time!

Peter got home from school and put on his Spider-Man costume. He had a whole week to get that assignment done, so Peter decided to make some rounds as everyone's favorite web-slinger!

Spider-Man swung through the valleys of New York City's skyscrapers until he found the perfect rooftop. I can see the whole city from here! he thought.

Hours went by without even one crime. This made Spider-Man happy, but Peter was frustrated. He could've been home working on his assignment. There's always tomorrow, Spidey thought.

TUESDAY—Peter was about to start his assignment when his phone rang. It was Mary Jane! He forgot about their date! His homework would have to wait.

Soon Peter and MJ were strolling through the local carnival.

With my Spidey skills, he thought, I can easily win MJ a teddy bear!

Krank! Krank! Krank!

"We have a winner!" yelled the carnival barker. And MJ had her prize!

WEDNESDAY — it was the middle of the week, and Peter was finally ready to start his Civil War assignment. But just as he was about to begin, a fire truck raced by outside his window with its sirens blaring.

Seems like trouble, Peter thought. And where there's trouble, there's Spider-Man! Peter quickly changed into his Spider-Man costume and rushed to the scene!

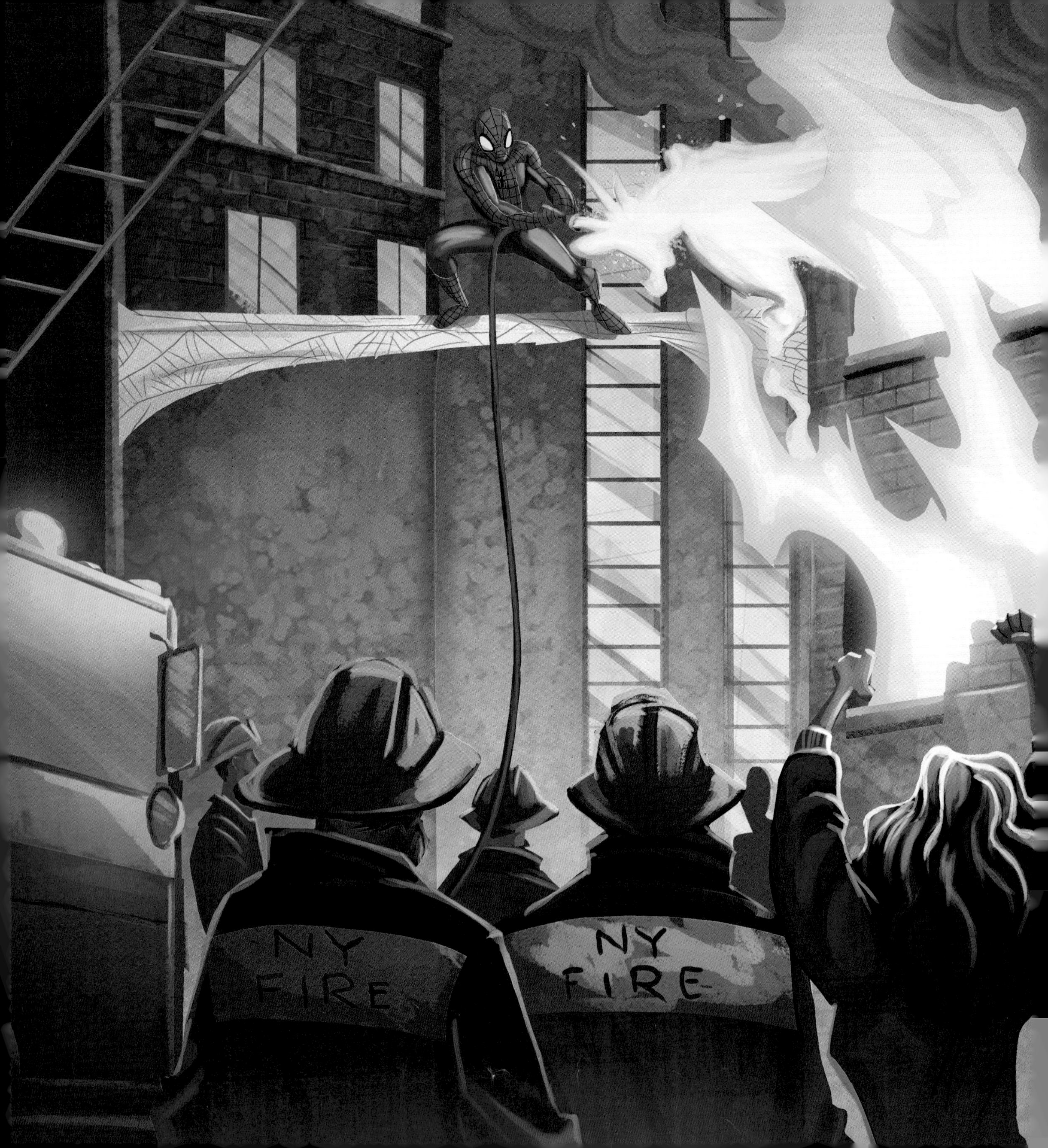
NY
FIRE
NY
FIRE

When Spider-Man arrived at the burning building, he knew he needed to act fast!

"We can't get our fire hoses to reach the top floor," a firefighter said to Spidey. "Think you can help us —?"

But before the firefighter could finish, Spider-Man was off! He quickly swung to the roof across from the burning building.

"Time for some web action!" Spidey said as he shot some webbing between the two buildings. Standing on the web-bridge he created, Spider-Man shot webbing at the fire hose below and yanked it up. Blasting the flames with the cold water, Spider-Man quickly put out the fire! Everyone cheered!

THURSDAY—It was a long week for Peter. And now he had to go to work at *The Daily Bugle*.

"Parker!" J. Jonah Jameson exclaimed. "Where were you yesterday when that building was on fire and Spider-Man supposedly saved the day?"

You've got to be kidding me! Peter thought, giving JJJ an awkward smile. He couldn't believe he forgot his camera! "I was doing homework, Mr. Jameson," he fibbed.

"I need a photo of Spider-Boy in action. By Monday!"

Peter's long week seemed to be getting even longer!

FRIDAY—As Peter headed out to get photos of Spider-Man, his stomach growled.

Then he remembered that he had promised Aunt May that they'd have dinner. Now JJJ's assignment would have to wait!

"Peter!" Aunt May said as he walked into the kitchen. "I knew you'd make it!

Peter smiled. "Me, too."

SATURDAY—Peter could not put off his assignment any longer, so he webbed himself in his room to work. After several hours, Peter's homework was finally done!

SUNDAY—With his school assignment done, Peter still needed to get photos for *The Daily Bugle*. Soon, the web-slinger was swinging through the city.

Suddenly, his spider-sense went off! But all seemed quiet. That's weird, Spidey thought. I don't see any—KACSSSHH! KREEEESHH!

Broken glass flew everywhere as the Rhino ran out of a bank with bags of money.

Spidey rigged his camera to a nearby building and swung into action.

"Hey, leather head," Spider-Man said. "You have an account with this bank?"

The Rhino let out a roar and charged full speed at Spider-Man! But the web-slinger was fast! He fired webbing into the villain's eyes, and the Rhino crashed right into a brick wall.

MONDAY—Peter woke up late for school and rushed to class. He quickly dropped off the assignment while the teacher's back was turned. He did it!

Meanwhile, at *The Daily Bugle,* J. Jonah Jameson paced behind his desk.

Suddenly, a breeze whipped through J. Jonah Jameson's office as papers flew off his desk, except for one.

"Man, that kid is fast," JJJ said picking up the photos of Spider-Man and the Rhino in action.

Boy, what a week! Peter thought, as he took off his mask and turned on the TV. It was finally time to relax.

"Breaking news! The Rhino has escaped!" cried a reporter.

Peter smiled, grabbed his mask, and swung into action. It was Super Hero time!

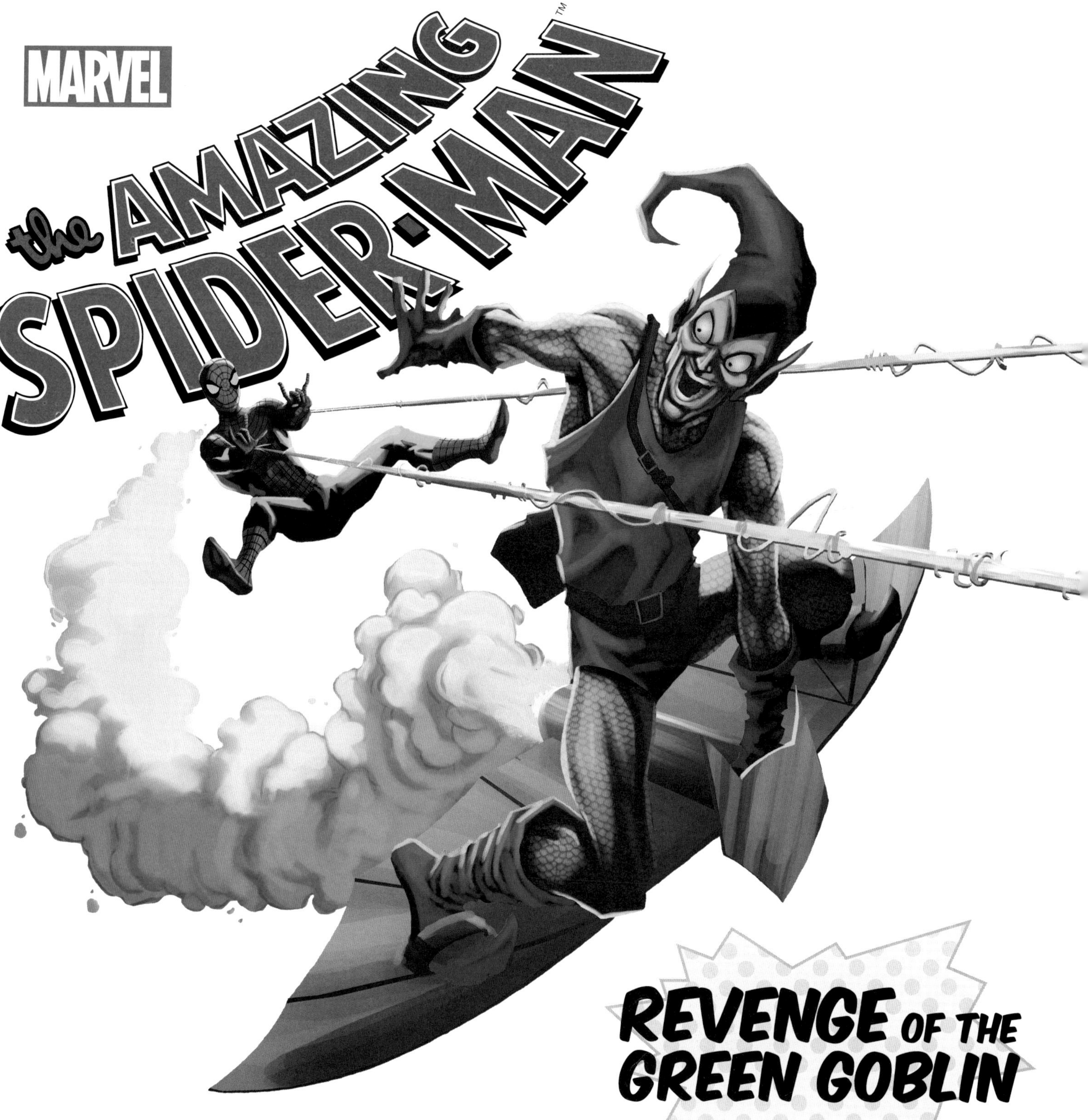
MARVEL
the AMAZING SPIDER-MAN™
REVENGE OF THE GREEN GOBLIN

Peter Parker was worried! He was the only person who knew that Norman Osborn had secretly been the Green Goblin. After the Goblin's last battle with Spider-Man, Norman got amnesia. He did not remember that he was the Goblin — or that he had discovered Spider-Man was really Peter!

Now, Peter had accepted an invitation from Norman to attend a theatrical performance starring Mary Jane. But something was wrong. Not only was Peter's friend, Harry Osborn, sick, but Norman was acting strange. He kept looking at an old, musty door next to the stage.

As they left the theater, Harry turned to Peter. "I feel sick," said Harry, as he collapsed into Peter's arms.

"We have to get Harry to a hospital!" said Peter, as his friends scrambled to help.

Peter was so concerned about his friend, that he almost did not see Norman running back into the theater. Could he be going back inside to check out that strange door?

After Peter made sure his friends took Harry to the hospital, he ran into a nearby building and took the stairs all the way to the roof.

"Time to see what Norman is up to!" Peter said as he changed into his Spider-Man costume.

Seconds later, Spider-Man used his spider-strength to kick open the theater door. He could not believe what he saw!

It was the Green Goblin!

Spider-Man could tell by the look in his eyes that Osborn remembered Peter's secret identity.

"Surprised to see me, Parker?" said the Goblin, calling Spider-Man by his real name. "This theater used to house one of my secret lairs! And now that I remember everything, I will squash you like a bug!"

"How many times do I have to tell you, Gobby?" said Spider-Man. "Spiders are arachnids, not bugs."

The Goblin sneered at Spider-Man and reached inside his weapons satchel.

He is madder and more dangerous than ever! thought Spider-Man. I cannot let him escape!

Just as Spider-Man tried to use his webs to snare his foe, the Goblin hurled a pumpkin bomb at the web-slinger. It contained a special gas that made Spider-Man fall asleep.

"Sleep now, Parker," said the Goblin. "We will soon meet again—for the last time!"

When Spider-Man woke up, the Goblin was gone. But Spider-Man knew that the fiend would soon show himself again. Meanwhile, Spider-Man went to the hospital to check on Harry. When he arrived, he looked through the window at his friend, who was asleep.

"Harry is getting better," said Spider-Man. "I will just change out of my Spidey suit so I can visit as Peter—"

Suddenly, the web-slinger's spider-sense started tingling. It was warning him of danger!

As pumpkin bombs exploded around him, Spider-Man landed
on a wall. But he was shocked to find out that he could not stick
to it! He started to fall.

"I can't stick to walls anymore!" said Spider-Man.

"You can thank my special pumpkin bombs for that, Parker!"
said the Goblin. "Now you will fall to your doom for all to see!"

"Not today, Gobby!" said Spider-Man.

Using his powerful legs, Spider-Man jumped off the wall and grabbed on to a nearby flagpole. With his incredible spider-strength, the wall-crawler spun around and soared through the sky. Spidey landed on the ledge of a building, ready for action.

Without a word, Spider-Man leaped from the rooftop and landed on the Green Goblin's shoulders! Stunned, the Goblin struggled as he tried to reach his weapons. But he could not! Spider-Man's grip was too strong.

"Curse you, Spider-Man!" said the Goblin.

"Let's take a little trip!" said Spider-Man. Using his hold on the Goblin, Spider-Man steered the goblin glider until they arrived at . . .

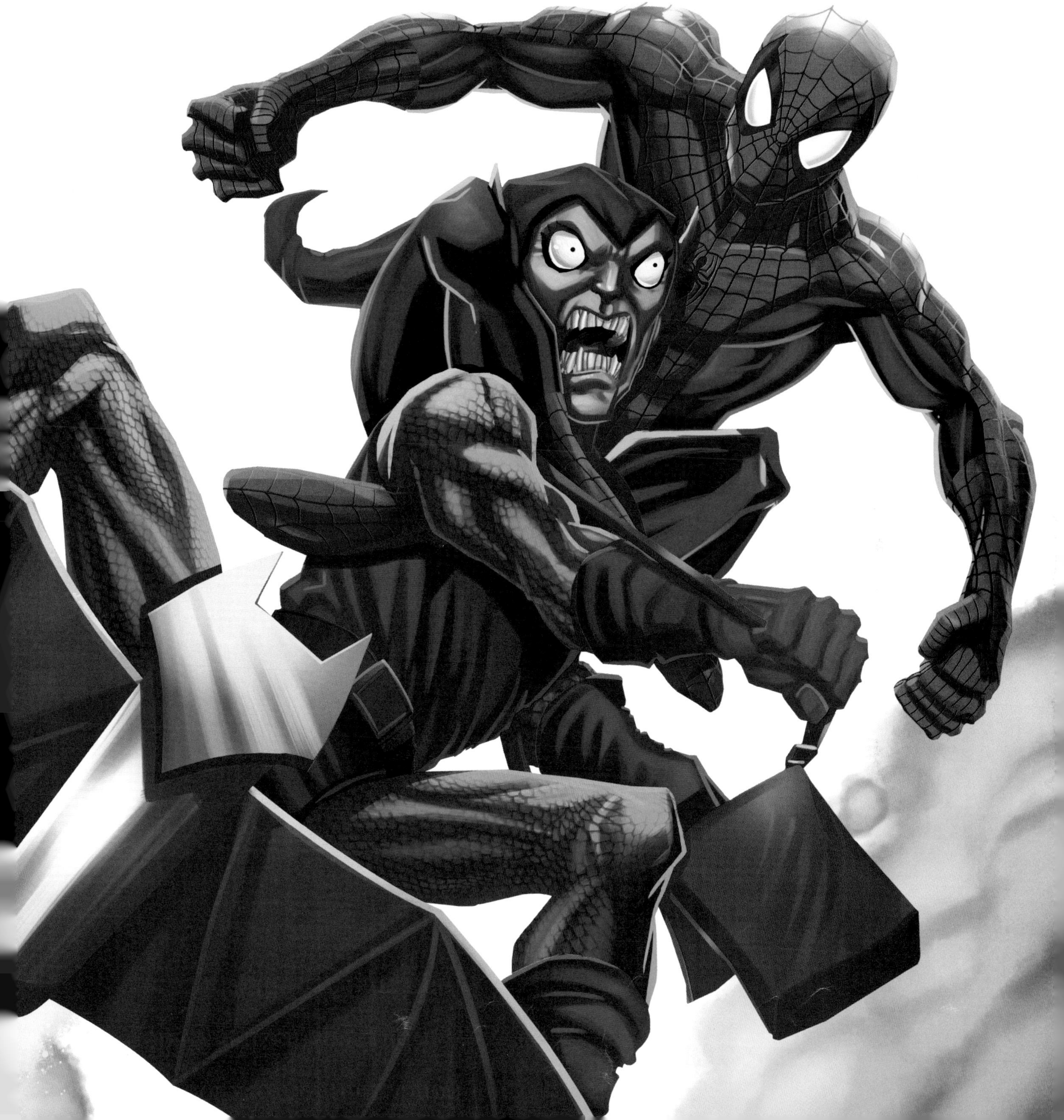

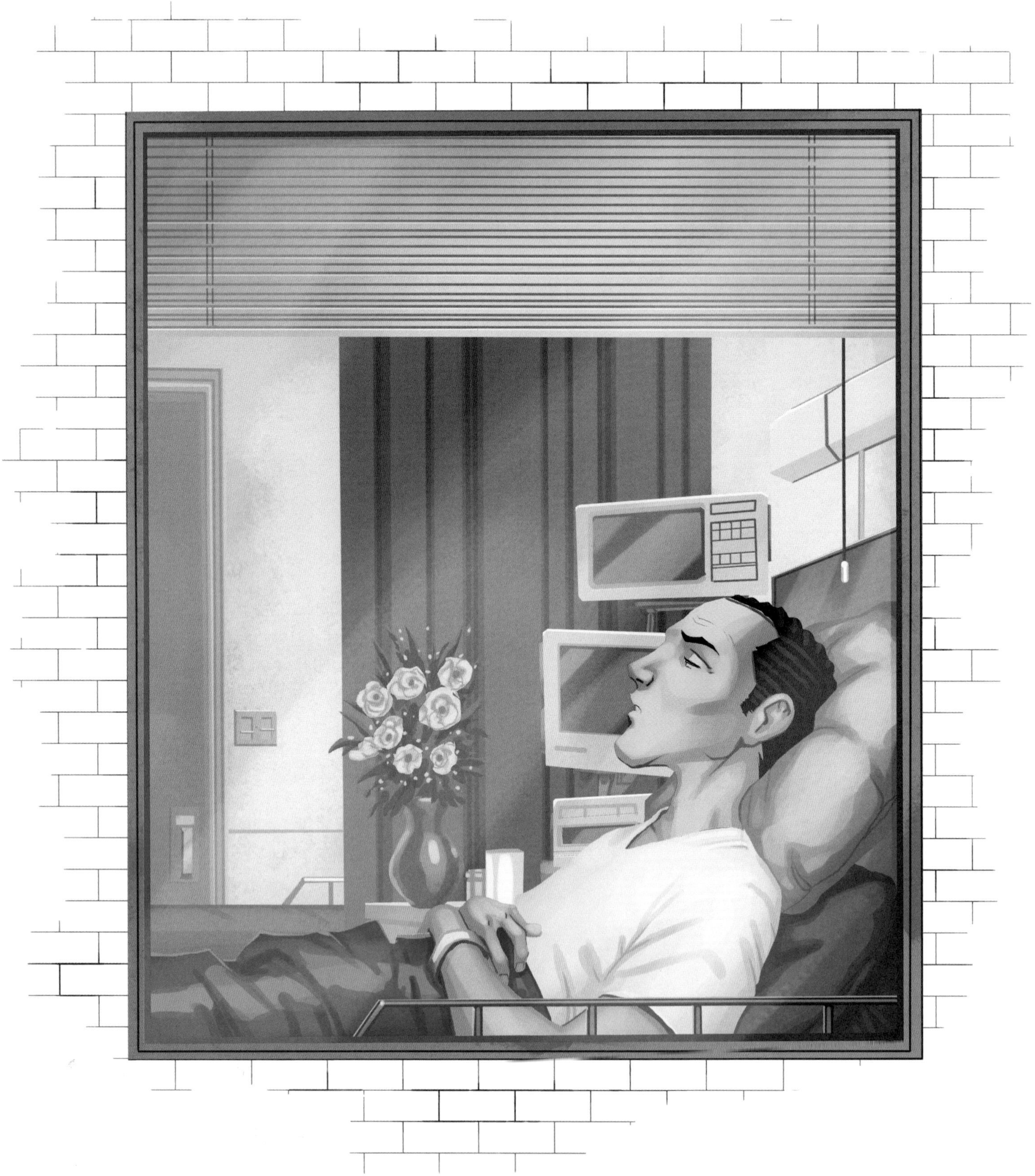

Harry's window! As the Green Goblin looked at Harry, sick in bed, something about him seemed to change. His eyes were full of concern. . .concern for his son!

"H-Harry!" said the Goblin. "My son! What is it? What is wrong with him? I—I must go to him. He's sick! He needs his father!"

Norman took off his mask. He wondered why he was wearing such a strange costume, and why Spider-Man was there.

The shock of seeing his son in the hospital worked—Norman no longer remembered that he was the Green Goblin!

"I must go to my son, Spider-Man," said Norman. "Thank you for bringing me here!"

Spider-Man heaved a sigh of relief as he took Norman's regular suit from the Goblin's satchel and handed it to Norman.

Norman had forgotten that Peter Parker was Spider-Man, too. Spidey's secret identity was safe once more, and the Green Goblin was gone . . . at least for now!

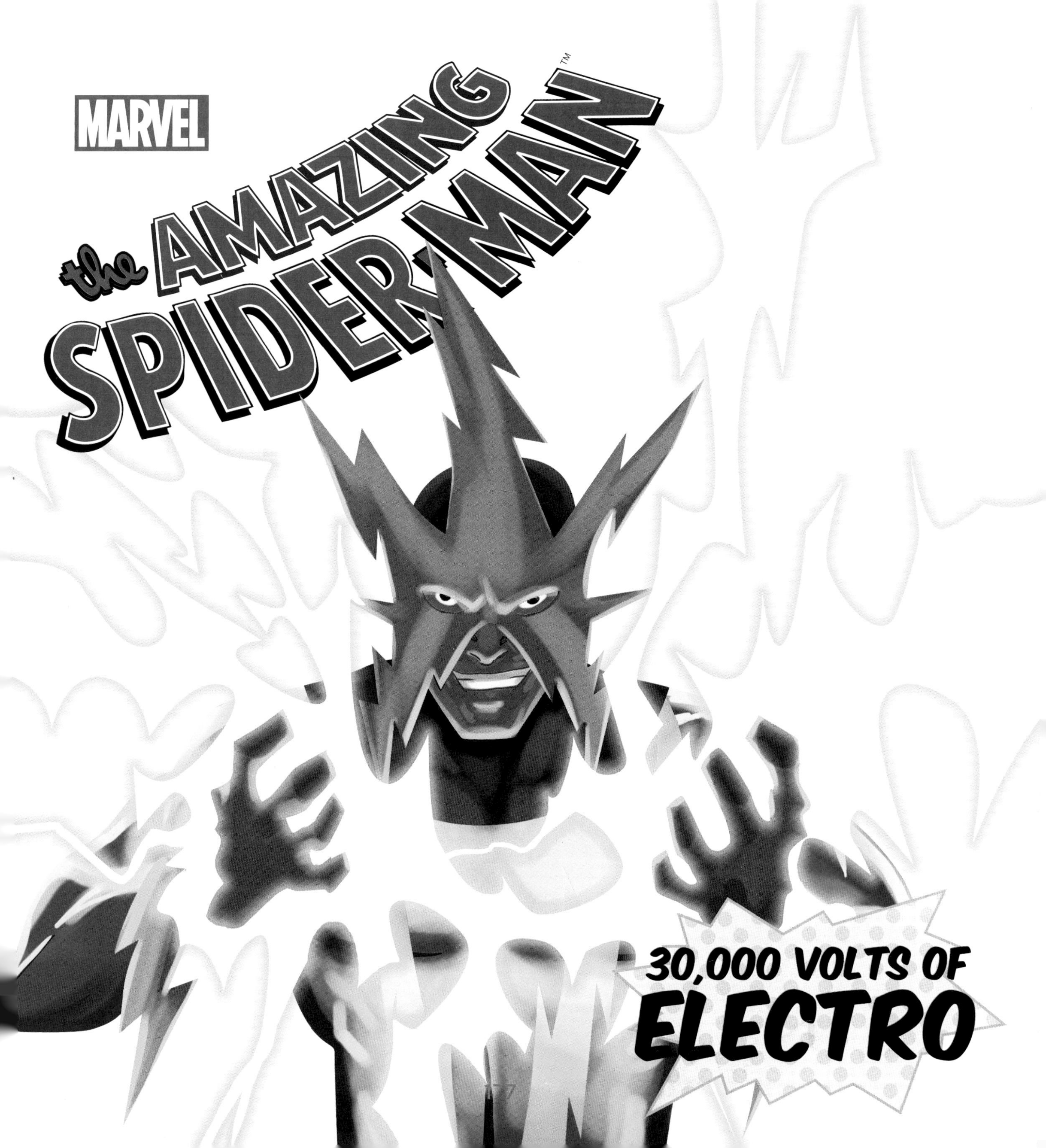
MARVEL
the AMAZING SPIDER-MAN™
30,000 VOLTS OF
ELECTRO

When he wasn't swinging around town as Spider-Man, he was average teenager Peter Parker. Peter liked science and math, and while some of his classmates thought he was a bit of a geek, he didn't want to be any different.

Across town, Peter Parker's boss, J. Jonah Jameson, was in a foul mood. That wasn't unusual, however. As publisher of *The Daily Bugle* newspaper, JJJ had a reputation for being one of the grumpiest people in the business. But today, Jonah actually had a good reason for his attitude.

Because today, the bank JJJ was in was being robbed right before his eyes! A new villain named Electro was making off with a small fortune.

As Electro escaped, JJJ ran after him. People loved to read about bank robberies, and JJJ was determined to get the whole scoop before any other paper. But by the time Jameson got to the window, Electro was gone. The only suspicious person around was...Spider-Man!

The next day when he showed up for his photography job, Peter saw that *The Daily Bugle* had a shocking headline.

Peter Parker couldn't believe his eyes. JJJ had always hated Spider-Man, but this was going too far. Just the idea behind the story was downright crazy. Why would Spider-Man wear a different costume to rob a bank? Peter decided the only way to clear his name was to find the real criminal.

Peter wasn't the only one surprised by the morning's news. In a different part of town, Electro's alter ego, Max Dillon, was getting a good laugh from the paper.

Just a few weeks ago, Max had been an ordinary electrician. But when a freak bolt of lightning struck him while he was working on some power cables, his body somehow absorbed its energy.

Max realized that he had become a living generator. He could shoot electricity from his fingertips. It was just the excuse he was looking for. He was tired of working for an honest living. So with one quick wardrobe change, the villain Electro was born!

Talk of Electro's daring robbery quickly spread through the city. As soon as he heard the news, Peter Parker knew it was time to act. But if Spider-Man was going to face an enemy with electric powers, then Peter needed a plan.

Spidey learned that Electro was planning on breaking into prison to find henchmen to work for him.

But the Amazing Spider-Man got there first!

"Howdy, Sparky," said Spider-Man, holding a metal chair. "Starting a prison riot looks like it's just tuckered you out. Why don't you take a seat?"

Electro didn't answer. Instead he shot a bolt of lightning directly at the hero. But unlike his enemy, Spider-Man came prepared. He knew metal was a good conductor of electricity, and that Electro's blast would be drawn to the chair rather than him.

Spider-Man also knew that a pair of insulated rubber gloves and boots would keep him safe from Electro's touch.

"What? You don't like my new boots?" Spider-Man said. "Is it 'cause they clash with my webbing? You could at least be polite about it, Electro. I mean, I didn't make fun of your giant lightning hat, did I?"

Spider-Man knew that if there was one thing that didn't mix with electricity, it was water. He quickly grabbed a hose off the wall and doused Electro. As the villain shorted out, Peter smiled beneath his mask. Looks like science class really paid off.

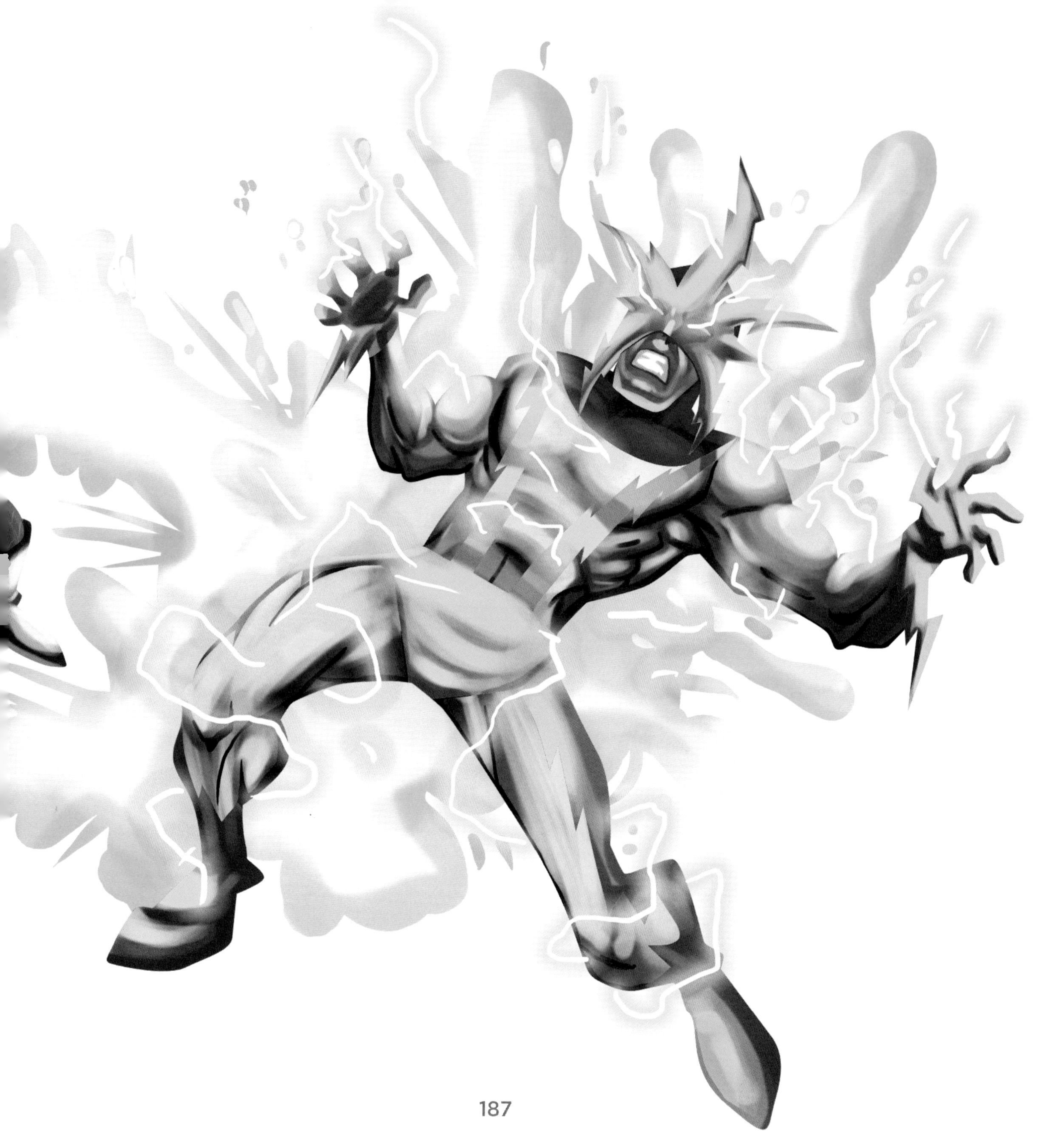

But with any luck, that wouldn't be the only thing that paid off today. Before he attacked Electro, Spider-Man had hidden his camera in a corner of the prison. Hopefully, he'd managed to get a couple of great shots that he could sell later as Peter Parker.

J. Jonah Jameson hated being wrong. But he liked making money. So when Peter Parker came to him with photos proving that Electro and Spider-Man were two different people, JJJ decided to pay Peter for the pictures.

After all, selling papers was the one thing that could put a smile on even J. Jonah Jameson's face.

Spider-Man was in a great mood. He had stopped Electro and cleared his own name. Plus, the money for his pictures would come in handy for paying some of Aunt May's bills. It seemed everything was going his way.

But even if it wasn't, Spider-Man knew deep down that he would probably be smiling right now anyway. All he really needed was a sunny day and a web to swing on.

MARVEL

the AMAZING SPIDER-MAN™

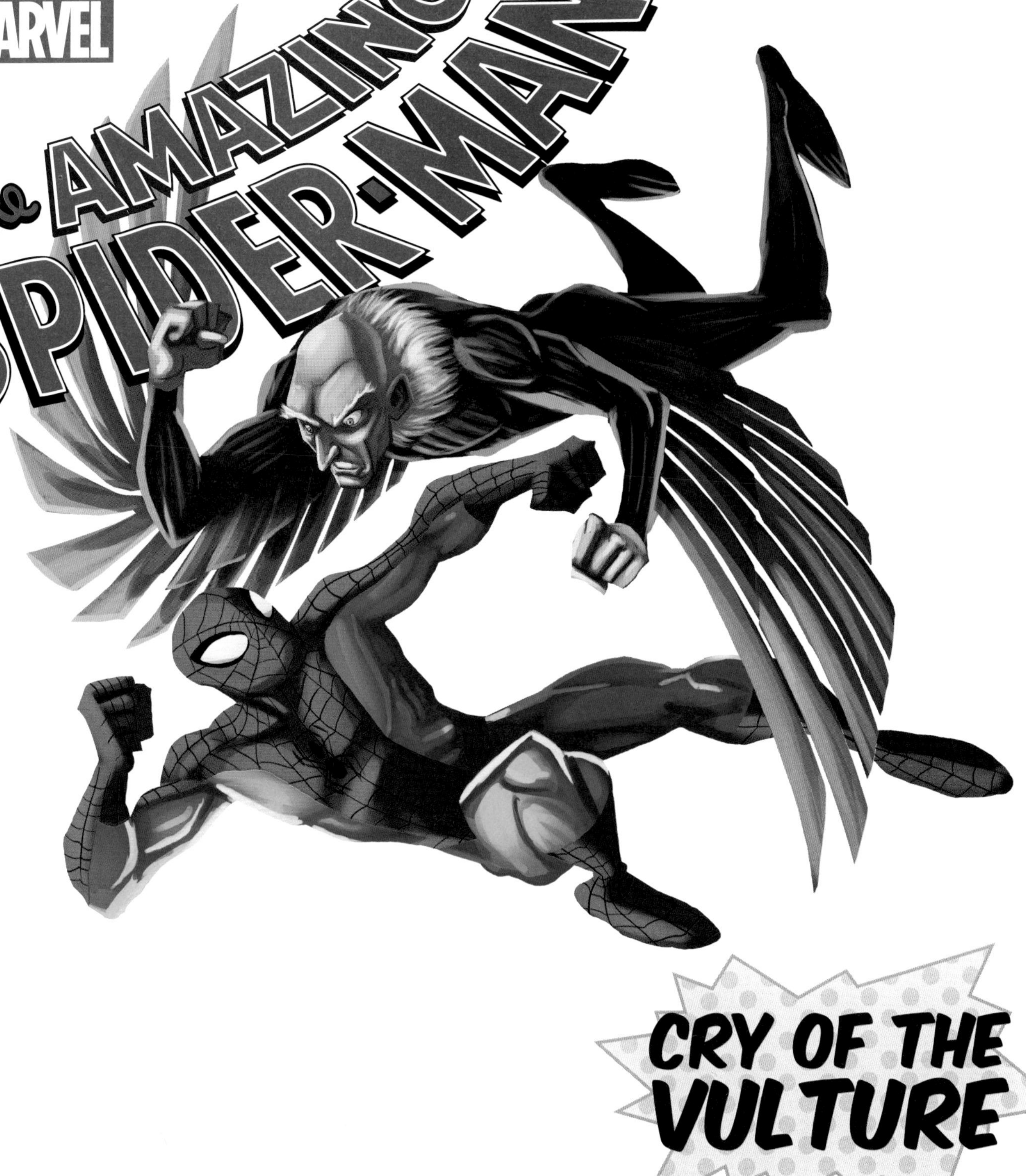

CRY OF THE VULTURE

"Can you imagine what this creep looks like up close?" one of Peter Parker's classmates said, pointing to an image on his phone. Peter looked closer. On the small screen was a picture of a man with green wings.

"A real photo of the Vulture would be worth some major money," Mary Jane said. "Too bad no one can get close enough. He's too fast! I heard he can fly without making any sound at all."

Peter quietly listened to the conversation. Something had to be done to stop this new flying villain. It looked like Spider-Man had a new adventure in front of him.

Meanwhile, the Vulture was planning his next crime. A famous jewelry store was going to be moving all of its jewels to a new location.

"It shouldn't be hard for me to get my hands on those gems," the Vulture said with a snicker. "And no one can stop me!"

While the Vulture was plotting, Peter had transformed into the spectacular Spider-Man. Minutes later, his spider-sense tingled. Something's coming, he said to himself. Suddenly, the Vulture appeared!

Catching sight of the webbed wonder, the Vulture sneered. "Well, look what we have here," he said.

Spider-Man took a step forward, about to shoot a powerful web at the villain. But the Vulture was too quick. With a flap of his giant green wings, he disappeared.

"Hey!" Spider-Man shouted. "Where'd he go?"

Then, as if in answer, the Vulture dropped out of the sky above. With a mighty shove, he knocked out Spidey. Then the villain tossed a large net over the fallen Super Hero.

Spider-Man had been captured!

The Vulture flew toward one of the city's many water towers. Opening up the lid, he dropped Spider-Man inside.

"With that wall-crawler out of my way, the city will be mine!" the Vulture said with a smirk.

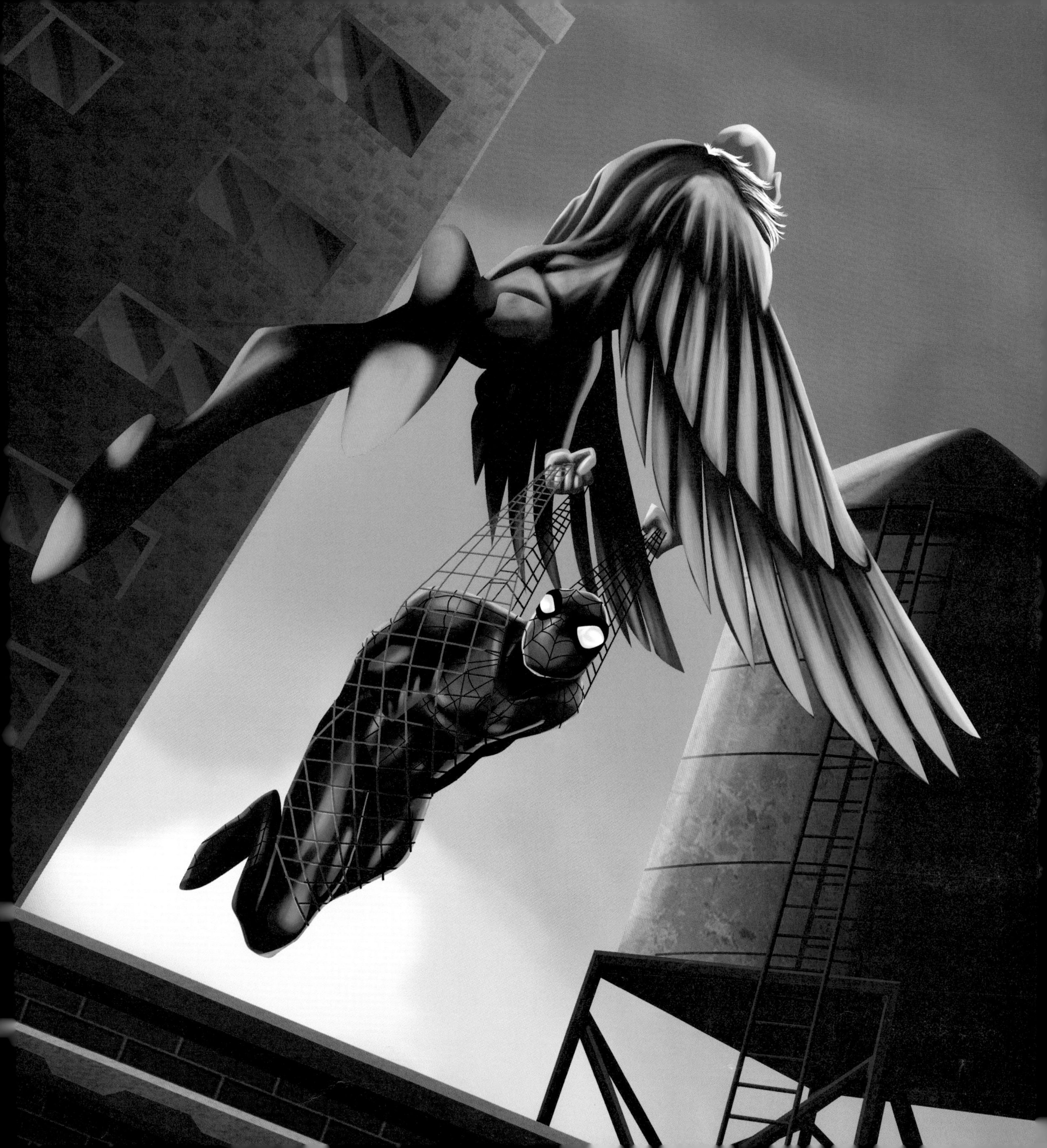

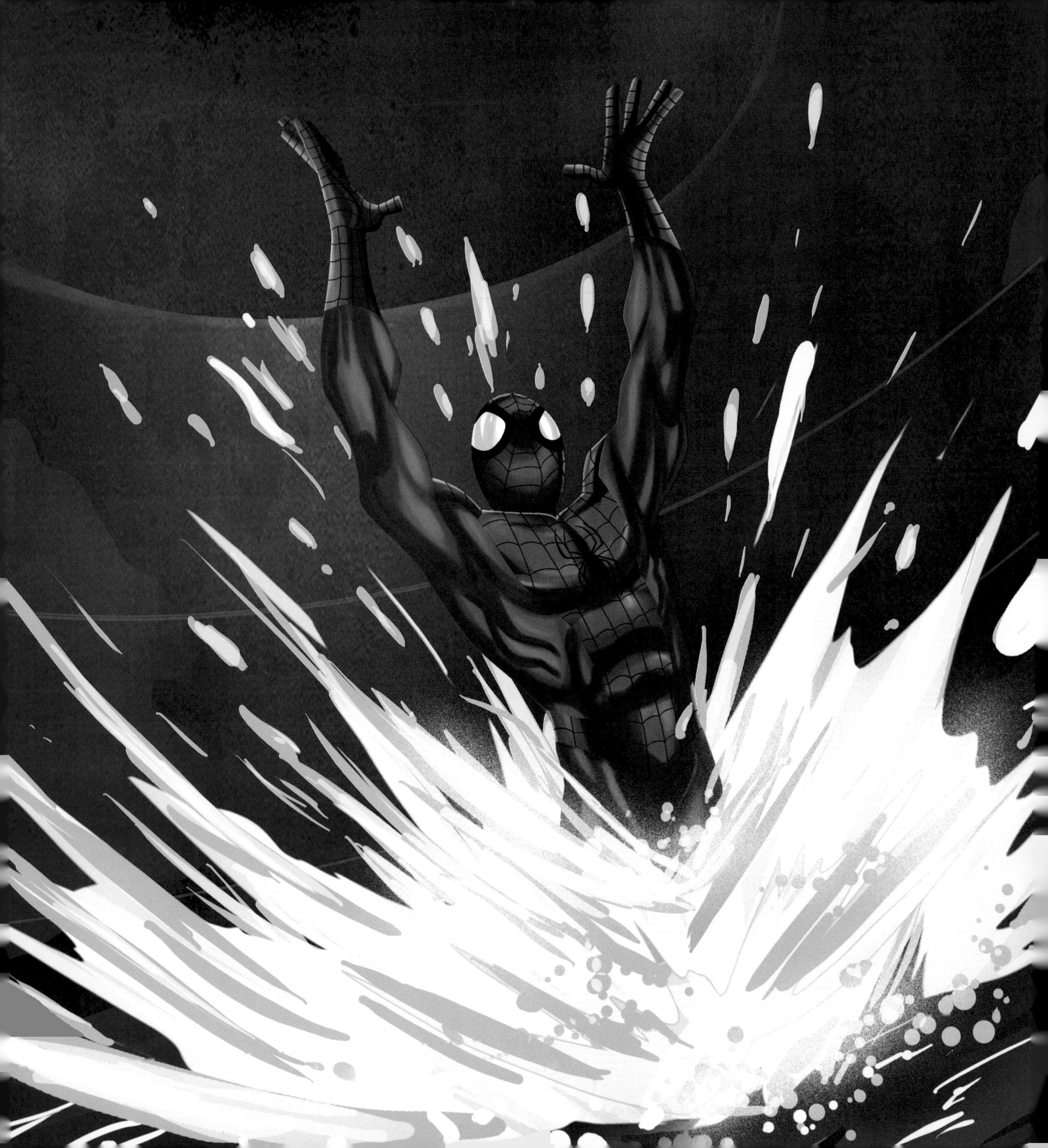

Spider-Man went numb as soon as he hit the cold water. Hoping to find an easy way out, he quickly looked around. But things didn't look good. The water tank's walls were high and slippery. The water was cold and dark. And there was only a limited amount of air. If he didn't find a way out of there soon, Spider-Man was going to be in big trouble. He knew he would just have to get out the same way he got in!

Taking a deep breath, Spider-Man dove down to the bottom of the tank. Then, using all his incredible spider-strength, he pushed off from the bottom. He shot up, up, up. Finally, he burst through the lid on the ceiling and into the sunlight. Spider-Man was free!

And now it was time to defeat the Vulture — one way or another.

Later, Peter sat in his room. Something was bothering him. How could the Vulture fly so quietly? His wings were clearly man-made. There had to be a way to stop the flying felon.

Suddenly Peter had an idea. If he was right, the Vulture wouldn't be flying for long. He quickly got to work.

A few hours later, he held up a small device that looked like a remote control. He smiled. The next time Spider-Man met the Vulture, the villian would be in for a big surprise.

The next afternoon, the jewels began their journey across town. There were police cars and helicopters. On the ground, officers stood at every corner, with their eyes peeled for signs of danger.

But nothing happened.

Finally, the jewels reached their destination. Three guards began to escort them into the building. And that was when the Vulture struck!

The villain burst through a manhole right under the guards' feet!

"Gentlemen," he said with a cackle, "I'll take those diamonds if you don't mind." Then, he swiftly yanked the jewels away from the guards and ducked back under the streets.

Quickly and quietly, the Vulture flew through the maze of underground tunnels. A few minutes later, he shot above ground, startling bystanders.

"This will give people something to talk about for years to come," he said with a laugh. But there was something — or someone — in his way. Spider-Man had found him!

The Vulture couldn't believe it. "That blasted web-head got out!" He circled behind Spider-Man. "I've got to get rid of him for good."

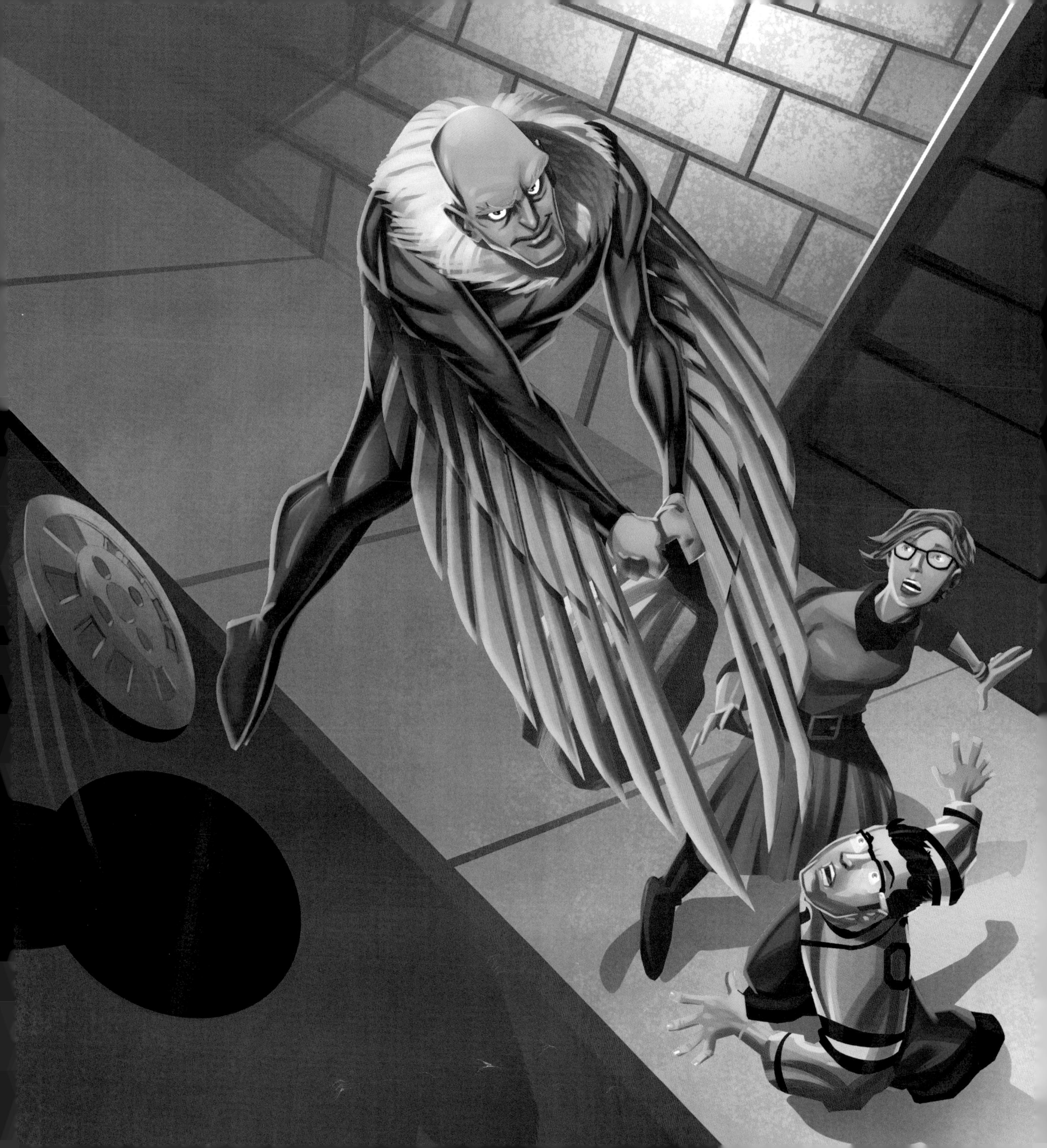

But Spider-Man had learned a thing or two from their last encounter. Relying on his spider-sense, he knew when the winged crook was about to attack. He aimed his web-shooters at the Vulture and fired a line. The web wrapped around the villian's ankle.

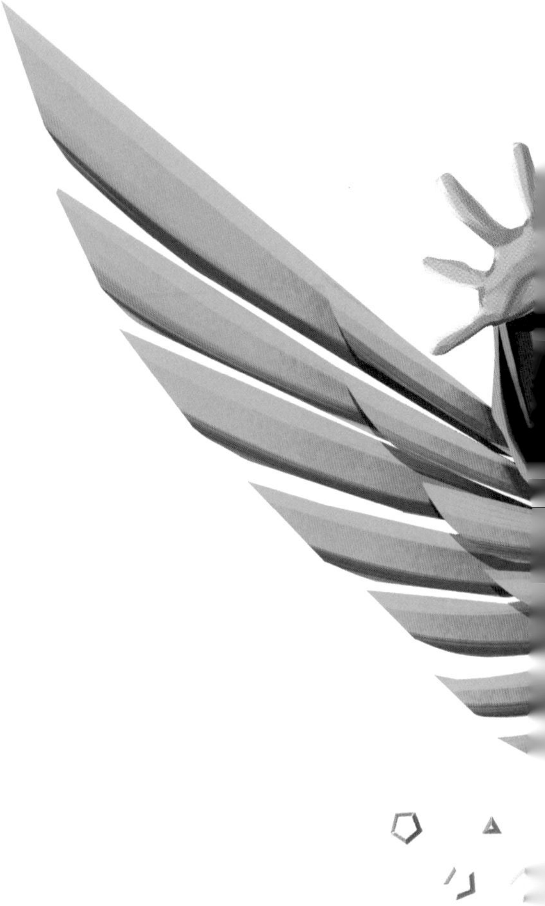

"Got you!" Spider-Man shouted. Then, he took out his latest gadget, a magnetic inverter. He knew the Vulture was harnessing magnetic power to help him fly. Once Spider-Man pressed the button, the Vulture lost control.

As Spider-Man web-slinged to safety, the Vulture fell onto the street below—landing right next to the police.

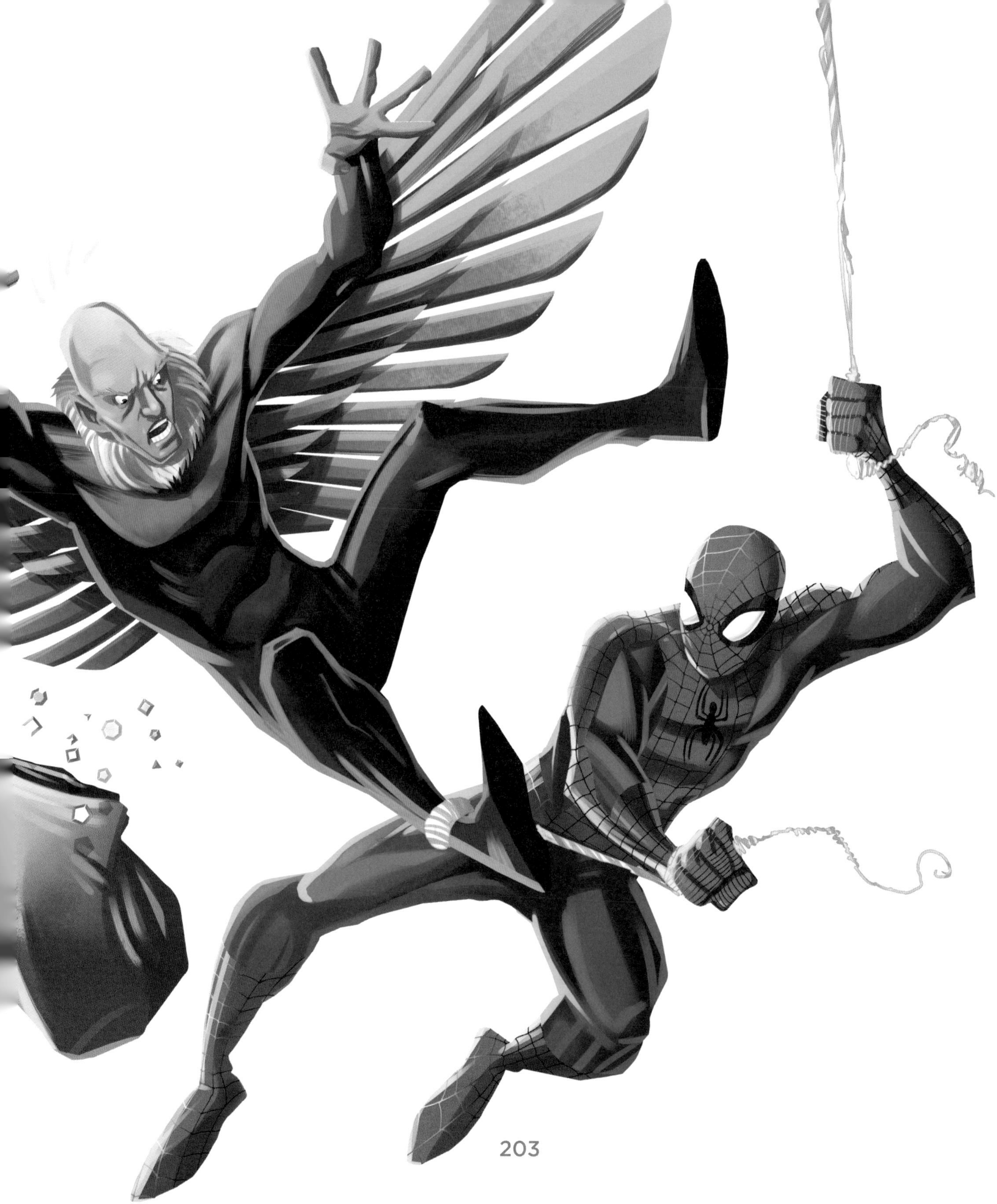

Spider-Man had saved the day.

But the Vulture wasn't done with Spider-Man yet. In his prison cell, the winged villain paced. "Sooner or later I'll develop a flying power that Spider-Man can't overcome," he snarled. "And then, Spider-Man, I will return!"

the AMAZING SPIDER-MAN™

MARVEL

THE TALE OF THE LIZARD'S RAGE

Dr. Curtis Connors was at the train station when he felt a strange, but familiar, sensation. He tried to think about how excited he was that his wife and son were visiting him at his new lab in New York. But when his right arm started to tingle, he knew he could not ignore the strange feeling any longer.

At the same train station, Peter Parker was helping Aunt May onto a train. *I could have sworn I just saw Dr. Connors,* Peter thought, turning around to catch a second glimpse.

"Mom, look it's Dad!" young Billy Connors said as he pointed. "Why is he's running away from us?"

The only reason he would is a terrible, unthinkable one, Mrs. Connors worried to herself. Just then, Dr. Connors started to transform into the fearsome monster known as the Lizard!

"It must be from my experiment earlier. It had some of the Lizard formula in it! My family can't see me like this again!" Dr. Connors gulped. He darted into a nearby subway tunnel.

After he dropped off Aunt May, Peter changed into his Spider-Man costume to investigate. Soon, he spotted Mrs. Connors and Billy, who were pointing to the subway tunnel.

Spider-Man followed Dr. Connors' tracks to the train platform. There he saw the Lizard bashing a giant hole in the cement wall with his powerful tail.

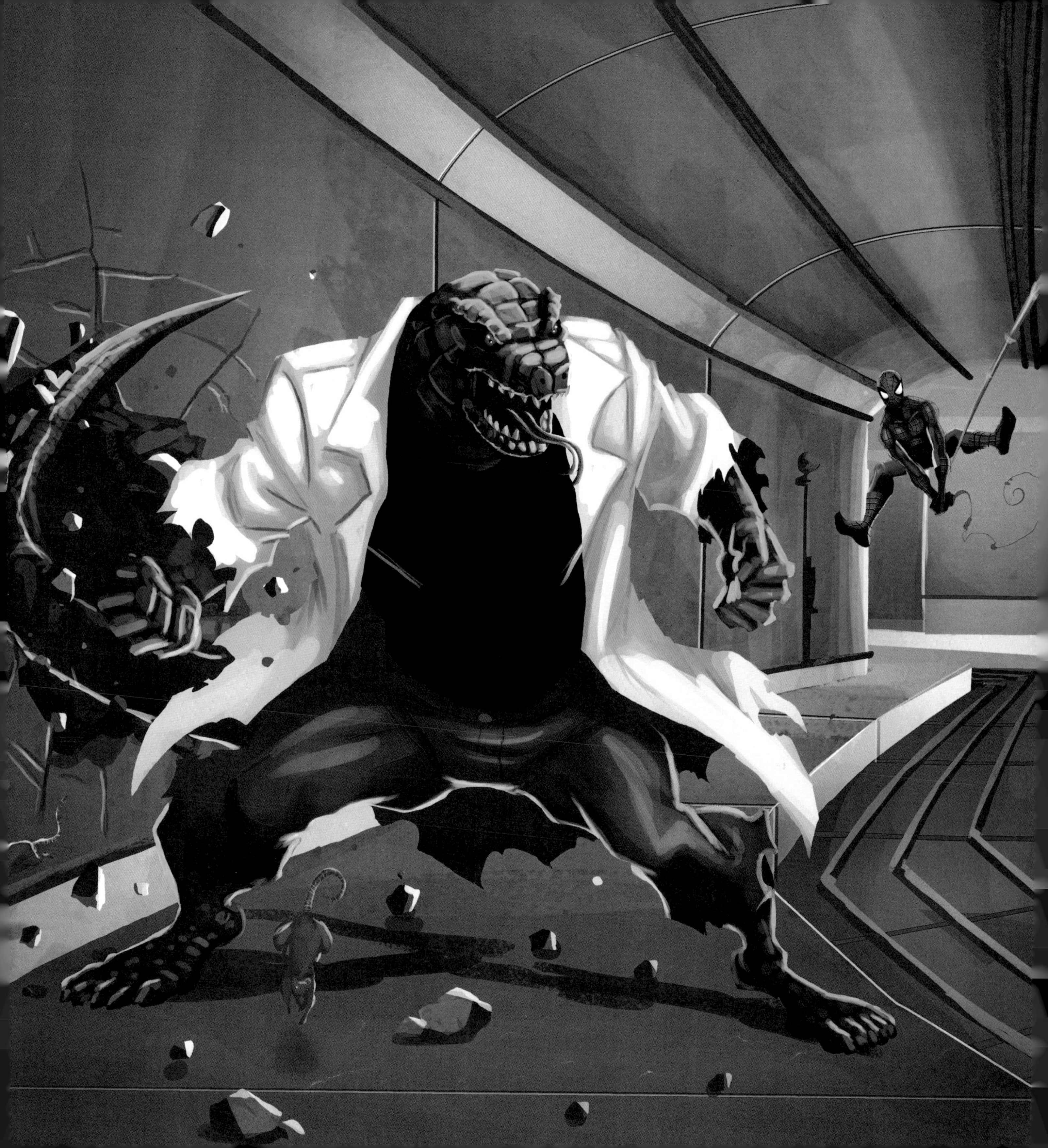

When the Lizard reached Dr. Connors' lab, he scurried up the wall with ease. But when he looked back, he saw Spider-Man was not far behind.

"It's you again! I should have known! You know what happens to the itsy-bitsy spider?" the Lizard asked. With one swift swipe of his tail, the Lizard knocked Spidey down!

Before it was too late, the web-slinger shot his web, swinging and landing on the other side of the building. That was a close call! Spidey thought.

Inside the lab, the Lizard searched for a special formula. "Once I find it, my army of reptiles would be unstoppable!"

After examining Dr. Connors' notebook, the frustrated Lizard threw it across the room. He couldn't read or understand the doctor's notes.

"It's pointless! It's just silly symbols and numbers!" the Lizard exclaimed as he leaped out of the lab.

Just as the Lizard left the scene, Mrs. Connors entered the lab. She saw Spider-Man, who had overheard the Lizard's evil plan.

"It seems like the Lizard completely took over Dr. Connors' mind! He doesn't even remember he is Dr. Connors. He is trying to find more reptiles. . . ."

"That means there's only one place where he could be: the zoo!" Mrs. Connors gasped.

Spider-Man searched the zoo until he spotted a trail of reptiles.

"I'm too late!" Spider-Man said as he quickly followed the reptiles to their leader.

Soon, he was surrounded. A hungry crocodile obeyed its leader's commands and lunged towards the web-slinger. Spidey had to act fast!

After shooting webbing at the crocodile's snout, Spider-Man swirled the beast at the other reptiles.

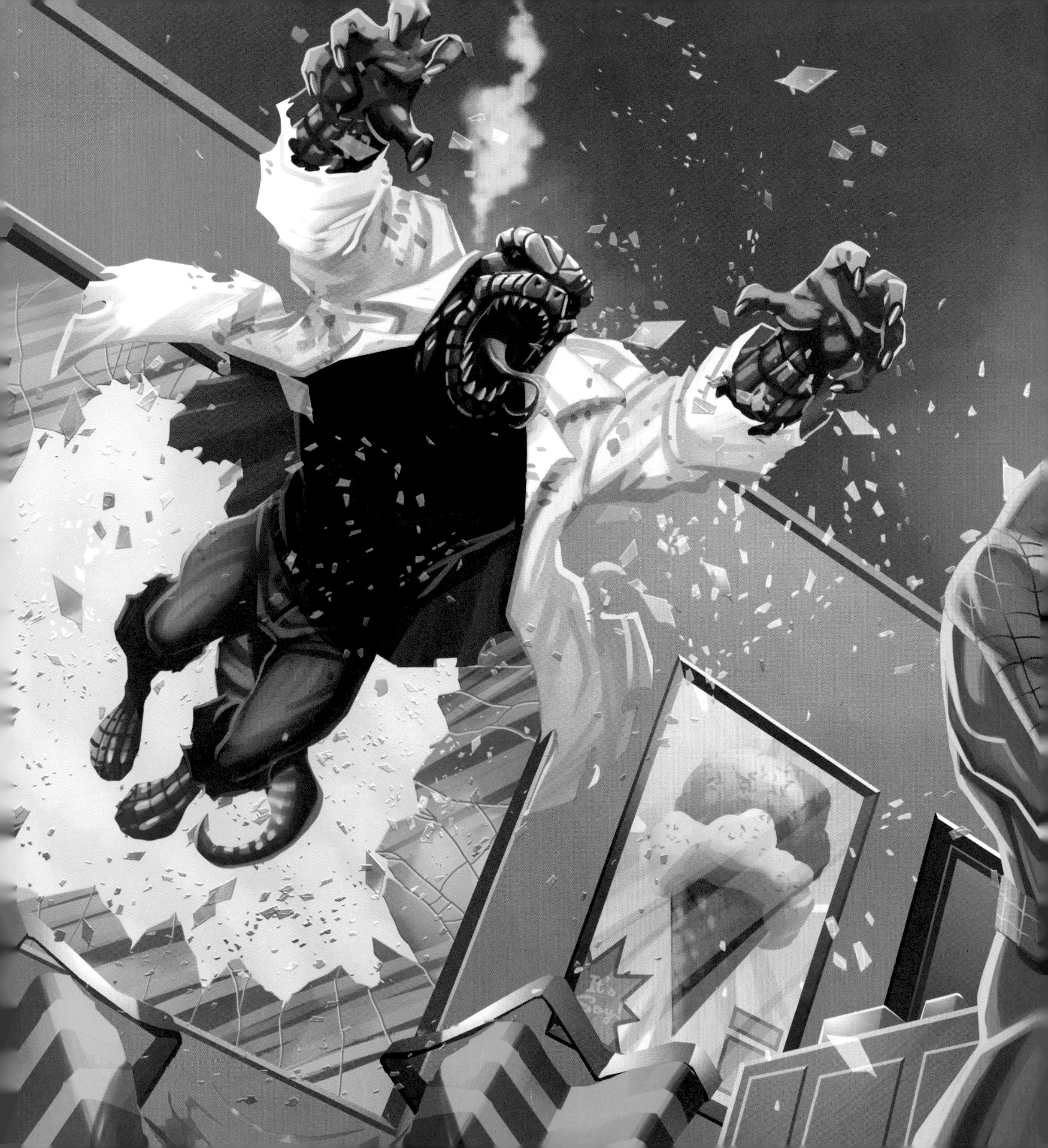
It's Soy!

I have an idea that might help me defeat this overgrown reptile, Spider-Man thought. He dashed into a nearby ice-cream shop and hid in the freezer room. He could hear the villain stomping toward him.

"I hope this works!" Spider-Man said underneath his breath.

In the icy room, the Lizard acted differently. When he charged at Spider-Man, he was sluggish and slow. "What's happening . . . to . . . me . . ." the Lizard stuttered.

"Oh, right. You're a big, bad, cold-blooded reptile! You're not warm-blooded, like me," Spider-Man said as he watched the Lizard collapse from the cold. "Now, let's make a web-cocoon so you stay warm enough to survive!"

After all, Spider-Man knew that somewhere underneath the ugly, scaly exterior was his friend Dr. Connors!

Returning to the lab, Spider-Man quickly got to work on an antidote. He glanced at the stirring web-cocoon. It would be dangerous if the Lizard thawed out!

"Who's there?" Mrs. Connors asked, arriving at the lab.

"It's Spider-Man. But stay back, it's unsafe!"

Not a moment too soon, Spider-Man poured the antidote into the Lizard's mouth.

Had Spider-Man saved Dr. Connors again or merely revived the Lizard?

As the lab door slowly opened, Mrs. Connors held her breath. Inside was Spider-Man and Dr. Connors! "This is the second time you rescued me! Thank you! How did you know I needed your help?" Dr. Connors asked.

"Let's just say a little spider told me." Spider-Man began his departure. He was very happy to stop the Lizard and reunite the Connors family again. He just hoped Mr. Jameson liked the photos he secretly took of himself fighting the Lizard more than the last time!

MARVEL

The Amazing Spider-Man

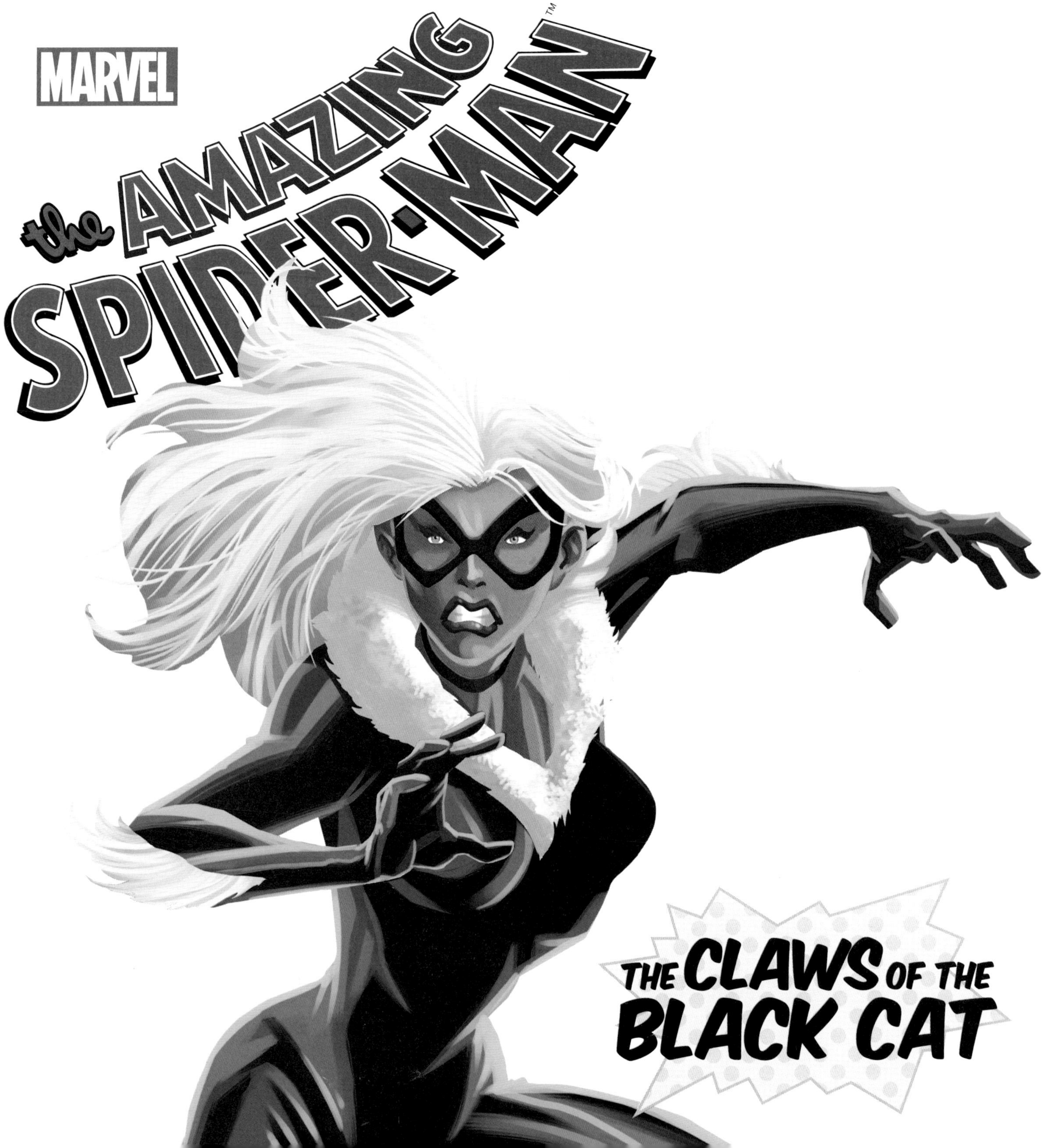

The Claws of the Black Cat

It was midnight, and two men, Boris and Bruno, were getting ready to rob a bank!

Boris was planting explosives on the wall of the bank while Bruno stood guard, looking down the alley to see if the police were coming.

But Bruno wasn't looking up. Suddenly, a dark figure landed in the alley. "Run!" Bruno cried. "It's Spider-Man!"

But it wasn't Spider-Man. It was the master thief known as
the Black Cat!

"The police are on their way," the Black Cat said. "Do you want
to stay here and go to jail, or do you want to work for me?"

The criminals knew they didn't have much of a choice. They
fled with the Black Cat.

In the morning, Peter Parker, photographer for *The Daily Bugle*, walked into the office. His boss, J. Jonah Jameson, was steaming mad.

"Parker!" Jameson cried. "How could you miss this? That menace Spider-Man saved two bank robbers from the police last night! I want pictures!"

"I really don't think Spider-Man would do something like that," Peter said. He knew for a fact that Spider-Man hadn't done anything like that last night. He'd been at home!

"I don't pay you to think!" JJJ barked. "I pay you to take pictures!"

Peter read *The Daily Bugle*'s story, which said that Spider-Man had helped two criminals escape. He figured out that someone else was swinging through the city high above the ground helping criminals, and he needed to find out who it was. He saw a masked woman dressed in black swing into a nearby warehouse and followed her.

Spider-Man was fast, but the Black Cat was faster! She
dodged the webs he fired at her and hid in the shadows. Spidey
looked all over the warehouse, but she was already gone.

Back at her hideout, the Black Cat up came in with a brand-new plan. Bruno and Boris were there. "Well, boys, now it's time to break into jail." she said.

"Break *into* jail?" Bruno cried. "Are you nuts?"

"Don't worry," the Black Cat said. "We won't be staying long. We just need to get an old friend of mine. His name is Gadget, and he can build us all the tools we need to rob every bank in the city!"

Peter Parker walked into *The Daily Bugle* offices with some pictures he'd taken with a camera he'd set up in the alley. They showed Spider-Man chasing the Black Cat.

"Here you go," Peter said as he handed the photos to Jameson. "Spider-Man chasing the Black Cat. She must have been the one who rescued those bank robbers from the police."

"They probably work together!" Jameson bellowed. "This is just two criminals trying to figure out how to split the loot!"

A television in the newsroom of *The Daily Bugle* gave
Peter the answers he was looking for. "—break-in at police
headquarters," the newscaster said. "Nothing was stolen except
the plans for East River Prison."

Spidey swung into action, and he arrived at the prison just as the Black Cat was lowering herself down the wall of the prison on a rope.

"Here, kitty kitty!" Spidey called.

The Black Cat spun around. "Back for more?" she asked. "You're in trouble, young man. Now, Boris!"

Just then, Boris triggered the explosives he had put in place. The wall of the prison fell apart, and Spidey fell right along with it!

While Spider-Man lay under a pile of rubble, Bruno grabbed Gadget from his cell.

Several corrections officers pulled the rubble off of Spider-Man. They thanked him for trying to prevent the jailbreak, but Spider-Man was embarrassed. The Black Cat had gotten away.

But Spidey knew exactly where to go. When Peter had looked up Gadget, he discovered his secret identity: a retired engineer named Miles Stitchson.

When Spidey arrived at Stitchson's house, he found Boris and Bruno leaving. "Hey, why don't you guys hang around until the police get here?" Spidey said as he wrapped them up in webbing.

The Black Cat was just coming out of the door as Spider-Man arrived on the doorstep. "Pizza's here! Somebody order a large with anchovies?" Spidey called.

The Black Cat jumped back. "How did you find me?" She yelled.

"It wasn't too hard to find the house of the guy you just broke out of jail," Spider-Man replied. "It's time for you to give up."

"Never!" the Black Cat cried. She leaped right at Spider-Man, but he ducked out of the way and she went flying across the porch. With incredible speed, she swung over the porch, and landed on the roof of the house. This time, though, Spidey was ready. He had covered the roof in sticky webbing!

"Stick around!" Spidey called. "I have a phone call to make — to the police!"

When the police arrived, and they were very happy to take Boris and Bruno into custody. But the Black Cat had gotten away again! She'd left her boots stuck to the roof and escaped.

"That cat really does have nine lives," Spider-Man said. "I have a feeling we'll meet again."

"Thanks for capturing Bruno and Boris and leading us back to Gadget," one of the police officers said to Spider-Man.

The next morning, Peter Parker walked into the offices of *The Daily Bugle*. "Well," he said to J. Jonah Jameson, "it looks like Spider-Man is a hero after all. He captured the bank robbers and the escaped prisoner."

"But he let the Black Cat get away! That wall-crawler may have everyone else fooled, but not me!" JJJ yelled. "And who wrote this headline, anyway?"

Peter picked up a copy of *The Daily Bugle* and smiled. It read "SPIDER-MAN: HERO!"

MARVEL

the AMAZING SPIDER-MAN™

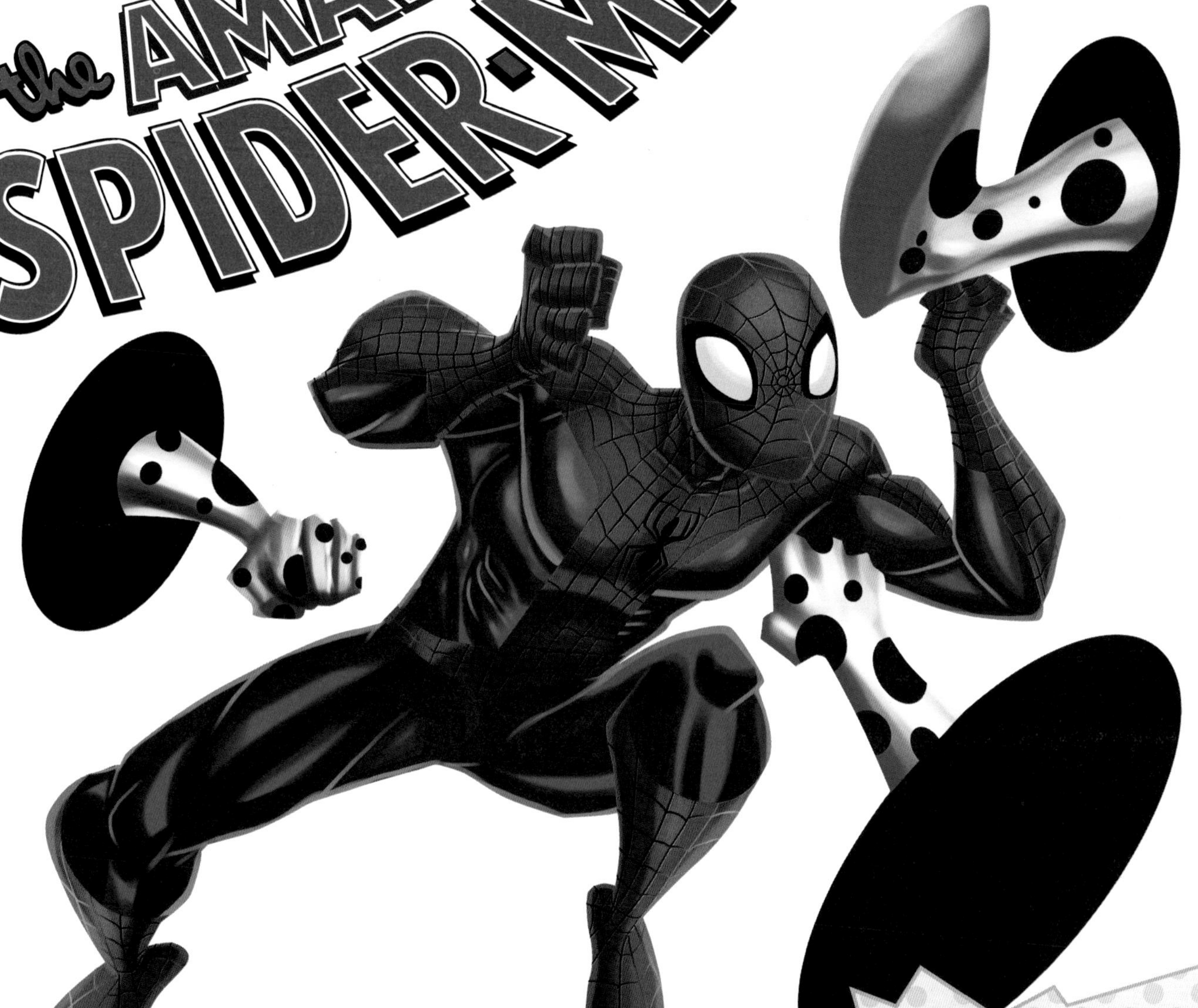

SEE SPOT PUNCH

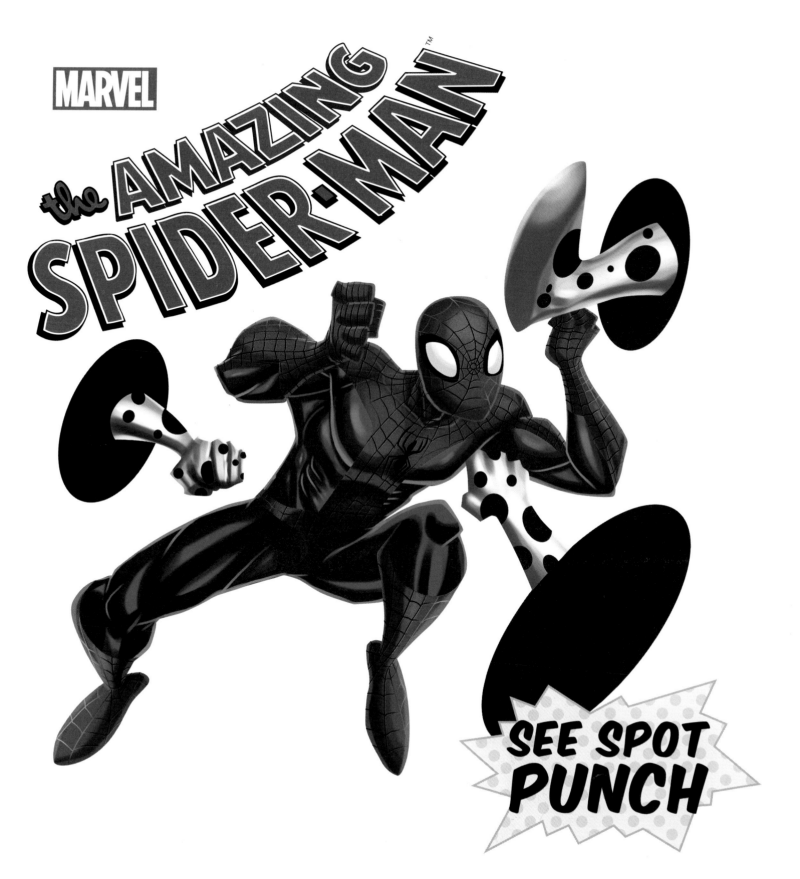

It was a rainy day in New York City, but that wasn't going to keep the Big Apple's newest villain from his crime spree! The teleporting thief called the Spot had robbed ten jewelry shops in two weeks.

The Spot would use his teleportation powers to appear in a store, take what he wanted, then leave. But Peter Parker, the Amazing Spider-Man, was determined to bring this thief to justice! He just had to find him first . . . even if it meant checking every jewelry store in New York City!

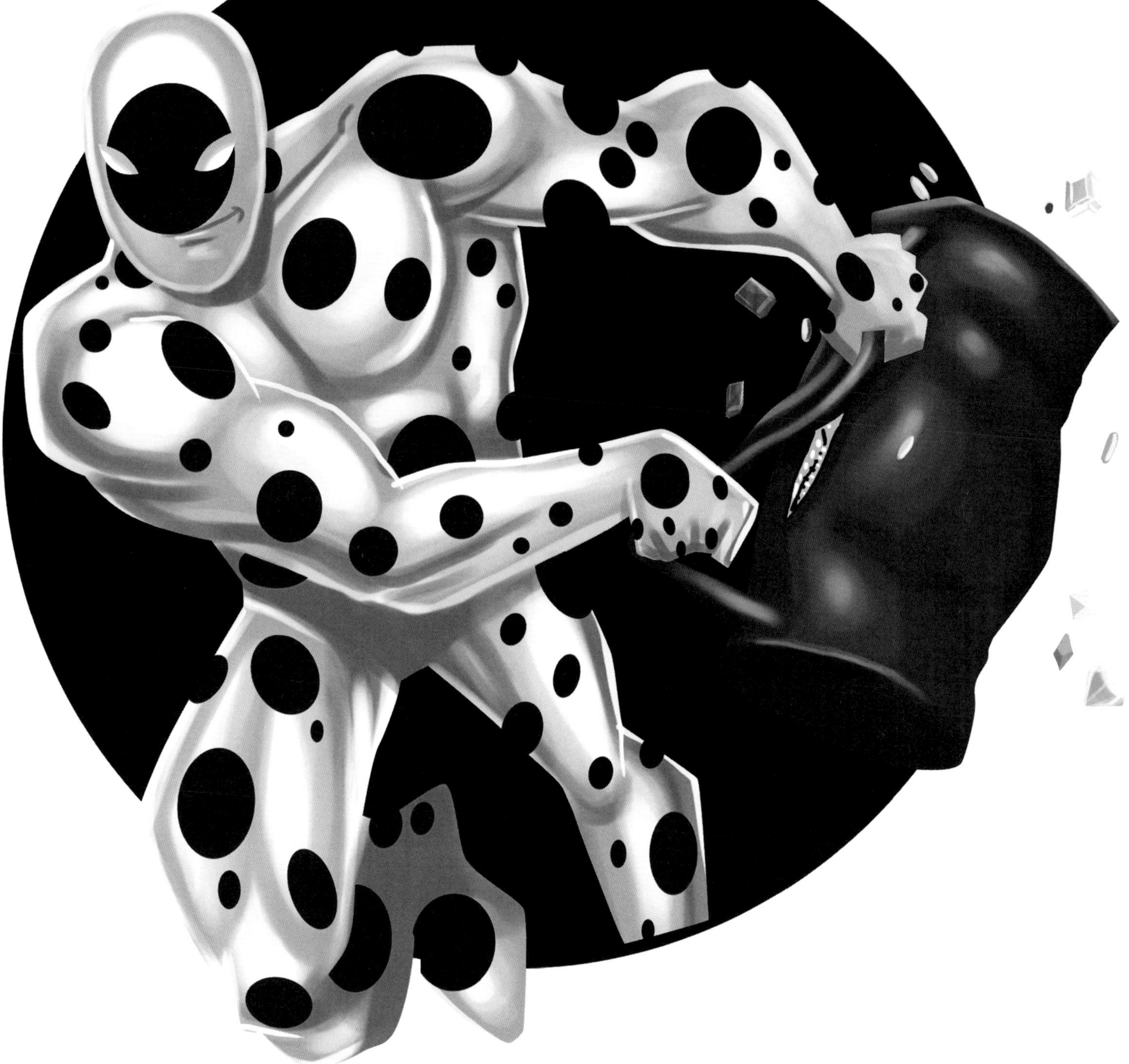

Meanwhile, the Spot appeared in another jewelry store, much to everyone's surprise.

"Greetings, greedy shoppers! I've come to take away all of your shiny gems!" Quicker than the eye could see, his hands appeared inside one of the jewelry cases and he filled his bag with diamonds and gold!

Just then, Spider-Man appeared on the scene! He kicked the Spot and made him drop the stolen jewels.

Spider-Man shot a burst of webbing hoping to stop the Spot. But a black portal suddenly appeared, and Spidey's webbing disappeared inside. It quickly came out another black portal, hitting Spider-Man right in the face!

"You snuck up on me once, Spider-Man, but you won't be able to do it again!" gloated the Spot as he disappeared into another black hole.

Spidey peeled the webbing off his mask.

"Thanks for saving us," one of the guards said.

"I can't believe he got away," said the wall-crawler. "But don't worry — I'm going to make sure his crime spree is stopped!"

But how can I stop someone who can appear and disappear whenever he wants, Spidey thought. He needed answers, and he knew just who to ask.

Spider-Man headed out into the rainy day to see his friend, Professor Franco. "Ever hear of an experiment that could create little black portals?" Spidey asked.

"I heard that Dr. Jonathan Ohnn was working on tapping into a new power source. It sounds similar to what you saw," the professor said.

What Spidey didn't know was that Dr. Ohnn had been trying to access another dimension. His experiment was eating up more power than he expected, but he would not shut it down. Suddenly, an explosion of pure darkness filled the room!

When Dr. Ohnn woke up, he was disappearing and reappearing in different parts of his lab!

What if I could control this new power? he thought. With some practice, Dr. Ohnn figured out that he had the ability to teleport from place to place. He could also reach out and grab something that was far away.

Dr. Ohnn realized that with these powers, he could take anything that he wanted, so he turned to a life of crime!

"The best way to stop him from teleporting is to disable his machinery," said the professor. "That should put an end to his disappearing act."

"All right, I'm going to go down to Ohnn's lab and see if I can shut down his powers," Spidey said as he headed for the window. "Thanks for the science, science guy!"

A rain-soaked Spider-Man snuck in through the roof of Ohnn's lab.

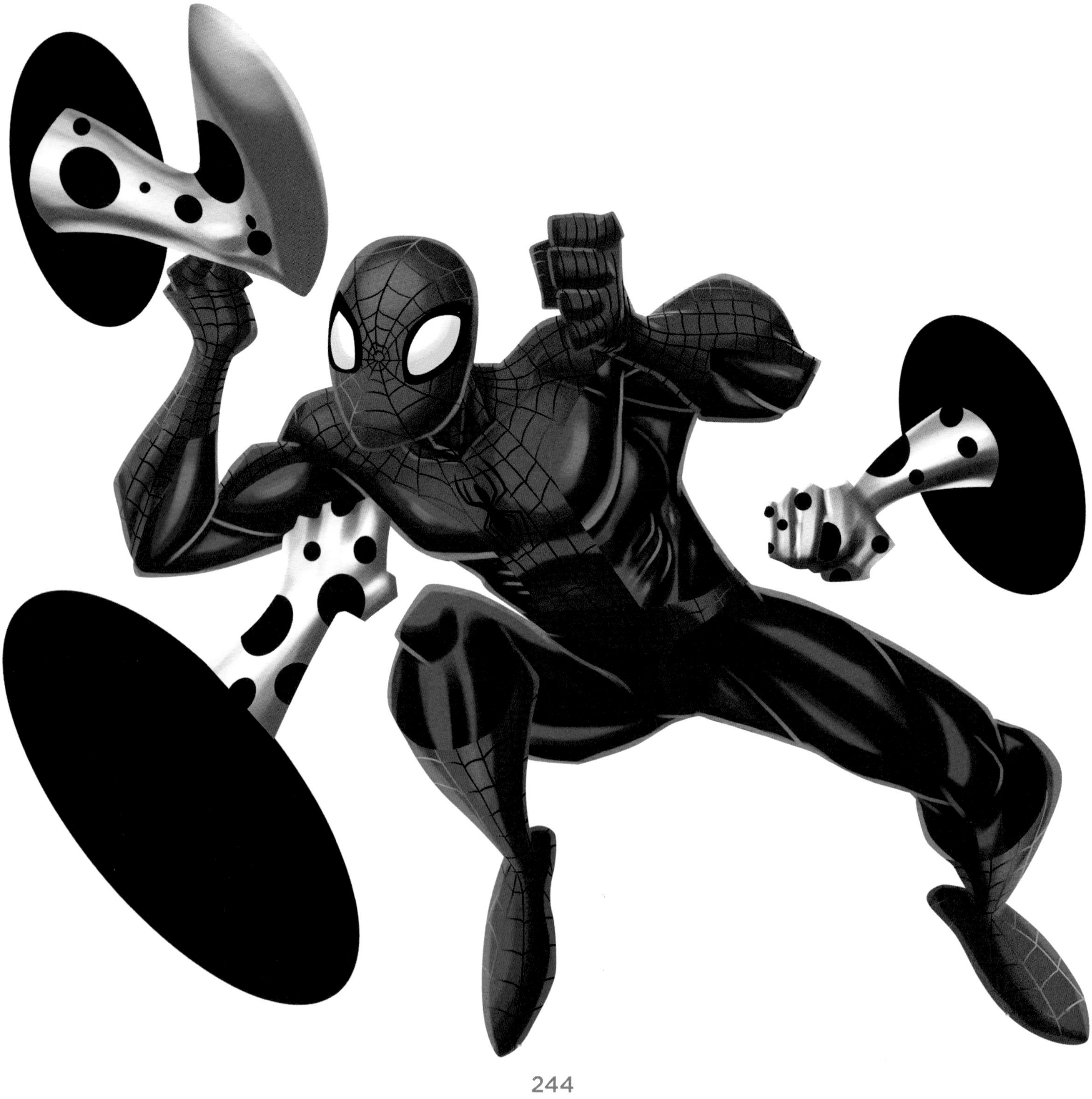

Spidey found the Spot tinkering with his machine. At the center of the machine, was a small black orb. "Okay, all I have to do is — *ah-choo!*" Spider-Man sneezed!

Hearing the sound, the Spot looked up. "So you were clever enough to track me down, but not bright enough to stay out of the rain, eh, Spider-Man?"

Suddenly, the Spot's arms and legs were punching and kicking at Spider-Man from every direction. Spidey swung down, landing next to the machine.

"No! Stay away from my experiment!" yelled the Spot.

"This experiment?" Spidey said, pointing. He reached to yank out the power supply. The Spot's arm suddenly appeared behind Spidey's head. But Spider-Man quickly pulled the Spot through his own teleportation portal!

"Gotcha!" Spider-Man said as he quickly shot webbing on the Spot, sticking him to the floor. "Let's see you teleport away while you're attached to the ground," said Spidey.

He reached out to the machine. "And I'm guessing this little doohickey is letting you teleport around the city," he said, yanking the power from the wall.

The small black orb disappeared. "No!" yelled the Spot. His disappearing act would be no more.

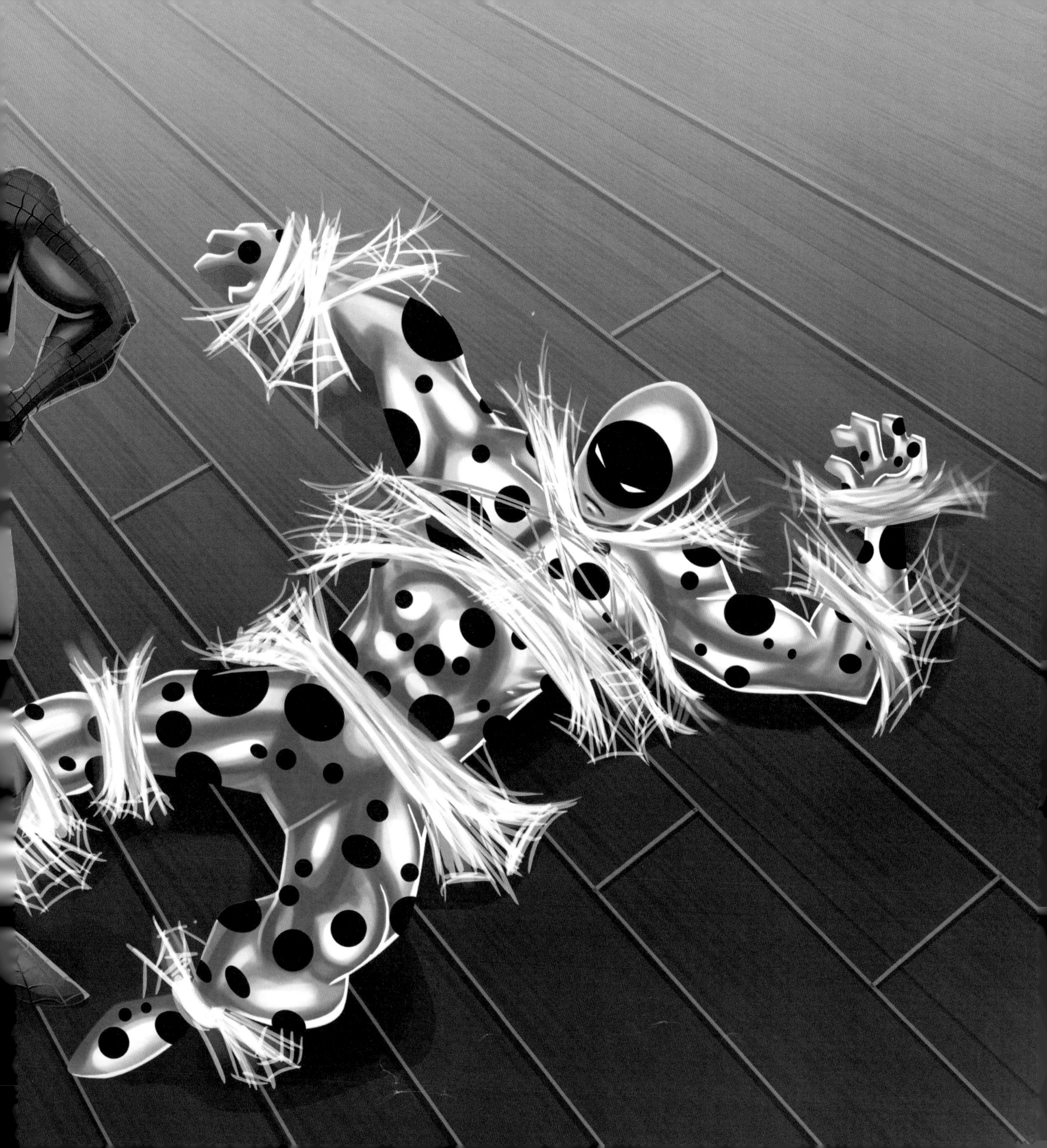

Spider-Man swung back out into the rain. He had defeated the mysterious Spot, but his night was just beginning.

Ah-choo! he sneezed again. "Maybe I should get out of the rain. I hope Aunt May will make me some chicken soup. I don't think anyone will find their friendly neighborhood Spider-Man impressive if I give them a cold. . . ."

MARVEL

the AMAZING SPIDER-MAN™

THE MANY FACES OF THE CHAMELEON

J. Jonah Jameson, much to Peter Parker's surprise, had decided to tag along on Peter's assignment for *The Daily Bugle*. Now Peter was trying to keep up.

Peter was shocked to learn that the Unity Day Parade had always been something JJJ enjoyed, ever since he was a little boy. What wasn't shocking was that Jameson was convinced Spider-Man was going to ruin the parade.

"That wall-crawling nightmare is going to swing in here and cause a mess," Jameson barked. "And when he does, Parker, I need you to get the photos."

But Peter was lost in thought. Peter didn't just put on his costume for fun — he always changed into Spider-Man to stop crime. And there wasn't a crime in sight. And even if there was, how would he ever get away from JJJ long enough to get a picture of himself in costume as the Amazing Spider-Man?!?

But then suddenly, Peter's spider-sense started tingling! He searched for any signs of danger. . .and then he spotted it.

The mayor had taken the stage, ready to give a speech. But what the mayor didn't know was that there was a window washer's cart tumbling down toward her!

Peter had to act fast — it was time to save the day, no matter how many people saw him doing it. He tried to leave without his boss noticing. But JJJ wasn't going to let Peter off the hook that easily. . . and with good reason.

"Parker! Take the picture!" J. Jonah Jameson shouted.

Peter turned, startled at the discovery that, somehow. . . Spider-Man was already saving the day! And no one knew better than Peter that it wasn't the *real* Spider-Man.

"That isn't Spidey," Peter explained. "He's swinging from a rope instead of a web-line!" But Mr. Jameson didn't care.

"He's brought this parade to a grinding halt, and he's raising my blood pressure. That's the Spider," J. Jonah Jameson growled. "Now get up there and get some pictures. For all we know, he's trying to kidnap the mayor!"

Peter bolted up the fire escape stairs toward the rooftops. Whoever this second Spider-Man was, Peter was going to have to thank him for helping out. But when he arrived on the roof, he realized that Mr. Jameson was right for a change. . . .

The fake Spider-Man really was kidnapping the mayor!

"Spider-Man, just what in the world do you think you're doing?!?" the frightened mayor asked.

"Why, holding you for ransom, my dear Ms. Mayor," the fake Spidey hissed through his mask as he sprayed her with knock-out gas.

"And then, all of New York will bend to the will of . . . THE CHAMELEON!" the villain said as he pressed a switch on his belt, revealing his true form.

"The only place the mayor is going is back down to the stage to finish her speech," a voice said from behind. It was Spider-Man! The real Spider-Man! Face-to-face with the hero, the Chameleon changed his strategy.

"When the Chameleon's charade is complete, the entire city will think Spider-Man is nothing more than a common criminal!" the villain hissed.

Just then, the Chameleon re-activated his Spider-Man disguise.

As the Chameleon jumped off the roof, the real Spider-Man made sure the mayor was unharmed.

"What's happening?" the mayor asked as she slowly awoke.

"Your not-so-friendly *fake* neighborhood Spider-Man tried to kidnap you, but you're safe now," Spidey explained.

"Then who are you?" the confused Mayor asked.

"I'm just your always-amazing, somewhat-spectacular, never-not-friendly neighborhood Spider-Man, of course!" Spider-Man answered. And in the blink of an eye, he was hot on the Chameleon's heels. Desperate to escape, the Chameleon leaped out into the open air and started bouncing from balloon to balloon!

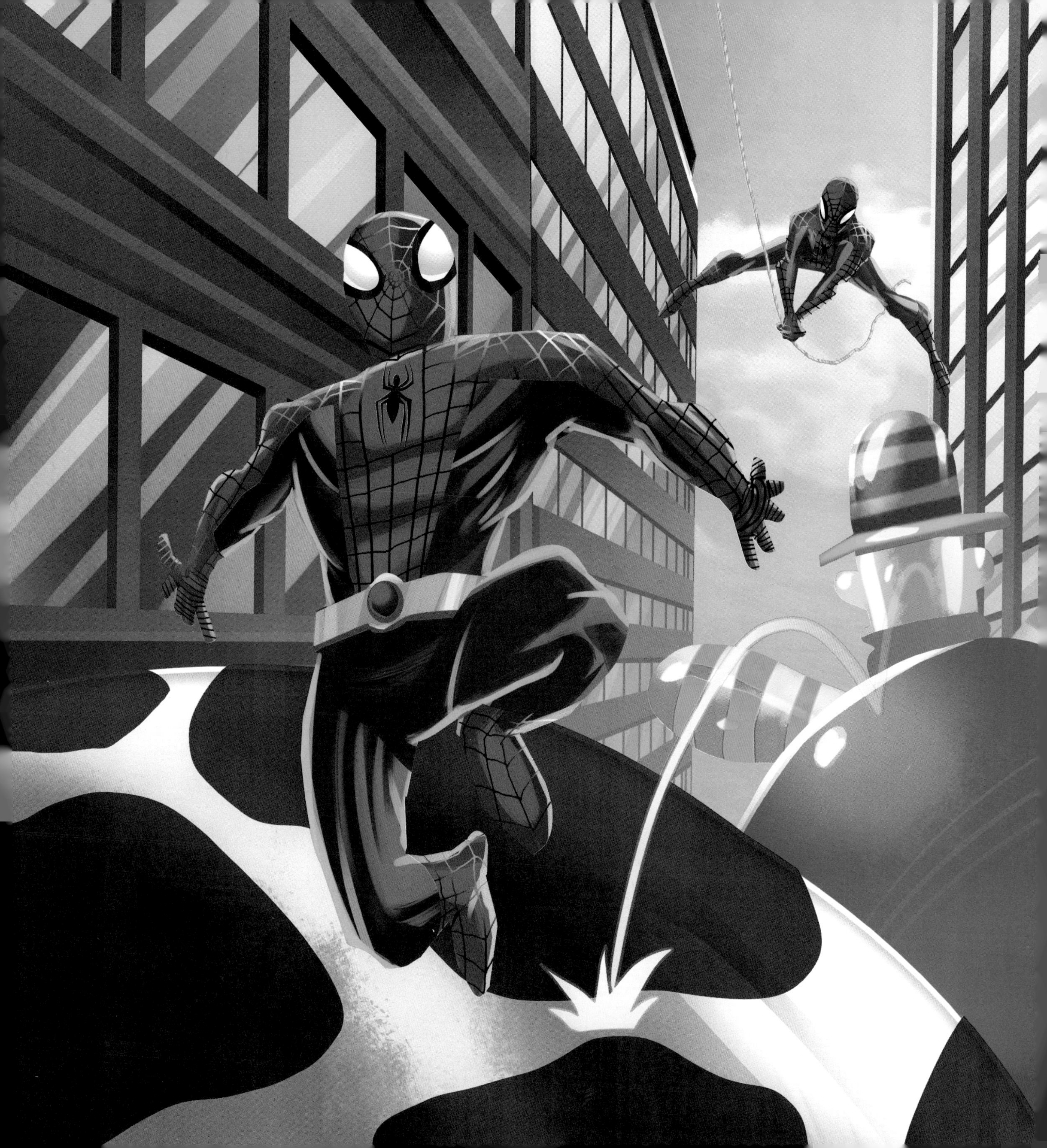

"You do know I can do everything a spider can, don't you?" Spider-Man called after the Chameleon, leaping along with ease behind him. But the clever villain had planned ahead— he knew he needed a distraction to escape.

"I thought you might say something like that, Spider-Man!" he called back, bouncing to the next balloon. "But can you spin a web big enough to save everyone on the street below?"

The Chameleon pulled a remote from his belt, then flipped the switch—an explosion caused a giant satellite dish to fall from a nearby roof, right toward the helpless crowd below!

"Spin a web? Any size!" Spider-Man said as he caught the dish in his webbing.

And then Spidey took aim at the Chameleon, who was trying to use the distraction to get away.

"Perhaps you've also heard I catch thieves just like flies," Spider-Man quipped as he snagged Chameleon in the back with another web-line, reeling him in like a fish.

"Look out! Here comes the *real* Spider-Man!" Spidey cheered.

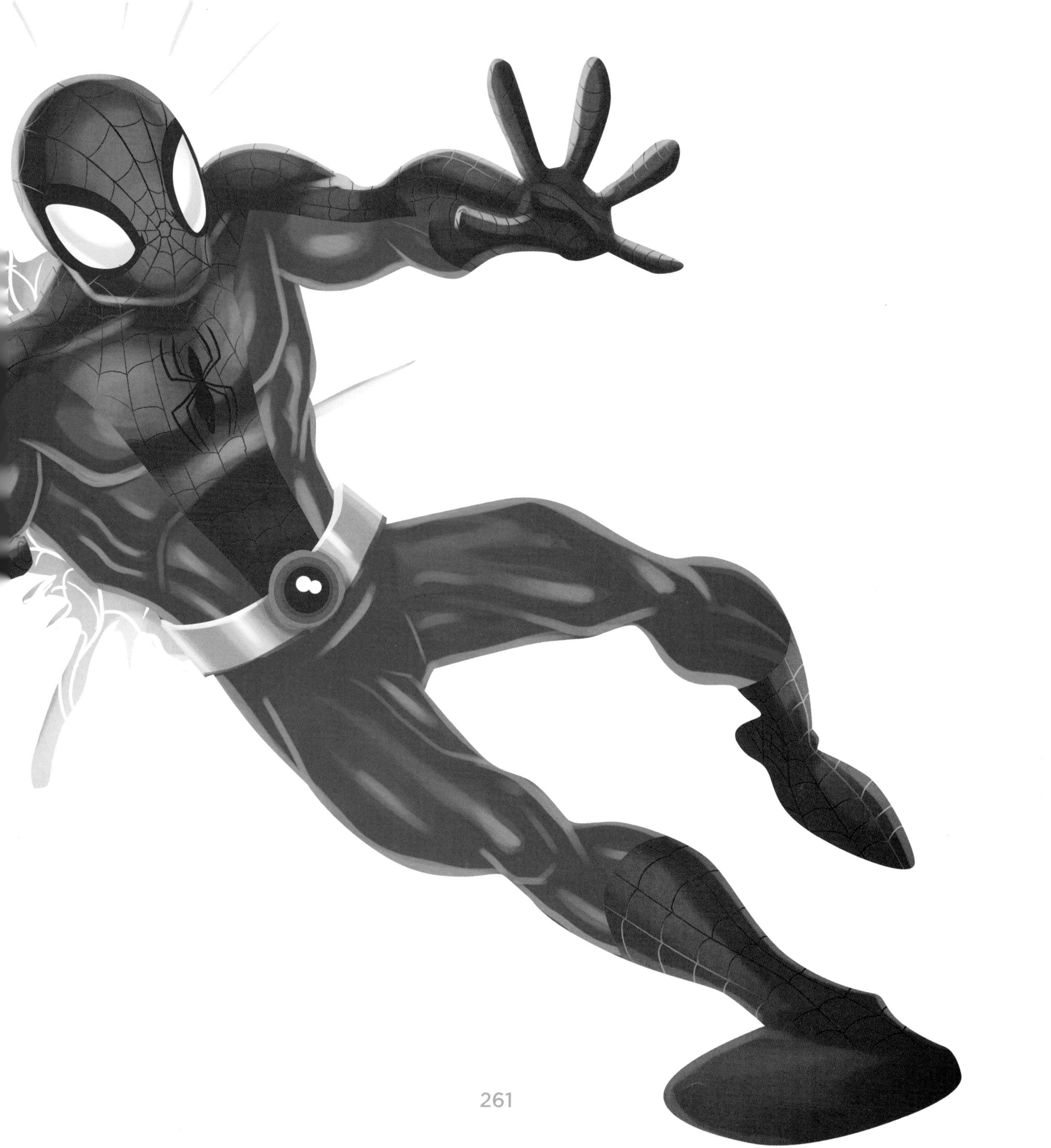

With one swift punch, Spider-Man smashed the Chameleon's belt, destroying the device the villain used to change his identity. As the Chameleon's Spider-Man disguise faded away, revealing the true villain within, the crowd cheered from below. Spider-Man had saved the parade!

Now, if only Peter Parker could save his job!

One quick change later, Peter pushed his way through the crowd, smiling as he saw the Chameleon being hauled away to jail by the police.

"It wasn't me," the Chameleon howled. "It was Spider-Man!"

"I'll bet it was," Mr. Jameson bellowed from the crowd.

"Guess again, Chief," Peter chimed in.

J. Jonah Jameson couldn't believe his eyes as Peter pulled photo after photo out of his bag.

They were all images of the real Spider-Man saving the mayor from the Chameleon. Peter had gotten his photos after all!

"Hate to admit it, kid," Mr. Jameson said, "but it looks like you just made the front page."

"Don't mention it." Peter blushed. "It's all in a day's work for your friendly neighborhood...Peter Parker!"

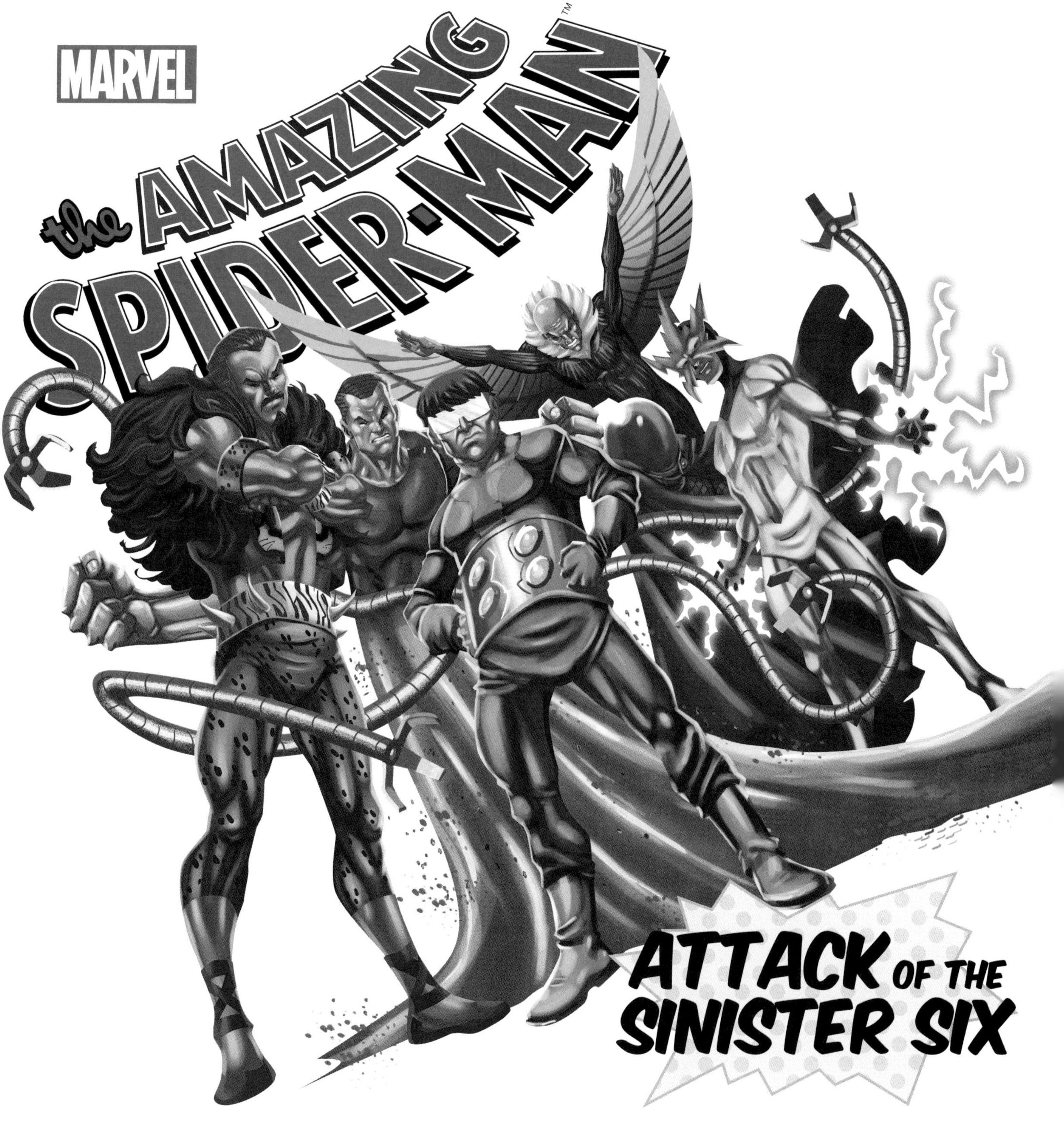
MARVEL
the AMAZING SPIDER-MAN™
ATTACK OF THE SINISTER SIX

Spider-Man was tired but happy. The past few months had been exciting — and very hard. Becoming Spider-Man was great. Fighting all those villains was not.

At least things seemed to be a little more quiet just now. He hoped it would stay that way. But he knew it probably wouldn't . . .

And he was right. Across town, some of Spider-Man's worst enemies were about to meet.

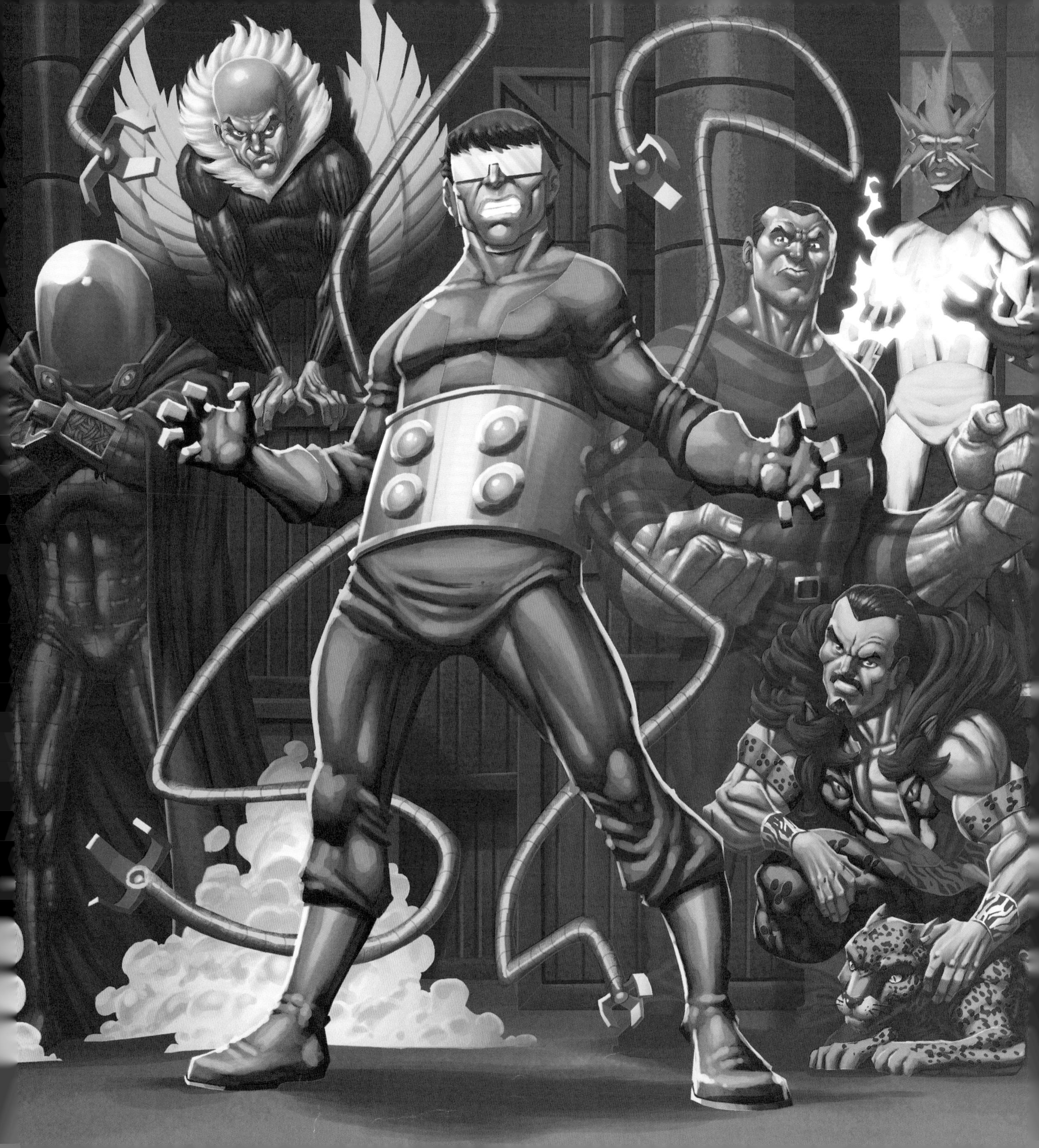

Doctor Octopus looked around at all the other Super Villains—Electro, Kraven, Mysterio, Sandman, and the Vulture!

"Each of us has fought Spider-Man," Doc Ock said. "And each of us has lost."

"So?" the Sandman growled.

"We all want to defeat Spider-Man," Doc Ock replied. "And if we work together, we can."

"You have a plan?" Mysterio asked.

Doc Ock smiled. "Oh, yes."

Outside *The Daily Bugle*, Aunt May and MJ arrived to meet Peter for lunch.

But Sandman was waiting! He needed two hostages to lure Spider-Man into a trap, and his sights were set on Aunt May and MJ.

Later, Peter learned of the news. "Kidnapped?"

"Saw it out the window," JJJ replied, handing Peter a note. "Says Spider-Man has to go to this address, or else."

Peter flew out the door. He had to rescue them!

The address led Spidey to an alley by an abandoned laboratory.

Suddenly, Spider-Man felt his spider-sense tingle. He twisted just in time. A bolt of lightning shattered the ground where he had just been standing.

"Electro!" Spider-Man said.

"How nice of you to remember." Electro smiled, stepping out of a doorway. "I've been looking forward to this."

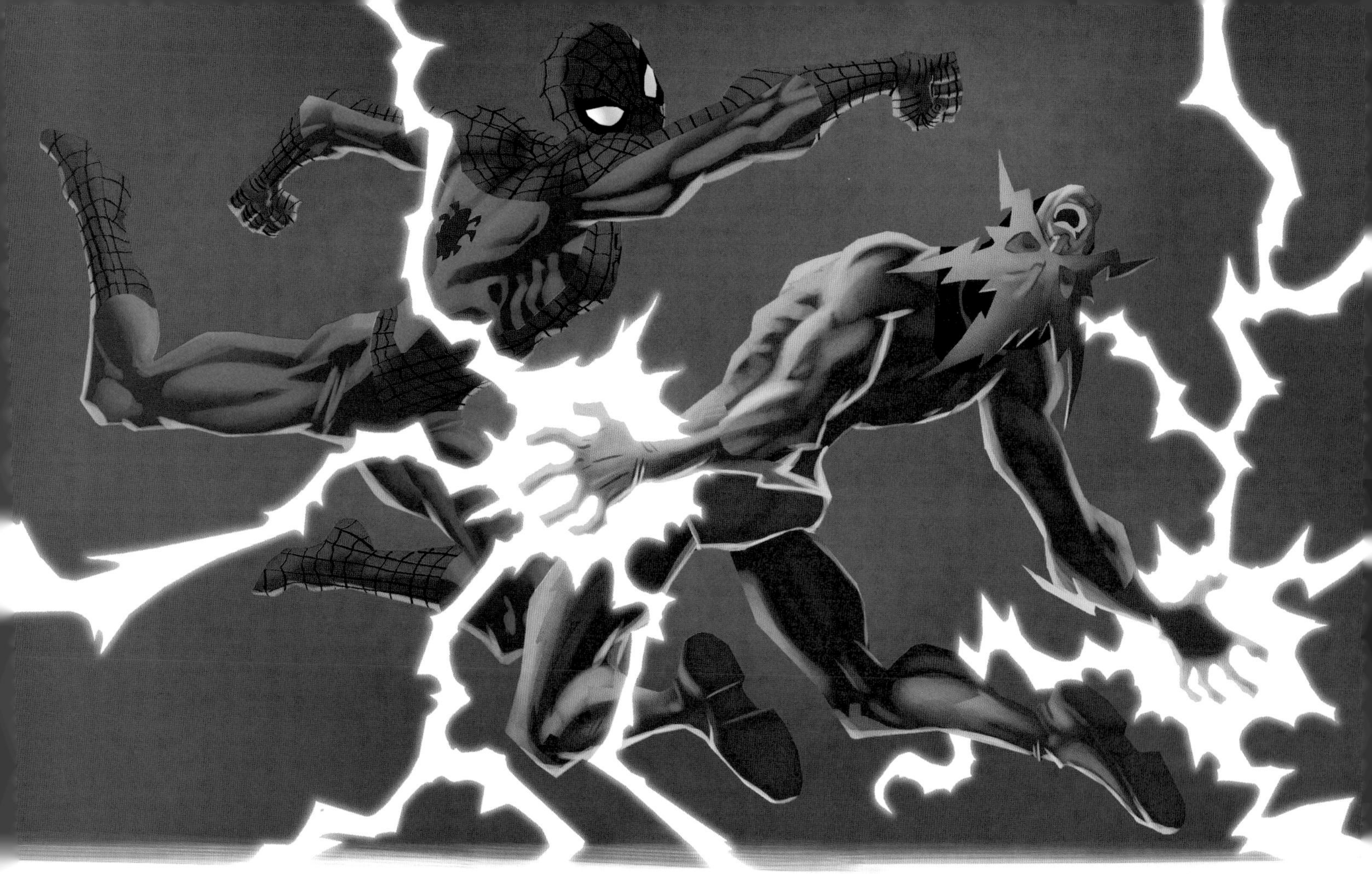

Spider-Man leaped back. He landed high up on a wall, then jumped down as hard as could.

The web-slinger's fist met Electro's chin. The villain was knocked to the ground!

"Sorry to be so serious," Spider-Man said. "I'm kind of in a hurry."

Spider-Man heard a low rumble. He looked up and saw a pair of leopards circling him.

"Kraven the Hunter, I presume?" Spider-Man said.

"You are correct," Kraven growled, stepping out from the shadows. "My beasts are hungry, and it's feeding time."

"Nice kitties," Spider-Man said, hopefully. "Spiders don't taste so good."

The giant cats' growls turned to shrieks as they leaped.

Spidey ducked, the cats barely missing him. "Almost!" he teased. Then Spidey shot a web that covered both leopards. Using his great strength, Spider-Man spun the leopards toward Kraven.

"Not again!" the villain cried as the big cats crashed into him. "Electro. Kraven. I wonder who's next!" Spider-Man said.

"We are," said a familiar voice. Spider-Man looked up to see . . . himself. Times three!

"Spider-Mans?" the real Spidey wondered aloud. "Or is that Spider-*Men*?"

He shook his head. "What am I talking about?! How can there be other Spider. . . other *ME*s?"

Spider-Man was stunned. There was no way he could defeat himself, especially if it was three against one.

"Wait a second," he said. Then he turned and burst through a large window nearby.

"How — ?" Mysterio cried. It was the only word he had time to say.

Spider-Man stood over the unconscious villain. "I knew they couldn't be real," he said. "Because as great as I am, even a Spider-Man has to cast a shadow."

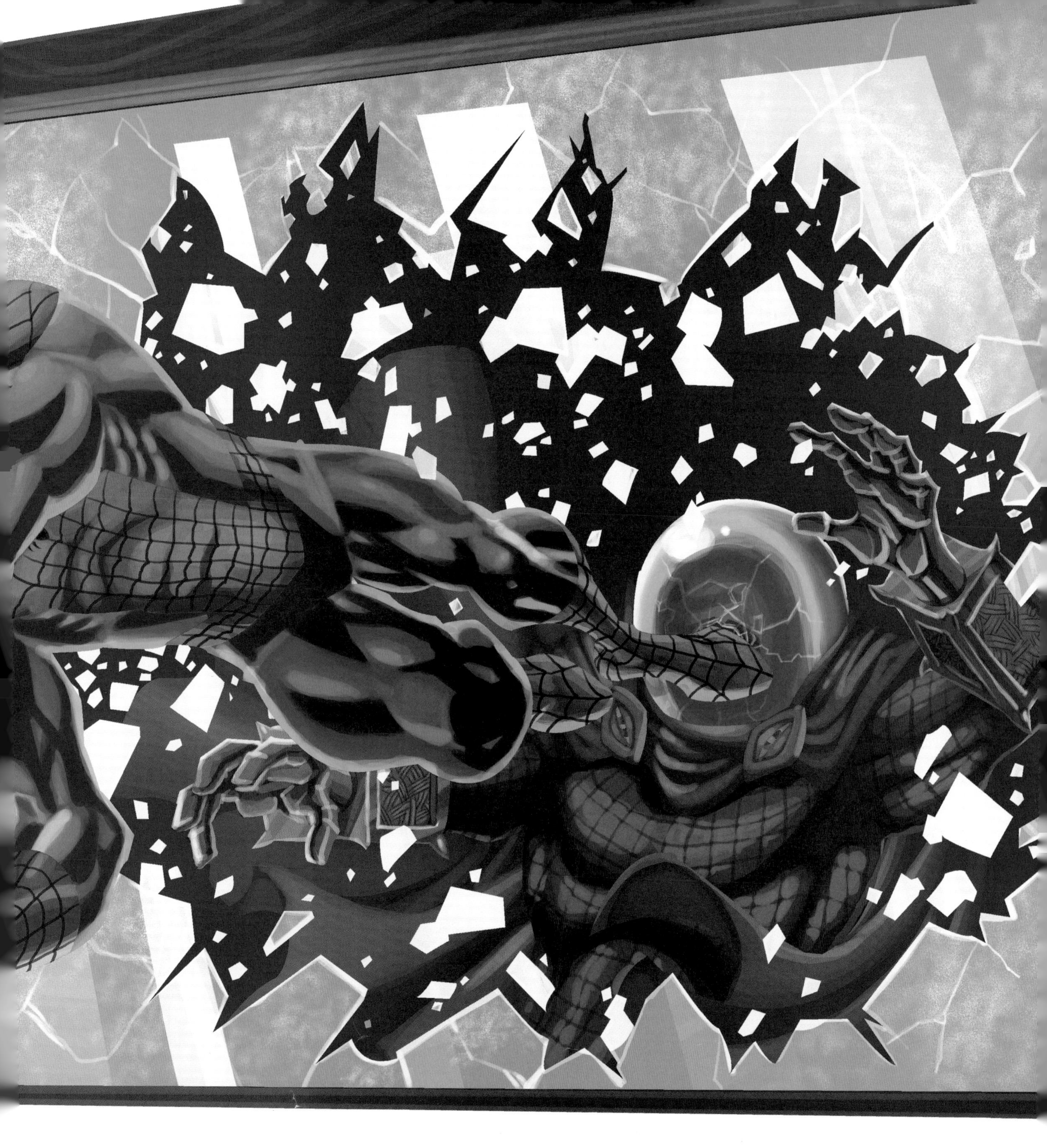

Spider-Man barely noticed a quiet hissing sound behind him.
He turned around to see the Sandman appearing.

"Oh, I'm sorry," Spidey said. "Was I standing on you?"

"In just a second, smart guy," the Sandman snarled, "I'm gonna
be standing on *you*." Spider-Man bashed into the Sandman,
and quickly shot a web off to the side.

"Ha!" the Sandman said as he hit the ground. "My sand can get out of any web."

"Heads up!" Spidey yelled as he pulled on the webbing.

"No!" the Sandman cried, as a truckful of cement mixture covered him. "You might be able to get out eventually," Spider-Man called. "But not for a while."

"Good thing he's not working alone, then," said the Vulture, as he slammed into Spider-Man.

"Oof!" said Spidey. "And you can quote me on that.

"I don't mean to brag," Spider-Man continued, "but when you've got reflexes as awesome as mine, well . . ."

Right before he smashed into the cement truck, Spider-Man reached out and grabbed the Vulture. He flipped the villain over his head, then jumped on the Vulture's back.

"This is how we ride them doggies in New York City," the web-slinger drawled. Then Spider-Man laughed. "Okay, I admit it — this is kind of fun. But I'm on a deadline, so . . ."

He wrapped the Vulture up in a web. "Don't go anywhere," Spider-Man joked.

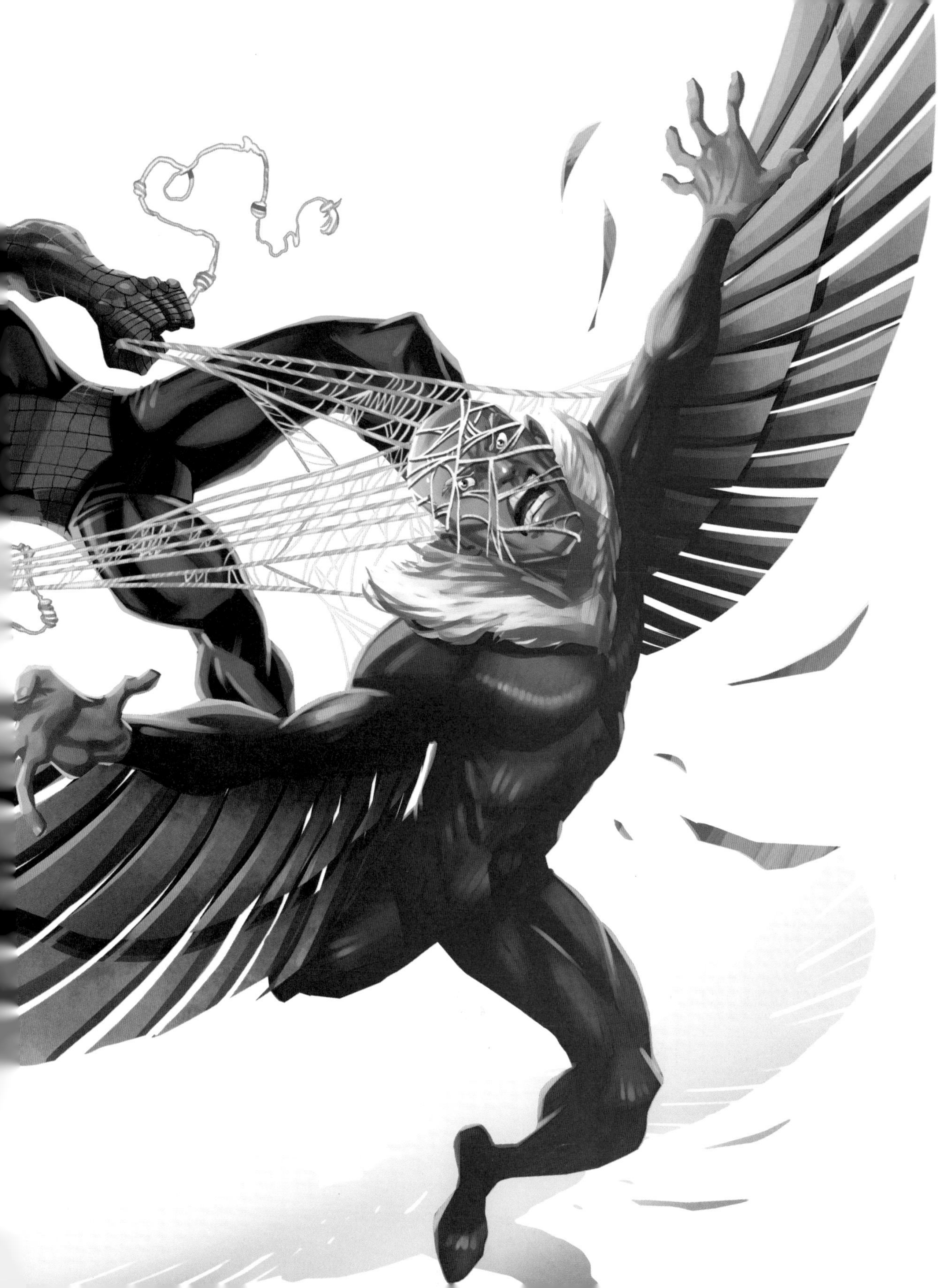

"Well," Spider-Man said, as he entered the laboratory, "that's five villains down. My guess is there's still one left to go."

His spider-sense tingled. Instantly, Spider-Man leaped up to the ceiling. Doc Ock's robotic arms whizzed by, just missing him.

"It doesn't take a genius to figure out who was behind this," Doctor Octopus sneered.

Spider-Man smiled. "Takes a nongenius to know one, Doc."

Doc Ock frowned. "I've had enough of your insults."

"You know, I disagree," Spider-Man said. "I don't think you've had nearly enough of them."

Spider-Man fired off a pair of webs.

"You know your spider webs can't hold me." Doc Ock snorted.

"That's true," Spider-Man admitted. "Not for long, at least. But they should last long enough for this."

He pulled the mad scientist off his feet.

"No!" Doc Ock screamed, as he fell into a large water tank.

"Oh, yes," Spidey said, watching the doctor's arms short-out and stop working. "Now to round you all up for the police."

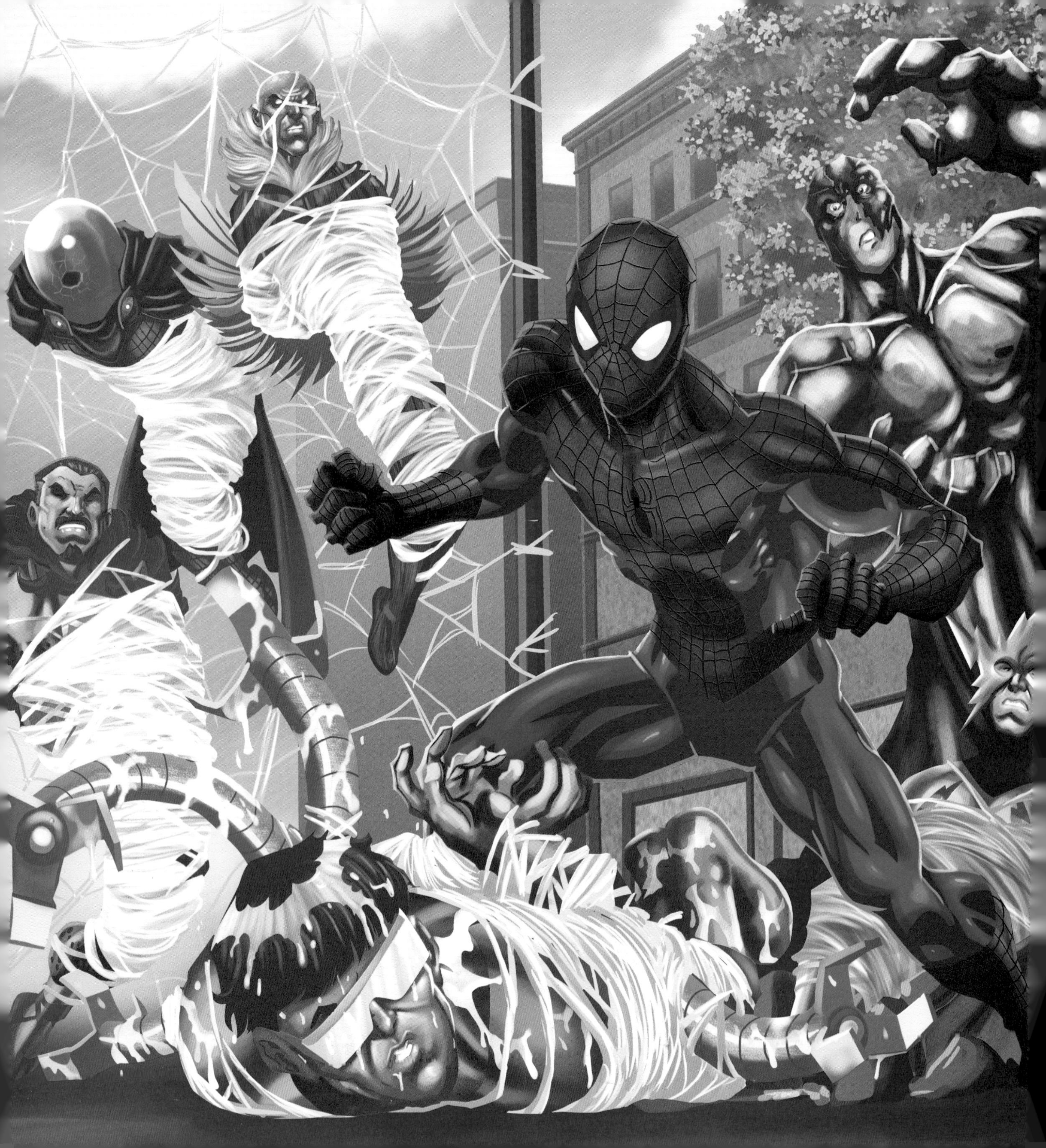

"*Oh, yes*,'" Kraven mocked from their jail cell. "'*I've got a plan.*' Some plan!"

"The plan worked perfectly," the Vulture grumbled. "If the plan was to get us all caught!"

"You fools think you could have done better?" Doctor Octopus grumbled.

"We could hardly have done worse," Mysterio said.

Doctor Octopus tapped his chin. "Hmm . . . next time we —"

"Oh, shut up!" the others yelled.

"Well, that was interesting," Spider-Man said, looking down at his city.

He smiled. "Aunt May and Mary Jane are safe, and all six of those sinister villains are safely behind bars." Spider-Man shook his head. "It's funny, but if they'd just worked together, I wouldn't have stood a chance. I guess it's a good thing they're all so selfish — they each wanted to be the one to beat me."

As he swung off, he laughed. "Villains . . . they never learn."

MARVEL

the AMAZING SPIDER-MAN™

WHAT MAKES A HERO?

It had been a long week for Peter Parker. He had helped put out a fire, caught a jewel thief, and fought *all* of the Sinister Six.

Peter sat on a ledge and looked out at New York City. It's not easy being a Super Hero, he thought. And it sure isn't easy being a teenager!

But how can Peter Parker — or Spider-Man — rest in a city that never sleeps?

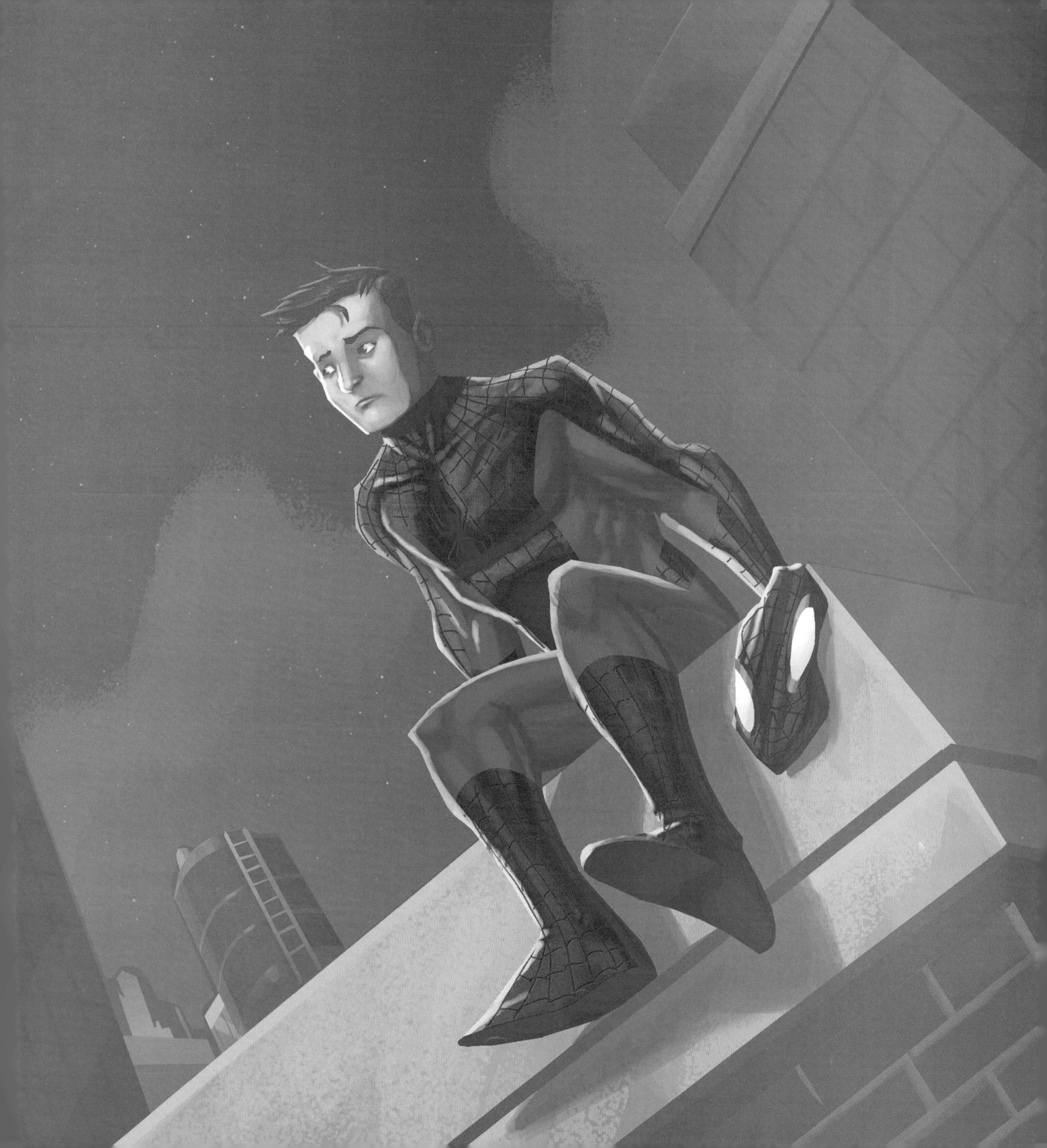

The next morning, Peter woke up in a bad mood. His body ached from the night before. He also had to finish an assignment for *The Daily Bugle* by the end of the day. A story without Spider-Man in it? Peter thought. So much for an easy assignment!

Peter grabbed his camera and headed downstairs. In the kitchen, Aunt May prepared a lovely breakfast and packed Peter a nice lunch. But he didn't notice. Peter trudged out the door, barely paying any attention to her.

Peter headed into New York City's Central Park. Suddenly, his spider-sense went off! But just as Peter was about to change into Spider-Man . . . a hand reached out and stopped the thief. It was a police officer! Peter grabbed his camera and snapped away as the police officer saved the day!

"What a great shot!" Peter said. "This will definitely make the cover of the *Bugle*. And no help from Spider-Man or *any* super powers!"

Peter looked around for more heroic pictures to take. He noticed a big brother helping his younger brother climb back onto some monkey bars.

Peter knew this too well: when we fall, we have to get back up and try again. Sometimes it's difficult to keep trying, but hard work pays off!

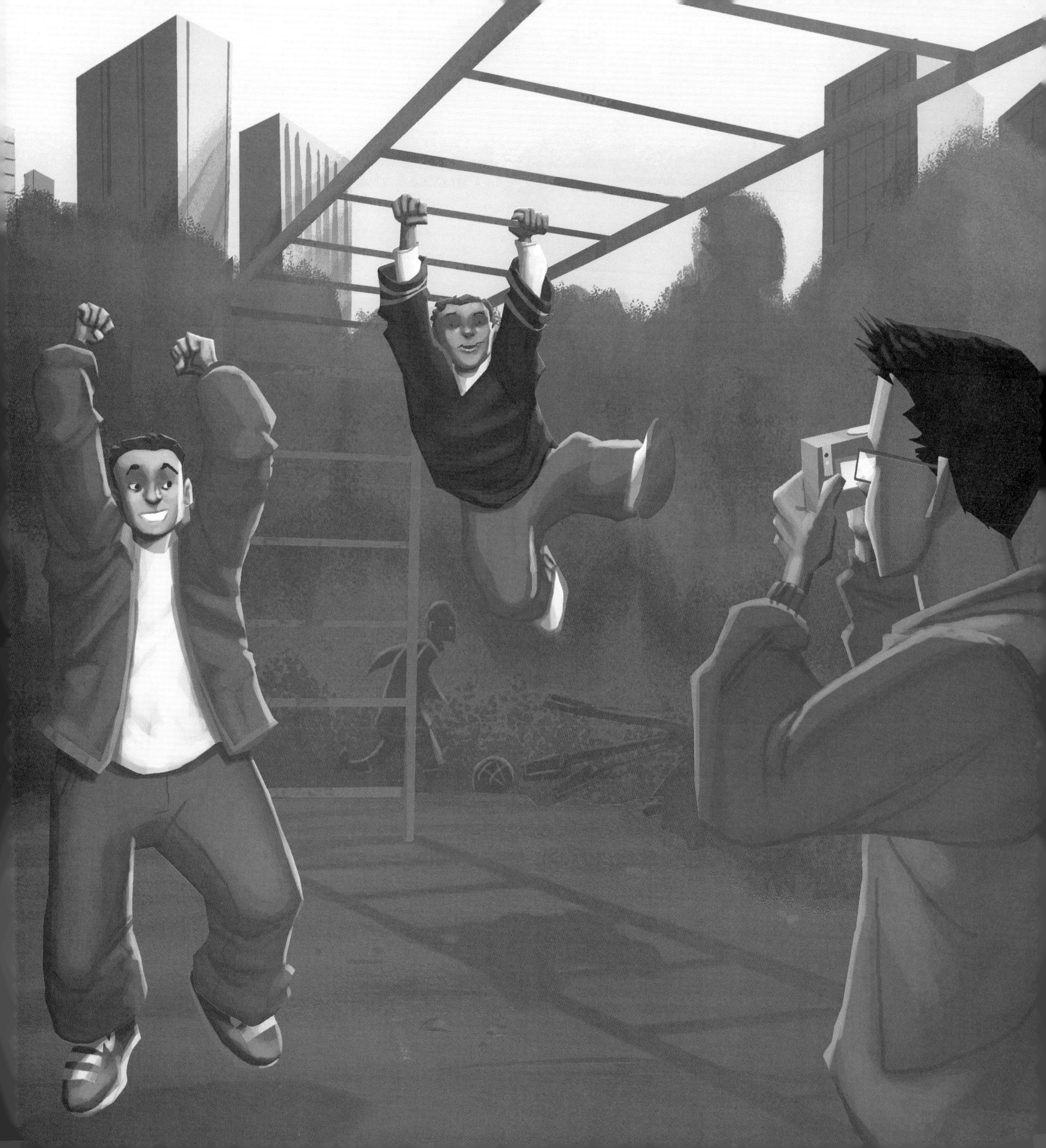

As Peter took more pictures, his spider-sense went off again.
He turned to see several fire trucks racing down Fifth Avenue,
their sirens blaring, their engines racing. Peter ran to the
sidewalk to snap photos of New York's Bravest. I better change
into Spider-Man and see if I can be of any service! he thought.

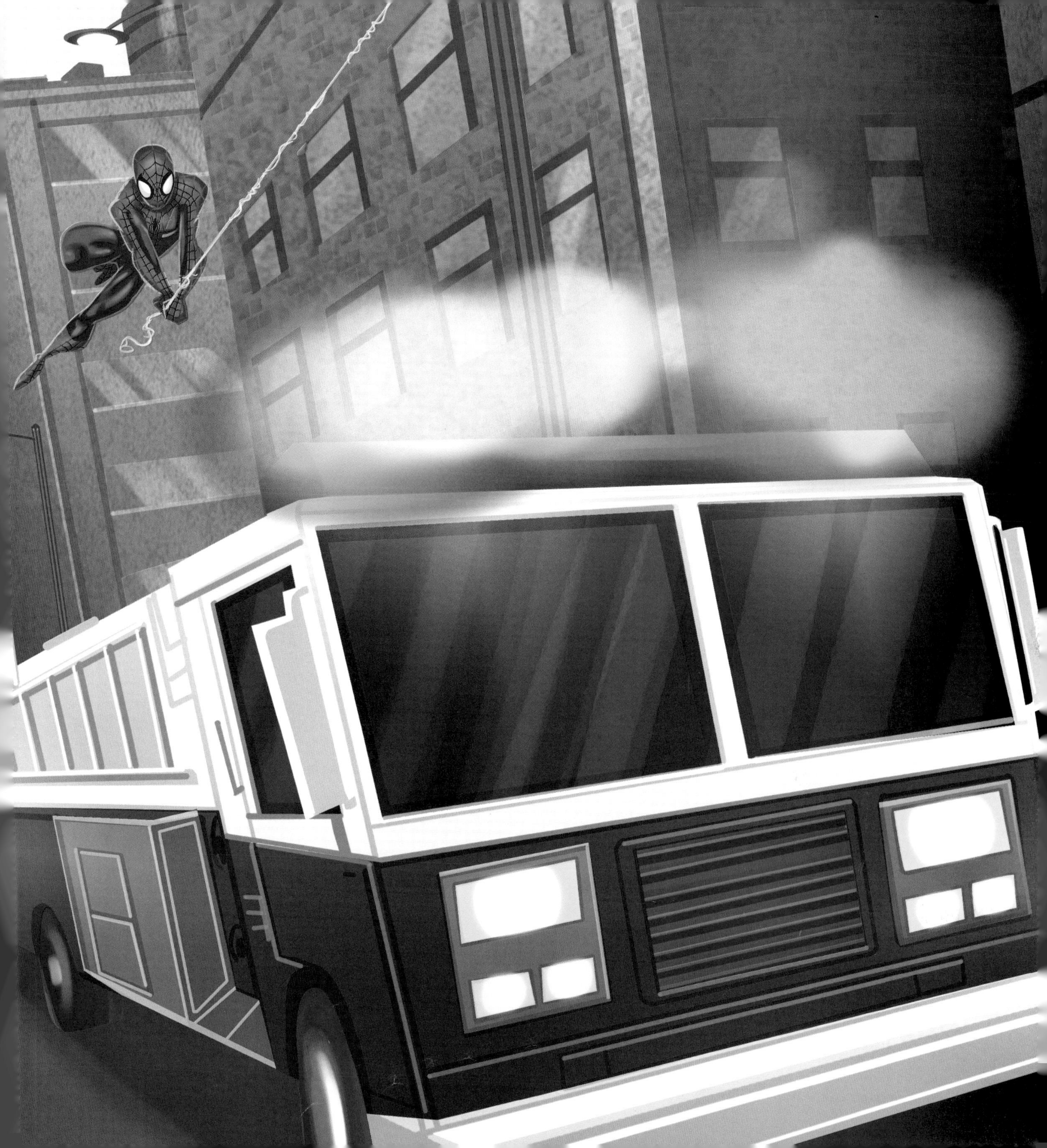

Spider-Man arrived at the scene and approached an emergency medical technician.

The EMT smiled. "Thanks, Spider-Man, but we have everything under control," she said as she helped someone into the ambulance. "The firefighters have put out the blaze, and we are taking these people to the local hospital."

And then it hit Spider-Man. There *are* other heroes!

But what makes a hero? Peter thought as he roamed the city taking pictures. Helping others? Standing up for what is right?

Peter made his way home and thought about all the pictures of the everyday heroes that he had taken. But something was missing. There was one hero he still needed a picture of.

"Smile, Aunt May," Peter said as he took a picture of *his* hero.

The next day, Peter decided to go back to Central Park. This time, he would relax. As Peter took in the sounds and sights of the park, something caught his eye. It wasn't a thief. Or a Super Villain...

It was a copy of today's *Daily Bugle*. Peter smiled.

WHAT MAKES A HERO?

Story by Tomas Palacios · Pictures by Peter Parker

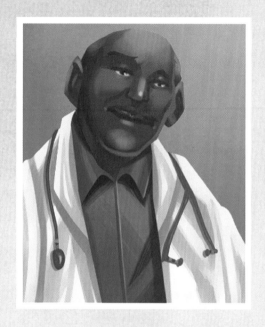

Every day, thousands of heroes in all shapes, sizes, and colors walk amongst us. They are police officers and firefighters and doctors and construction workers. They are mothers and fathers and sisters and brothers. They are the people who lend a hand. They are the people who always do the right thing. They are the people who help, and they are all around us. Who knows... the next HERO could be YOU!

DAILY BUGLE

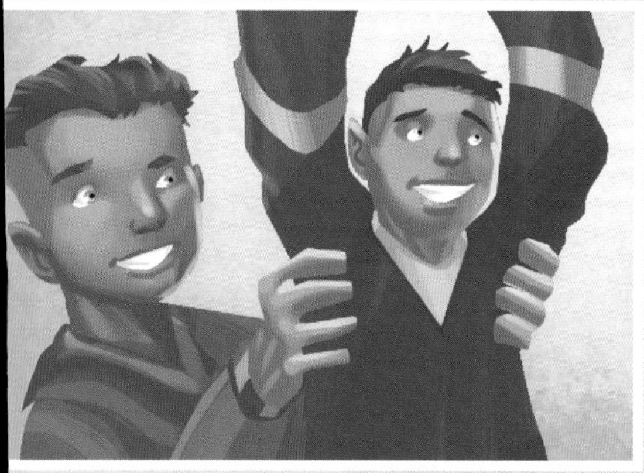

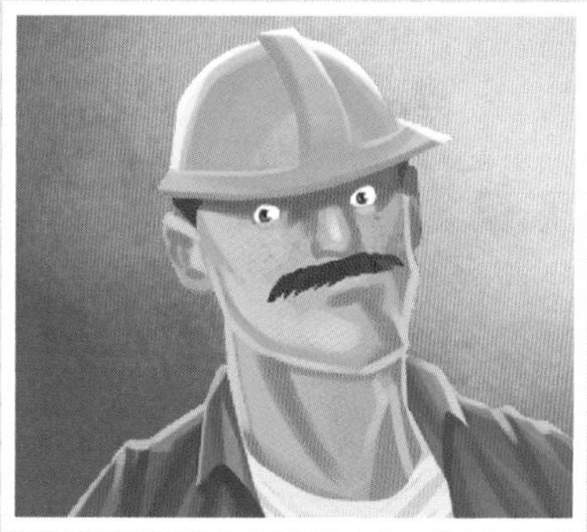

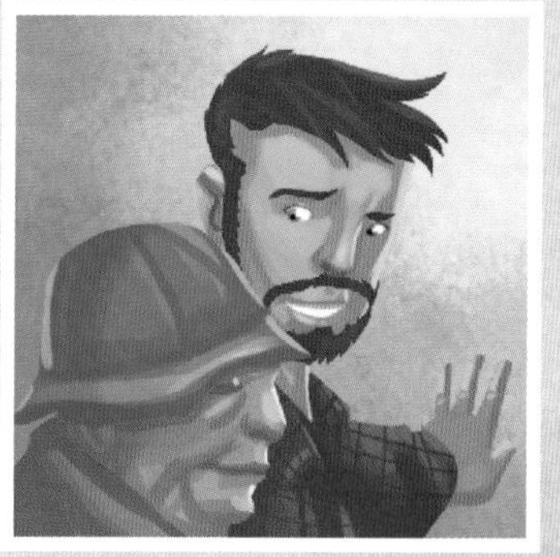

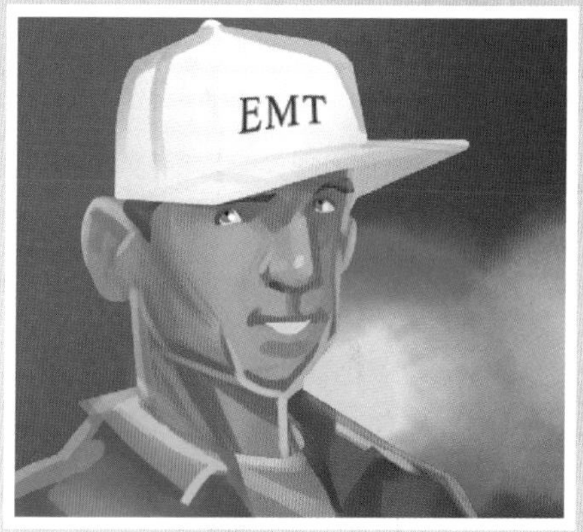
EMT

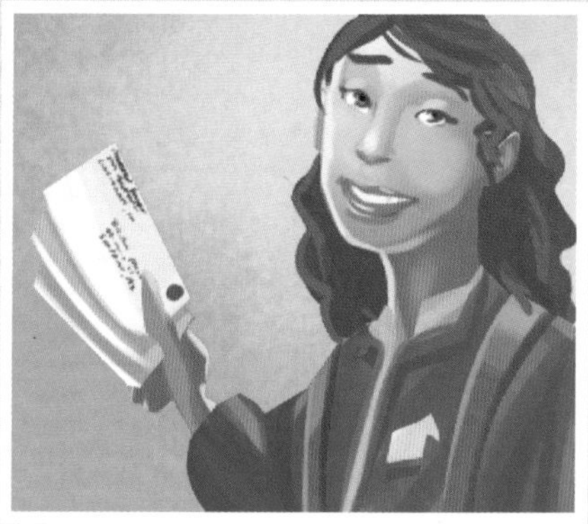

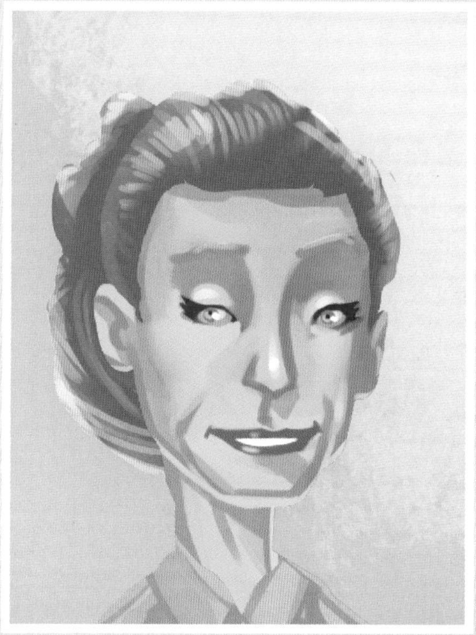

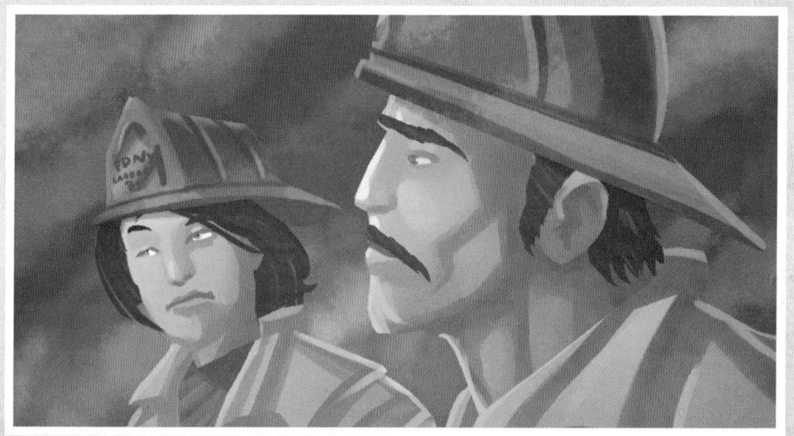

Peter learned a great lesson that day: Spider-Man can't be everywhere at once. But it's good to know that when he's not there, others will be, and that is truly amazing.

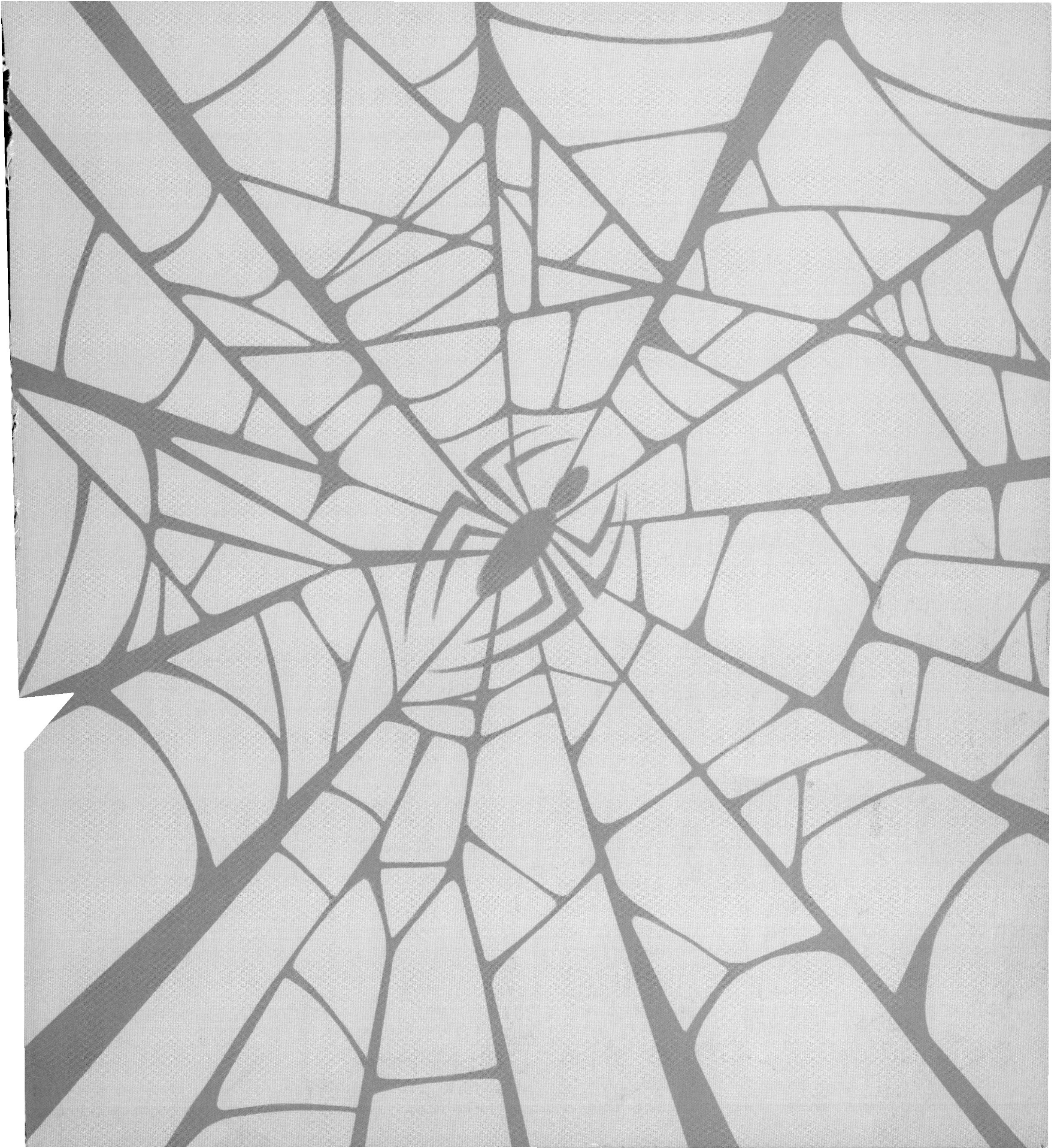

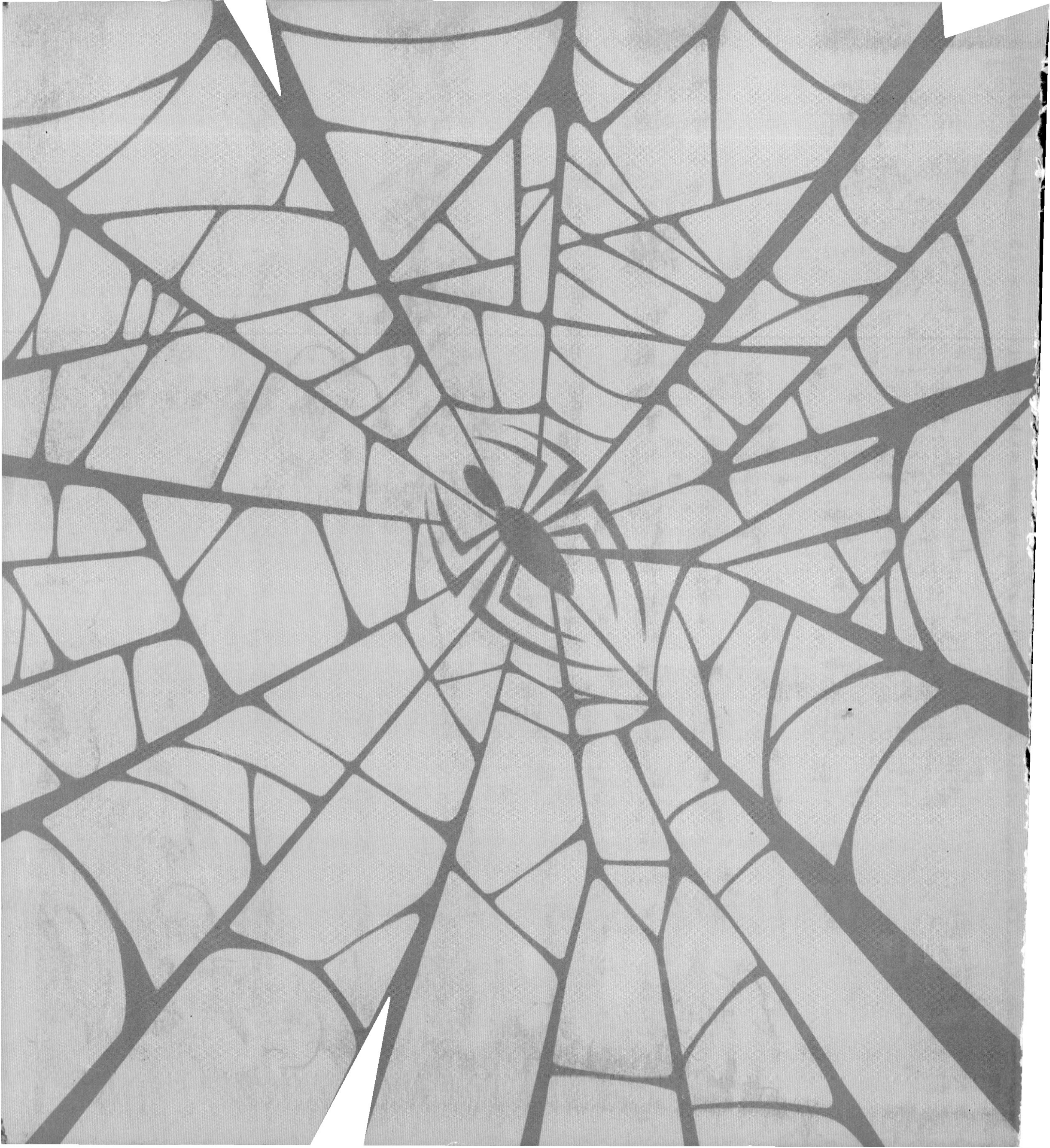